UNWRITTEN SECRETS

Ronald Frame

Unwritten Secrets

TELEGRAM

This edition published in 2010 by Telegram

ISBN: 978-1-84659-084-9

A full CIP record for this book is available from the British Library.
A full CIP record for this book is available from the Library of Congress.

Printed and manufactured by Thomson Press Ltd. (India)

TELEGRAM
26 Westbourne Grove, London W2 5RH, UK
2398 Doswell Avenue, Saint Paul, Minnesota, 55108, US
Verdun, Beirut, Lebanon
www.telegrambooks.com

Montag

Monday

2008

The taxi dropped her off at the end of Graf-Rhena-Strasse.

'I want to walk,' she told the driver.

They were in Hietzing. A long, quiet road of villas and apartments shaded by linden trees.

She stopped outside the building where she was expected. It hadn't been easy tracking down an address. She'd had to employ all the resources of the record company's New York offices and their German headquarters. But at last the information she needed came through: an address in Vienna and a phone number.

She'd had to leave a voicemail message. A reply reached her from Vienna at 3.30 a.m. Eastern Time. An elderly voice, which wasn't Ursule Kroll's, told her in German which day she could come, at what time, and to be punctual. The tone was unwelcoming.

So after nearly thirty years, Mariel Baxter thought, what's new?

Now here she was.

A man in a green loden coat was holding the front door open for her, and had raised his hat. That was what she used to appreciate Vienna for, its good manners. Even if people didn't like each other, they kept up appearances. The man with silver hair was smiling at her, while also carefully scrutinising her. That too was a feature of the Vienna she recalled from 1980: how everyone watched everyone else.

She thanked him, and walked from the vestibule into the hall.

Her surroundings smelt airless. White lilies, not fresh but wax, stood on a console table. A bronzed mirror inset in an alcove showed her looking apprehensive.

She was alone.

Her reasons for being here, why she had felt it necessary to come, were uncertain even to her.

She took the elevator up. (She'd been told the apartment was on the third floor.) The walls were tapestried – with the Vienna Woods, or something older? – and the floor was a square of thick blue carpet. The elevator rose so slowly she thought it might have stopped. Would anyone know, would anyone hear her calling out?

Finally the door opened. The whole building felt hushed.

She stopped outside apartment 3-1 and hesitated before ringing the bell. It sounded muffled and far away. She tried to see through the panel of frosted glass set in a wrought-iron grille.

She thought of ringing again, then she saw movements. A figure approached.

A bolt was pulled back, and a lock was turned. The door was opened cautiously.

It was hard to see against daylight at the far end of the corridor, which made the foreground seem all the darker.

'Is this—?' Mariel asked.

An elderly woman stood staring at her. Her face was shadowed.

It *was* her, wasn't it? They hadn't met, or even spoken, in all the time since.

Yes – Mariel could make out in the gloom – yes, she still had the high cheekbones. And the sweep of hair, no longer grey but white. She was more stooped, and narrower. But in an instant the woman had raised her chin, and her American visitor recognised her, incontrovertibly, from that one imperious gesture.

'It's me, Fräulein Kroll!'

That was just how the words came out.

For a few seconds they both seemed to be transported to another apartment in another street, and a girl standing at the door, clutching a sheaf of sheet music. 'It's me, Fräulein Kroll!' The woman had responded in the same way, saying nothing, as if she couldn't decide on the wisdom of letting her pass through the door.

'Come in.'

Mariel Baxter snapped back to the present. She had been granted entry.

The door was closed behind her. She couldn't think what to say. The silence of the apartment confused her; she felt she was losing her train of thought, which had led her all this long way back here.

She followed Ursule Kroll.

With the merest sigh, some petals dropped from an arrangement of pink Albertine roses as they passed.

Various rooms opened off the long corridor. Mariel glanced in as they were passing. They were crepuscular, thanks to heavy drapes and net curtains.

She was careful to keep to the runners of carpet and not to step on the parquet floor. They moved almost noiselessly. This was a more modern apartment than the previous one in the middle of town, maybe 1920s, but the ceilings were high and seemed to swallow sound.

The accommodation felt dimensionless, and she began to feel disorientated.

Ursule Kroll indicated where they would go – between double doors, into a spacious drawing room.

Mariel looked about her, wide-eyed. The other apartment, by comparison, had merely been a rehearsal for this one. Some of the furniture she thought she recognised. It was a masterly mixing of baroque and some Biedermeyer. Good-quality pieces, as a woman who must have been rich in her heyday could have afforded to buy herself. Mirrors repeated the room, magnifying it to vastness. The paintings were mainly landscapes, nineteenth century, as well as some Jugendstil. Seating was of the traditional high-backed variety. (Kroll used to have back pain, and would say that such troubles never really went away.)

The room made Mariel feel that she was on a stage, in a play.

'Take a seat, will you?'

When she first came to Vienna on her studentship, she had thought Kroll would speak little English. It turned out that she spoke it, if not like a native, then fluently, and with a commendable accent. So much about Ursule Kroll, she quickly discovered at that time, wasn't as it appeared to be.

Mariel realised they weren't alone. A woman was standing at the door.

'My visitor has arrived, Brigitte. We shall have coffee now.'

The woman was staring at her. Mariel smiled vaguely in the housekeeper's direction. The gesture was not reciprocated.

'I remember Brigitte,' Mariel said when the woman had left the room.

It was an altered Brigitte. Like her employer, she was a slighter figure with rounded shoulders, and slowed by time. Her straggling hair was thin on top.

'Brigitte says there's too much she has to remember,' Kroll replied drily.

The coffee was brought in. It was served with old-fashioned deference, in silence. Again Mariel felt uncomfortable – not with the social situation, because she was being waited on, but because Brigitte kept glancing in her direction. Mariel couldn't tell if she recognised her; the woman hadn't used her name, or spoken a single word to her.

'Thank you,' she said, as the milk was stirred into the coffee in her cup.

Kroll waited for her cup and saucer to be handed to her.

'That's all, Brigitte.'

The housekeeper looked at her employer; her eyes might have been passing her a warning.

'We have everything we need, Brigitte,' Kroll said in German, dismissing her.

Brigitte's parting expression was reserved for their visitor. It seemed to be pleading with her to be kind.

Mariel was left with this image of mute concern.

She's an old lady, treat her with care.

Somehow, though, one continued to forget about age with Kroll. She was still intimidating, still demanding, still – in her quest for perfection – inflexible.

'You're looking well,' Mariel said.

'Well, I'm not,' Kroll replied, as adept as ever in English.

'What's wrong with you?'

'Oh ...' Kroll shrugged her shoulders. 'I'm two hundred years old. I'm as old as those songs I taught you how to sing.'

Mariel smiled hesitantly, looking away for an instant.

'I live quietly now,' Kroll said. 'As you can see.'

'Yes.'

Mariel nodded, meaning to be bright, polite.

'Without surprises.'

'Would you prefer me to go?'

'You are now my guest. The famous Mariel Baxter.'

Mariel felt her own smile tightening.

'I didn't read anywhere that you were coming.'

'This is a private visit.'

'To do what?'

'See *you*.'

Kroll raised an eyebrow.

In the background, Brigitte was busy in the kitchen.

'New York is your home?'

'I live in New York. I live there more than I live anywhere else. It's my base. Has been.'

'Your charmed life,' Kroll said, not hiding her scepticism.

Mariel didn't reply.

'You never really see any of those places where you sing, I expect.' The slyness crept back into Kroll's voice. 'Modern singers have a miserable life.'

'If I feel like being a tourist, sightseeing – I go. I can afford it.'

'Am I supposed to be impressed by that?'

'I can't guess', Mariel said, 'what might impress you.'

This wasn't quite how she had envisaged this conversation going. She had assumed it might be awkward, but not to this degree.

'You disappeared,' Kroll said.

'I left Vienna.'

'Without telling anyone where you were going.'

'I didn't think anyone would be much bothered.'

'What about inconvenienced?'

'I wasn't really worried about that.'

'Only about yourself?'

'Oh, I think I needed to think about myself.' Why not tell Kroll the harsh truth? 'Self-preservation, wasn't that what you taught me?'

'*Die Transzendenz.*'

Another pause.

'Transcendence,' Kroll repeated.

'I can translate,' Mariel said, unable to disguise her irritation, and feeling that this conversation was getting away from her. 'I know what the word means.'

'They say you don't suffer fools gladly.'

Silence.

'You've never sung in Vienna.'

'No.'

'Salzburg twice. Graz once. And once at the Schubert Festival at Feldkirch.'

'You keep track of me.'

'Not Vienna,' Kroll persevered. 'They must have invited you here?'

'Oh yes. Several times.'

'Maybe you *will* sing in Vienna.'

Mariel simply shook her head.

'Why not?'

Silence.

'Now', Kroll said, 'you have students of your own—'

'No, I don't.'

'But you teach?'

Was Kroll being mischievous now, Mariel wondered.

'I've never taught.'

'I presumed—'

'You presumed incorrectly.'

'No one has asked you?'

'Oh, I've been asked.'

'You said no?'

'I said I was too busy.'

Kroll didn't seem inclined to believe her.

'Anyway,' Mariel added, 'students now are hopeless.'

'Every generation thinks the same. I thought it of yours.'

'Of me also?'

'You were a little different.'

'"A little"?'

'Sufficiently different, then. Enough for me to do something with you.'

'I was a commodity?'

'A raw substance. It was a refining process.'

'Base into gold.'

Kroll's eyes narrowed.

'Your voice has minted very nicely, I gather.'

'Do you resent me for that?'

Kroll's ready smile lacked warmth.

'Why should I resent you for anything, my dear?'

Mariel Baxter

Mariel's special scholarship had been scraped together from several funds. There was only a modest amount to spare in those straitened times, and it was too late to apply for any of the sources of money in Vienna. She would be allowed to sit in on a couple of classes at one of the city conservatories, but she couldn't be officially enrolled without one of the recognised exchange scholarships.

This arrangement would allow her the rare opportunity – the great PRIVILEGE (with caps), as Professor Donsbach kept calling it – to study with Ursule Kroll, and would cover the cost of her accommodation and basic living expenses for a year.

'It's the best I could do for you, Mariel. A one-off. When I heard that Miss Kroll might have a vacancy—'

Take it or leave it?

She reached out and, with both hands, she grabbed it.

Mariel had done a little homework. It was difficult to find out much about Ursule Kroll. She had become one of the big stars in Germany in the late 1930s. She was perhaps the pre-eminent lyric soprano during the war. But after 1945 her career was over; it didn't go into a decline, it just suddenly stopped.

She had never performed in the States, and so she was written off by many of the American reference books. It didn't appear to matter to them that Kroll had given definitive performances in the great German operas, which were still the staple of the Western musical world. Nor did they take into account her seemingly incomparable recitals of lieder. She hadn't come to the New York Met, and she hadn't made any broadcasts, so she had failed the standing criteria for success. Even in Germany, the period of the Reich and the war were sketchily written up. Professor Donsbach, an evacuee from Austria, had told Mariel that Kroll had subsequently received less of her due in her homeland, which must have pained her greatly.

'Whatever her politics might have been, she really had the field to herself. Take it from me, she was first-rate. I think you should study with her. Your voices have tonal similarities, she could teach you a great deal. She has always taken on one or two students. She's a tough teacher, she has high standards – very German, very Prussian – but that's the best way, believe me. If she likes you, you'll have the time of your life. What she teaches you will be the making of your career.'

Kroll was a byword for Teutonic excellence, Mariel realised. And demanding, even harsh. But Kroll wasn't on the musical radar in late 1979. When Mariel mentioned the name to people, they'd say, 'Ursula who?' Perhaps she might be better off going to one of the wartime stars here in New York, who had done very well with the repertoire several thousand miles away from its roots.

'It's up to you,' Professor Donsbach had said, but Mariel knew that wasn't really the case. It got to the stage where she was sitting in a diner on Dartmouth Street thinking, if the sunshine on the floor reaches across to the leg of that table, then I'll go. Before it could, though, a fire alarm went off and all the customers were hurried out on to the sidewalk. By the time she remembered it was too late, Professor Donsbach had wired Vienna to tell them she would be coming.

Ursule Kroll's apartment at that time was on Schlehengasse, half a mile or so from the conservatory where she used to take classes. On the ground and first floors were lawyers' offices, and on the second floor a doctor's consulting rooms. Both premises had discreet plates by the doors, with names and degrees and profession. On the fourth floor there were two doors on opposite sides of the landing, with the word WOHNUNG attached to one and the more rarefied RESIDENZ to the other, which was Kroll's.

Downstairs, there would be continual comings and goings: clients, staff, delivery men. (It was a very different atmosphere from the morgue-like block on the linden-lined Graf-Rhena-Strasse.)

A small brass plate announced:
KAMMERSÄNGERIN
PROF. DR URSULE KROLL

The music room in the apartment was at the end of the corridor, and Mariel had had a chance to glimpse into the other rooms. The walls were hung with paintings, and there was even a tapestry. The furniture was the grand sort she used to see when her parents dutifully took them to museums in Columbia or Augusta. It couldn't have been more different from her own home in Red Hills, with its 1950s Kon-Tiki memorabilia, burned-leaf carpets and shag pile rugs.

A few times she caught Kroll examining her as she looked at her surroundings.

It was there in the music room, four flights up, that Ursule Kroll spoke forthrightly, laying her cards on the table.

'I haven't taught an American before.'

'No?'

'You are the first.'

Mariel giggled from nerves.

'This amuses you?'

Mariel felt her smile fading fast.

'Why – why have you taken me, Miss Kroll?'

'It would be easier to tell you why I haven't taken Americans before. Because they can be frivolous and only want to play. Because they think they know best.'

'Not all Americans are like that.'

'Then it's up to you to show me I'm wrong.'

'Yes, I shall.'

Mariel realised she sounded too sure of herself.

Ursule Kroll stood, hand on hip, staring through her.

'I – I might just be like the others, though.'

'You might be, yes. In that case, you will have proved I was correct.'

Mariel felt confused, overcome by the experiences of the past ten days she'd spent travelling and settling in. Even living away from home in Boston hadn't prepared her for this.

'I *have* heard you.'

'Heard me? How?'

'They sent me cassettes. Did you think I would accept you if I didn't know how you sing?'

True, Mariel hadn't thought of that.

'That is why you are here. To learn from me.'

'Because I wasn't very good?'

'Because you sing very—.' Kroll stopped herself. 'You are not the same as the Americans that people here tell me about. Too big for their shoes.'

Mariel let go of the chair, and pulled herself taller.

'I think, the two of us, we have much to do together.' Kroll didn't smile. Singing was a serious business. But she did permit herself a couple of nods. It was approval of a sort.

'And I think, young lady, we can achieve good results.'

Mariel could only hope and pray.

Kroll's appearance complemented her manner. Cultivated, suave, decorous, restrained. Mariel could imagine her in a high wig and crinoline gown – of the finest silk, of course – watching the antics of her fellow humans from behind a spread fan. She still had her high cheekbones, and retained a firm jawline: that meant she was in full control of her eyes and her mouth, and neither could betray her. The time with Kroll had already opened a window on a different world for Mariel. The past. People there lived closer to nature, and to the raw elements. They were also closer to the truth of *human* nature, hence their efforts to disguise it through courtly intrigues and witty stage badinage.

Each day Mariel took a tram to go back two centuries. For 'dislocation', understand 'emancipation': at least, according to Kroll. Who would have chosen this era in preference? Life used to be lived more *intensely*, when people followed the weather and the seasons, going to bed at dusk and rising at first light, making the most of what every day brought them.

'What I am teaching you,' Kroll would explain, 'we Germans call "the unwritten secrets".'

Mariel stood attentively, waiting.

'They are passed down from teacher to pupil. The pupil in turn becomes a teacher, and the same secrets are passed down to a new pupil. And so on.'

Mariel nodded.

'All the way back to the beginning. It started with the composer. So the secrets come to us, spoken in *his* voice. But only by that one line – teacher and pupil – the special line, which comes from the source.'

'Yes,' Mariel said. 'I see.'

'You must never betray the trust.'

Mariel held her breath. She was aware that this was a moment of unique significance in her life, an initiation.

As the first weeks passed, Mariel remained fascinated and intimidated, even appalled, by Kroll.

She resembled one of those aristocratic *grandes dames* in the final phase of their glory shortly before the French Revolution swept away such overbred and cynical specimens. She was a relic. Her autocratic manner ill-befitted their egalitarian age. She judged entirely by her own exacting standards. She didn't pity or excuse others or herself, she didn't take refuge in blame. She deplored weakness: it was the sign of a bad character. *This is how I am, she proclaimed.*

There were others like her, scattered throughout Vienna. They lived away from the vulgar gaze, their paths crossing on park promenades or in the hushed, dimly lit public rooms of palast-hotels.

Mariel envied her the experience of a world less ordinary than this one, and at the same time she realised the woman was out of date and unconnected. Her grandeur could easily be misconstrued as superciliousness. But that was other people's fault, Kroll would have thought, because they wouldn't take responsibility, because they couldn't accept absolutes.

Mariel had encountered nobody like her.

Ursule Kroll

Ursule Kroll. Born Maria Semmelrogge.

Her father became factor of a small estate in Wendland, Lower Saxony.

Little Maria Semmelrogge found her voice in a box. The little gilded casket had a mechanism that was triggered when the lid was raised, and it was to the pretty tunes inside that she sang.

She sang herself to school, if her sister Elsa wasn't there to accompany her. She sang whatever she felt like singing, which might be a proper tune or something she made up to express what she was feeling and match her mood. People listened out for her coming.

She started to think she remembered being snatched from her bed in the middle of the night, and meeting gypsies by the light of their campfire, in front of their gaudy caravans, and having a spell cast on her, and then being spirited back home again. But when she encountered some Romanies one day, they looked unfriendly, dirty, not exotic at all. They spat and swore at one another, and then she wasn't so sure, and the memory faded, just as the pattern on the rug in the bedroom at home she shared with Elsa had worn away to the bare cord.

She couldn't sing in the church choir because she was a girl, but her father and brother did. They couldn't hold a candle to her, old Frau Roetzke in the village told her, which made Maria feel guilty.

Her own mother envied her, and didn't compliment her, but at the same time she wanted people to hear, and so Maria would sing at birthdays and festivals and harvest suppers. Old Frau Roetzke left her a small bequest in her will, meant as just enough for her to go to see singers on the stage, in a proper theatre, some time when they came to Hamburg.

A company from Munich presented an operetta. Kálmán's *The Gypsy Princess*. Maria sat, entranced, beside her mother, unable to take her eyes off the stage. For days afterwards she sang snatches of the *Csárdás* melodies, and played out all the roles by herself. That experience was bound to wane in her memory, she realised, just like her dream of the gypsies. But she knew she wouldn't forget what it had felt like to be suddenly liberated, to believe she was among the colourfully dressed characters on the brightly lit stage, to be inside the inn and by the village fountain, living inside the welter of cheerful music that hardly paused to draw breath.

Count Niklas-Schwarzenberger had married again, and his young wife had given birth to twins, and soon after to a third child. Besides her children, music was the Countess's abiding love. She invited professionals to their castle, and entertained friends with concerts. She hired tutors for the children, so that they too would discover the pleasures of music.

One day she had Maria come to the castle. Maria, in her fourteen years, had never been inside the castle walls. She had walked past it every day on her way to and from school, trudging along a muddy lane which bordered the gardens. And some old damp-spotted prints of it hung on the walls of her parents' tied-house, but none showed the rooms inside.

Once she had been admitted to the stately interiors and seen them with her own eyes, there was no going back to her ingenuous state.

Maria was able to study the Niklas-Schwarzenbergers at close quarters. How they stood, sat, dressed, how they ate, drank, used their napkins. The etiquette of conversation. She was looking in on their lives. She didn't know the people or events they reminisced about, or the places they'd been, but she did register their tone of voice and how they responded to one another's remarks. Their values eluded her at times – why they approved or disapproved of things – but she observed their facial expressions, and how they would disguise what they were feeling behind neutral politesse.

She made the most of her time. She didn't just presume that invitations to her would follow, one after another. While she did receive invitations she capitalised on her access to the household; she didn't mistake it for intimacy, however.

Sometimes she almost forgot that she was there. She would have to be asked a question twice or three times, and she would be embarrassed.

'You are far away, Fräulein.'

No, that wasn't true. She was very close, in fact, but vanishing into the conversation, into the history of Schloss Esterhofen and the Niklas-Schwarzenbergers' Austro-Hungarian ancestry, into the beauty of material objects.

Mariel Baxter

Mariel's landlady, Frau Werfel, had known all about the arrangements with Ursule Kroll.

'She will spoil you for anyone else. She will work you hard, but you will find that only *her* lessons matter. The classes at the conservatory, they will seem like a waste of your time.'

There were any number of cafés she could have gone into, but the name appealed to her.

Café Glockenspiel.

It was just far enough from Schlehengasse to make her feel she had this distance between them, but she could find her way back to the apartment – in this warren of a city – without too much difficulty, steering herself by the spire of the Stephansdom.

The Glockenspiel came at a price, but that only reminded her that it was a cut above the rest. She could only afford a coffee; she made it last, and would rein back on spending throughout the rest of the day. Mozart looked benevolently down on her. A crowded mural depicted characters from the operas, very nearly straying into one another's *mise en scène*. Sometimes Mozart or Haydn would play through the wall speakers: something uplifting (since those two composers invariably were), never to obtrude or distract but as an accompaniment to clear thoughts.

She would put off returning to the pension in Penzing for as long as possible. She lingered in the narrow streets of the Old Town, window-shopping and spending nothing. She ventured into a few of the specialist record shops, or those which were the least uninviting, not to buy but to satisfy her curiosity.

In one, which mostly dealt in classical music, the owner seemed to take pity on her. He had a few American customers who knew their rare German labels. He had learned English from a one-time GI who married his aunt and then skipped town when another wife from Berlin showed up. He laughed as he recalled the man's effrontery and stupidity.

Mariel mentioned Ursule Kroll. The owner picked out several record sleeves for her.

'They leave the shop as soon as I get them in. New or second-hand.'

He called them 'new', athough they were actually old stock bought up from bankrupt businesses.

The post-war labels were obscure ones.

'Terrible, what they did to her.'

'Who?'

'Your lot.'

'What did they do?'

'They fucked her career.'

His American uncle had been a man of few, pithy words. Mariel nodded, hearing the anger in the man's voice.

She searched through the record sleeves to see what Kroll had looked like when she was younger. She would have been in her forties when the final picture covers appeared, in the late 1950s. The stern coiffure and countess's exalted mien were firmly in place. She was a paragon of Aryan sophistication. The credited photographer was mostly 'Studio Fayer, Wien'. Kroll looked up or down or sideways. Only in one did she look directly at the camera, and her eyes revealed a strange sadness absent from the rest of her austere poses.

Tomas, the proprietor, played her some tracks from one of the discs, a recital of Mozart arias, on her third visit. He must have known that she wouldn't be buying it, and even teased her, telling her how much he'd charge a fan here for the privilege of owning it.

Kroll's voice of twenty years ago was spirited out of the hi-fi.

The Marriage of Figaro.

'*Dove sono i bei momenti.*'

The voice had lost a little of its lustre, but even the top notes rang true. They both stood rapt.

'Those dames,' Tomas said when the record had spun to a halt, 'you feel they really believed in what they were singing. Now with singers—.' He shook his head. 'Shit, man, it's all style.'

Ursule Kroll

Conrad Niklas-Schwarzenberger was the elder son of the Count's first marriage. Tall. Blue eyes and wavy fair hair. An open face; a refined yet virile profile. Exemplary manners. He hovered about Maria, attending to her needs.

Maria responded, as she felt any girl in her right mind would, like a plant shoot breaking the dark soil and rising to the light.

Whenever she sang at the Schloss, she was singing to him. If – as happened once or twice – he was absent, she would close her eyes while she sang and imagine he was there.

It became routine for him to accompany her as far as the end of the driveway after those evenings of entertainment. If it was raining he would drive her home.

It gave them a chance to talk for a while longer.

'Everyone will be waiting for you,' she would remind him.

'Let them wait.'

She would be thinking of the Count and Countess, and of one guest in particular, Frau Duringer from Bremen, who was always darting her eyes towards him when she thought no one else would notice.

Conrad kissed Maria on one occasion, on the hand, then on the wrist, sending pulsations all through her, a sensation she'd never had before.

The next time he kissed her cheek and asked her to please stay in the car with him. But Maria's instinct was to hold back, not to give him everything he wanted. For a few moments, saying goodbye and waving, she felt that the triumph was hers; then, as the minutes passed without him, she grew less sure.

Maria was careful what she said to Conrad about Christine Duringer.

'My father feels obliged to invite her. He knew her husband well. My stepmother would rather he didn't. She has these notions, and nothing will move her. Unlike us, the Countess isn't required to explain herself.'

And that was that.

The widow, whatever her host's wife thought of the matter, continued to be invited. She would be there among the company listening as Maria sang. She would sit demurely, quite still, but just out of the Countess's range of vision, so that she was able to swivel her eyes undetected to the dashing son. Unseen, that is, except by Maria. Once when Maria was singing, she looked across and caught the woman trade a colluding smile with the heir to Esterhofen. Momentarily Maria's voice wobbled, before recovering its strength – and for the remainder of that song and throughout the next, her voice blazed like never before.

Maria didn't forget. Couldn't, wouldn't forget. She had let her voice betray her. It mustn't happen again. The voice somehow had to operate independently of her feelings.

That would take years to master, but at least she'd had the first intimation of what she must master.

Maria hadn't had a chance to speak privately to Conrad since the evening of the kiss in the car. The Count was unwell, and Conrad was having to assume the host's role, so that she had to make do with brief social chit-chat.

When Conrad was then called away 'on business' his stepmother took over those duties. Maria was desperate to know when he would be returning, but felt she could only ask vaguely after his health. She noticed Frau Duringer looking more dour-faced than ever, and frankly bored by the singing.

She received a letter from Conrad, from Berlin. He told her he'd met the composer Kálmán, but Maria was more impressed by the fact that he remembered she'd once seen *The Gypsy Princess*. She imagined him sitting down to write to her, stealing time to do so, and was gladdened to know that she could occupy his thoughts even though he was so many miles away. She kept the letter in whichever pocket was closest to her heart, carrying it around with her for weeks.

The distance seemed to lessen between the Schloss and the tied-house, where she still shared a room with Elsa. In her dreams she moved easily about the castle, into rooms she still hadn't seen; there was nowhere she couldn't go, with Conrad at her side to guide her and whispering into her ear, and it felt more like home to her than home was.

Conrad returned with a new stallion, a purebred Morgan from a stud farm in New Jersey.

'America?'

'They shipped him to Lübeck for me.'

He invited Maria to the stables, for a private viewing.

When she got there, he put his hand on her arm quite firmly.

'You can see it first.'

She wanted to say yes, but she saw through that ruse, and felt afraid. She pulled herself away.

'I'm late for a music lesson,' she called behind her.

Before another of the Countess's soirées, she intended apologising to him. How else would she be able to sing, unless she removed all strain and could control her voice? She saw his car heading towards the stables in the middle of the afternoon. She followed it on foot.

She heard them before she saw them. Conrad and Frau Duringer.

Voices.

'You're imagining it, Christine.'

'Am I?'

She was saying something else, accusing him.

'That's absurd,' he was telling her.

'Then prove it.'

Maria knew what she would find when she hazarded inside. Frau Duringer was lying on her back in the straw, dress round her hips, with her legs up on his back and her hands buried in his fair hair. Conrad Niklas-Schwarzenberger, trousers round his ankles, was riding her like one of his cross-country hunters.

'Harder! Faster!'

Maria was transfixed.

Conrad's naked buttocks quivered as he drove up into the woman.

Maria stood watching them for fifteen or twenty seconds before she could think to look away. She felt she was going to retch. The sudden movement made Frau Duringer look over, and Maria saw an expression not of bewilderment or shame, but of simple indifference, of being somewhere else and too far away to come back.

Mariel Baxter

'Karen?'

Mariel looked up.

'Pardon me—?'

One of the Glockenspiel regulars had come over to her table and was speaking to her in English.

'You're Karen?'

'No. No, I'm not.'

'Oh, sorry. Mistaken identity. I'm really sorry.'

'It's nothing,' Mariel said.

The English girl was doing a circuit of the room when the young man came in.

'Zoë!'

'Where've you *been*, Ben?'

Mariel registered the names. Ben was complaining about hating work; Zoë was telling him he couldn't get something interesting to translate *every* time, and he was saying *anything* interesting would do.

It was a jazz night, and he had to head off to the club.

Mariel didn't look away in time, so that Zoë noticed her listening to them. Zoë smiled over at them, shrugged, waved goodbye and walked off with Ben.

Ben – after a backward glance – appeared to be asking her something.

Who was that?

The window of the sheet music shop on little Blücherstrasse was covered with protective yellow plastic, but the sheet music on display had curled nevertheless and everything about the place laid Mariel's spirits low.

The music there, though, was cheaper than anywhere else. She was reluctantly headed there when the door opened and out stepped a customer with a pigskin satchel over his shoulder.

He looked round at her, then away, then looked again.

He smiled.

Mariel smiled back.

Then she remembered where she'd seen him.

She returned to the Glockenspiel.

She was at the counter, choosing a pastry to substitute for a meal, when she caught sight of a pigskin satchel.

A man's voice, speaking with an English accent, made her turn round.

'Another conscript! Come to sign up?'

It was him!

'What d'you say I introduce you to the others?'

'I—'

'Yes?'

'Sure!'

Brendan. Helga. Miguel. Gita. Karl. Zoë. Ilan. Elena. Aldo. Lucien.

'Have I left anyone out? I don't think so.'

'Yourself.'

'Oh yeah. I'm Ben!' he said, and Mariel laughed along with him.

They called themselves 'Die Gruppe'.

Her introduction was as simple as that.

She had come back to the Glockenspiel because she had hoped this would happen. She felt she had been programmed to return. On the corner of the street a stone caryatid on the façade of a building had seemed to be keeping watch for her.

A number of customers were none too delighted about the noise from the bunch of foreigners. But the owner's daughter-in-law was now in charge, and she would have been glad to see the back of those elderly regulars who occupied a table each and lingered for hours over a single cup of coffee.

Frau Edel was of the opinion that the young people livened up the premises. They spent more too. They breezed in, huddled round a couple of tables and suddenly would be gone again.

Ben would walk with Mariel to the tram stop, where they would stand talking, Mariel secretly wishing that the tram would be late.

Only once did she feel that she'd made a fool of herself. On the subject of jazz, Ben's big thing.

'You just hope for the best, I guess?'

'What?'

'Well, it's all kind of accidental, isn't it?'

She didn't know why he was laughing so hard.

'In a way, yes, we *do* make it up. But it's like getting on one of those,' he pointed to her approaching tram. 'You have a pretty good idea of where you're going.'

She'd been dating someone back in Boston.

David was her first boyfriend, her only boyfriend.

He was in one of her classes.

Vienna became the insoluble problem between them. He seemed to think she should have considered him more.

'But it's a great opportunity.'

'For you, Mariel.'

'Yes, for me. But we can—'

Keep in touch, she meant.

David was chasing jobs in various places. Nothing was settled yet.

'It's at the other end of the world,' David told her.

'That's Australia,' Mariel corrected him. 'Or the Cape of Good Hope. Or Japan. Not Vienna.'

'Well, let's not bother with the geography lesson, okay?'

It was the sarcastic and demeaning tone of that remark which *really* got to her, which as much as anything helped to finish what they'd had going.

'Ben's something else,' Miguel explained to her, 'that's what you've got to understand. He's mellow. Just like Miles.'

'Miles?'

'Ahead. Miles Smiles.'

'Pardon me?'

'Davis.'

'Yes?'

'Miles Davis.' Miguel impersonated blowing a trumpet. 'Ben's a jazz bird, right?'

Mariel felt she could breathe more easily around Ben. He was a little older than the others, more savvy about life. He gave her space. But she also knew he rode shotgun for her. One of the Gershwin tunes he played was 'Someone to Watch Over Me'.

His hair curled down to his collar. (David was a monthly trim man.) He wore shirts with frayed collars (she thought of David in his polo necks), jeans with stringy cuffs (she remembered the sharp crease in David's woollen Lord & Taylor trousers), plimsolls or second-hand wing shoes (David was only very formally casual, in polished buckskin moccasins). Ben had watches on both wrists: a cheap one to keep local time, and a good Swiss one (handed down from his great-uncle) on East Coast time, where those who hired his labour were.

His maleness was more evident than David's. Five o'clock shadow, dark hairs sprouting over the open collar of his shirt, and on the backs of his hands, a tang of sweat which frankly exhilarated her. (David liked to test the new colognes in the big stores, and showered twice daily all year round.)

There was nothing mean about him, Mariel thought, he'd have spent his last few marks on her. He had an energy which wasn't like David's nervous stuttering sort, and she felt she could tap into it and get a charge from it. He had an aura of worldliness about him, but he was one of life's optimists and didn't waste time being cynical.

'*Oo Bop Sh'bam!*'

One day when they were walking along the street together, Mariel realised the two of them were proceeding precisely in step.

Ursule Kroll

A few weeks after the episode in the stables, a professor at the University of Tübingen, who also happened to be one of the Countess's favourites, was seconded to the Hochschule für Musik in Hamburg.

They wrote out of the blue, FOR THE URGENT ATTENTION OF FRÄULEIN MARIA SEMMELROGGE, asking if she would consider applying for a music scholarship.

Once she had been admitted, she went with her good news to the Countess, to thank her.

'It's my son you should thank, Fräulein Maria.'

Conrad had absented himself again, to Berlin and then to Rome, without Maria having set eyes on him since that evening at the stables.

'Before he went off, he asked me if I thought it was the best thing he could do for you. I said he should ask you himself. Did he not?'

'No.'

'"It's the least she deserves," he said. 'I'm not quite sure what he meant, are you?'

Maria smiled. To her, the matter was resolved: it couldn't have been clearer.

She wrote him a rather formal letter of thanks, using the Esterhofen address.

No doubt he was seeing the Merry Widow Duringer at every opportunity he – or she – could find. That woman had sunk her claws into him. Her character was highly undesirable, which probably made her all the more alluring.

The aristocracy had their own way of doing things.

There would always be a distinction between them and lesser mortals. It wasn't up to her to apply her morals to the time-hallowed order of behaviour observed in castles and manor houses, and in those apartments – even townhouses – in cities where their paramours were kept.

In time he would become engaged to the daughter of an Essen ironmaster, whom Maria would remember from the musical evenings as rather drab. The young woman's fiancé was a man with his finger on the historical pulse, and Maria wondered if there hadn't always been close contact between the two.

Conrad was pragmatic to a fault. He wouldn't commit himself, as others had, on the matter of politics, which had to be conducted out of the Countess's hearing. He wouldn't shake his head at developments – the fermenting unrest – in the big cities, so that in the future there would be no one to recall or denounce him for reactionary talk and monarchist sympathies.

Even more than Maria had appreciated, Conrad Niklas-Schwarzenberger was a consummately adaptable man, made for these current times.

'Ursule,' she replied when they asked her at the Hochschule which name she wished to be known by. They examined the letter they had received from her, and the recommendations which accompanied it: those referred to her as 'Maria'.

'No, I use my middle name,' she fibbed. (She had no middle

name.) She had decided in an instant, but she felt she had already known for a long time that she was someone else.

She didn't care much for the name Maria. If she'd been planning a modest career, teaching children or the like, then it wouldn't have mattered. But on a concert programme it would look too ordinary.

On one of the central streets from the train station, she had stopped to look in a modiste's window. The garments on display were Paris-made. The lettering scrolled on the window announced 'Madame Ursule'. She'd caught a glimpse of the said Madame Ursule inside, deigning to give her attention to a customer. The woman ostentatiously consulted the watch hanging on a chain from her waist. Ursule looked round, to find a street clock. She mustn't be late. Hurrying off, she took away a picture in her head of the sort of life the Christine Duringers of this world might enjoy in this city, making a detour between a visit to a beautician and a lunch rendezvous, dropping in to inspect the season's arrivals and to earn the approval of the svelte and curvy-hipped Madame Ursule.

At the conservatory Ursule Semmelrogge, now an exhibition student, would be under the tutelage of none other than Sabine Hebbel.

Hebbel had understudied Lehmann as the composer in *Ariadne auf Naxos* in Vienna, and five years earlier, in 1911, Minnie Nast's Sophie in the Dresden premiere of *Der Rosenkavalier*. It was said that Strauss intended writing a new main role specifically for Hebbel (Hecuba? Or Diana?), if he could lure von Hofmannsthal back into the opera house, and if his other ever-faithful divas could be trusted not to sabotage his efforts. It was also claimed – by one aggrieved party or another – that the young pretender had failed to please him in some regard, and that she and the master had had a falling-out.

Sabine Hebbel appeared in other opera houses, in roles not written by Strauss. She was considered to be one of the doyennes of lieder singing, when her repertoire did include Strauss. The

Hecuba–Diana rumours, despite coming to nothing, trailed her like some menacing doppelganger she couldn't shake off.

She left Vienna for Hamburg, and it was there that she decided to settle.

She took on a few pupils, and in time became more famous as a teacher than as a stage singer.

That seemed to be her destiny, and she had the maturity to accept the fact.

Mariel Baxter

They talked, Die Gruppe, about everything.

About Stockhausen, Pop Art, Berio, Op Art, Berlioz, *Empire of Passion*, spacecraft travel to the sun, Steve Biko, pomegranates, Frenchman Levy and Levi's, blue suede shoes, Casanova, Polaroid cameras, President Carter, Brezhnev, disco, Thai food and tie-dyes, Marquez, Waldheim, KFC, minis, midis, maxis, Aesop, the Fonz, Hildegard Knef, Gregorian chant.

They argued, but never to the death, and not enough to leave blood on the floor. In fact they never talked about any subject for too long. Once there was Beat, and then it all hung out, but already – ahead of their time – the attention span was shortening. There was just too much of everything to forcefeed into the mincer (Zoë's term), and the jaw jaw (her term also) never let up.

Zoë. With an umlaut.

She wrote her name in confident, arty, outsized letters, with two circles over the 'e'.

Long blonde hair. She rode a red bicycle with a cane basket on the front. She had the willowy elegance of a certain well-bred type of Englishwoman.

Zoë was here as part of her modern languages course at Cambridge University. In a guidebook to England Mariel found in a bookstore, cows grazed in a meadow and King's College Chapel rose through the morning mist behind like some vast mysteriously beached ship; quadrangles were colonnaded and creeper-clad; a flat punt, steered by a barefoot student in a straw boater, passed beneath the Bridge of Sighs.

Aah ...

Zoë was friendly and open. She didn't advertise her own expertise in the German language or her understanding of all things Viennese. But anything which Mariel wanted to know about, Zoë generously told her.

She was a specimen Mariel wasn't familiar with. Private boarding schools, self-deprecating so far as her intelligence was concerned, a skier, a sailor. Mariel would have felt intimidated by her if she hadn't been so agreeable. Given a free hand to choose an alter ego for herself ...

Ben didn't ask her, who's this Ursule Kroll?

'You've heard of her?'

'Of course I have,' he laughed. 'Don't look so surprised!'

'Well, I *am* surprised.'

'Why?'

'Almost no one else has heard of her.'

'I'm not everyone else, though.'

'No, I know you're not.' She smiled at him, taking his arm. 'I'm very glad you're not.'

On her way from Schlehengasse 19 to the Glockenspiel, Mariel would stop at a certain fountain and splash her face with clear water from the stone bowl.

She experienced the shrill coldness of mountains, snow and ice. She pictured a torrent tumbling from a glacier as it thawed. Later the same rushing water ran past a mill, turning the old creaking wheel while a lover stood on the bank yearning for what wasn't meant to be.

Mariel enjoyed Die Gruppe's youthfulness, living from hour to hour and not plotting the future. The past was just something massed in stone, lifeless and inert like the big government buildings they sprinted past or pedalled past on their bicycles.

No Ursule Kroll. No Mozart, no Schubert, no Heine or Goethe.

Freedom!

Ben. Zoë. Ilan. Helga. Aldo. Lucien. Karl. Elena. Miguel. Gita. Brendan.

A couple of her compatriots, Elly and Seth, floated in and out of their arrangements; but the three of them seemed to have decided separately that the American herd mentality didn't apply to *them*.

Time with Die Gruppe went straight to Mariel's head. She didn't need wine or beer, or strong coffee, or the substances which Aldo bought from a man near the Franz-Josefs-Bahnhof. They spoke most of the time in English, usually talking over one another and veering from topic to topic.

They knew their own physical attractiveness. Even if their looks weren't their selling point, each of them had exuberance and health, the firm, unlined skin of youth.

Youth excuses so much that is questionable in a person's character. Youth is what every older person craves, even if they deny it. (There's a vampire inside every man or woman past the age of thirty.) Mariel wanted to rejoice in hers, quite blatantly.

She had a sense that they all felt, in a vague way, they could have achieved anything. Anything at all. Their potential was unlimited, boundless, inexhaustible, never mind that they weren't certain yet what their true calling was.

Zoë was tall and slender. Mariel envied her her height, and that air of disciplined will which kept her a size 10. And those perfectly regular, perfectly white teeth. All a matter of metabolism – and birth and genes, of course.

Life was unfair right from the start.

Brendan, the Irish member of Die Gruppe, told her that Ben and Zoë had had a serious falling out about something. Elena had heard them quarrelling.

'Was there anything between them?' Mariel asked.

'Why?'

'Well,' she could only think to reply, 'why not?'

'Zoë is upper-middle, at least.'

'Upper-middle what?' Mariel asked.

'Class.'

'Oh.'

'Ben is lower-middle, at best.'

'That matters?'

'Maybe not to an American.'

Zoë told her, 'I *knew* you'd like Ben.'

Mariel felt her face reddening.

Zoë smiled.

'Ben and I look out for each other, Mariel. We met on the train here. He was sitting in my reserved seat. He said he hadn't noticed. Anyhow I turfed him out, and that's how it started.'

'"It"?'

'Becoming buddies. Sparring partners, if you prefer. He's annoying as hell sometimes. We're too much alike, I guess. You two are—' Zoë thought what the correct word was. 'Complementary. Yes.'

'We are?'

'Don't think I haven't noticed how well you get on!'

'Yes?'

'You're not going to deny it?' Zoë laughed. 'You thought I wouldn't approve?'

'"Approve"?'

'Shock, horror!' Zoë laughed again, shaking out that ash blonde hair.

'I'm a newcomer,' Mariel said.

'Beginner's luck and all that!'

One day, during a sudden downpour, Ben covered them both with his trench coat and they ran along the street like that, a four-legged creature scuttling for shelter.

Standing inside a doorway, watching the cascade of drops, Mariel asked him about himself.

Ben told her a little of his history. It sounded odd to her, as if he was offering a translation from a book he'd read. Perhaps he was right, and it didn't really matter very much in his case, eight hundred miles away. (How much less, then, did her story – an ocean and half a continent away – signify? She had to think twice even to remember the colour of David's eyes.)

Ursule Kroll

'I presume', Fräulein Hebbel said, 'you are intending a proper profession in music?'

She didn't give her new pupil time to respond.

'A smaller surname could expand to fill the same amount of space on a poster. But the letters would be bigger, and I think it would look more important.'

Fräulein Hebbel chose for her. 'Kroll'.

The name had been abused, Fräulein Hebbel explained, stolen by Kestenberg for the second house at the Berlin Staatsoper. Now they'd closed it, for not being German enough, and about time too. Her own mother's name was Kroll, and this way they would be honouring it.

So Ursule Kroll she became.

Fräulein Hebbel, who was affiliated to two conservatories, had taken on another new pupil that semester.

Ursule and Alina might not have met, since they were attending classes at their different, rival institutions in the city, but for a mix-up one day. They both arrived for a lesson at the same time. Fräulein Hebbel was full of apologies.

'I think I must take you both together today.'

Normally Fräulein Hebbel was the most precise of persons,

checking and double-checking times and the music to be studied. This seemed quite untypical. (It did occur to Ursule that it might not have been an accident.)

But now they had been introduced, and this allowed them to have the measure of each other's voices, which they wouldn't have been able to get by any other means. (Maybe, Ursule wondered, Fräulein Hebbel had a hunch they would get along?)

Following their first encounter, they went walking along the Neuer Jungfernstieg. Alina introduced Ursule to a couple of her friends they passed, and she invited them all to her aunt and uncle's home the following Sunday.

The rooms of the Fleissners' apartment on Tiergartenstrasse were filled with light.

White walls. Sofas and armchairs fitted with white covers. Chrome and glass side-tables and tubular chairs. Rugs with geometric patterns laid on polished woodblock floors.

Ursule was charmed by her very contemporary surroundings. They made her feel like a different person. Well-born, and intellectual. She imagined herself tall and thin, and as elegant as the luxuriantly dressed figures who stooped with limber grace on the front of a white Art Nouveau cabinet.

The drawing room fireplace dated from the same period. A mosaic of coloured stones and little mirrors spun daylight back at her.

The Fleissners had welcomed her as if they'd known her all her life.

They met most days after that, Ursule and Alina.

Ursule was happy just to be seen with Alina, who would be turned out in the latest fashions. She pretended less with her than with anyone else she'd met here. She forgot which one of them had done it first – hooking an arm through the crook of the other – but the gesture had become a very public display of their mutual affection.

Sunday afternoons were usually spent with Alina's uncle and aunt. Ursule had her own seat, 'Ursule's chair', which they kept for her; and they knew which food she liked best, although she enjoyed whatever the couple chose to serve their guests.

Sunshine fell through stained glass panels in the windows, throwing jewels at their feet.

It was Alina who taught her how to dress, to try heels and ankle straps, which cocktails and wines to be seen drinking. The information was imparted in the lightest manner, with an open heart.

Ursule studied everything – how Alina wore her woollens over her shoulders, knotted in front, how she could somehow look natural in a photograph when she was consciously posing for it (more difficult, then and always, to pull off), how she smoked a cigarette (Egyptian) by hardly inhaling at all, how she plucked her eyebrows without leaving that silly expression of surprise on your face which an inexperienced pair of tweezers could do, how she dashed off her signature (without lifting the nib from the paper), how she let laughter ripple up out of her throat.

That silvery way of laughing wasn't easy to copy. Some mannerisms just seemed too much like Alina Giebisch to imitate. Two hands to shade her eyes against the sun, or the little skip-step on the pavement whenever she jumped topics in a conversation.

A diplomatic frank. A sheet of notepaper, bearing the inscription: GERMAN CONSULATE, GUADALAJARA, FEDERAL REPUBLIC OF MEXICO. *Dear Maria.* And a signature at the bottom, *Conrad N-S.*

The envelope was addressed to *Fräulein Ursule Kroll.* (So he had ways and means of knowing such things.)

Halfway through the letter he wrote, *I don't doubt that, being an intelligent young woman, you will be able to read between the lines.*

What about? Not his best wishes for her future, surely, nor even his regrets that he wouldn't be able, from this distance, to hear her sing.

She used that intelligence he claimed to find in her to translate the rest.

He was advancing up the greased ladder of the diplomatic corps, while presenting all the right credentials. Perhaps the newly established progressive Cardenas administration in Mexico might prove willing brothers?

Espionage involvement, did that mean?

Nothing about Frau Duringer. Might she have expected there would be? No, probably not.

Mariel had no hopes on that score, and no real regrets. She and he had gone their own ways. Hamburg was her life now: Schubert, and Strauss, and wanting to put the tied-house on the Esterhofen estate behind her, and memories – other people's memories, because *she* couldn't recall it – of the little girl singing up in the branches of apple trees, and the tedium of life in Wendland so flat to the horizon.

The Fleissners wanted her to feel at home.

It wasn't home, but Ursule could imagine it being so, more easily than the Schloss Esterhofen. There, she had always been aware of the distinctions. What freed her at the Tiergartenstrasse apartment was what the Fleissners called her 'art'. Her talent was fully recognised: she was a pupil of one of the best singing teachers in Germany, and she spent hours of every day in the company of the finest composers and poets the world had ever known. Somehow that put her on a par with the Fleissners, or so the couple believed. They knew living painters and writers and composers, and could afford to furnish their house however they chose, they could discuss any play or concert you cared to mention, played records inside their cabinet gramophone, and they still – inexplicably to Ursule – considered that she deserved their munificent hospitality.

It wasn't in Alina's nature to be cynical, or even unduly reflective. She was easy-going and likely to be surprised by any special praise that came to her. She sang without seeming to give the business much thought. Fräulein Hebbel called her 'lazy' to Ursule, but to Alina the woman would say that Ursule 'tried too hard' and 'strained'. She told Ursule that Alina found her inspiration on the spur of the moment, as if the lessons were neither here nor there to her; meanwhile she told Alina that her friend couldn't sing without her music and notes and was forever criticising herself.

Fräulein Hebbel exaggerated. What was the point of it? Whose side was she on?

Alina shrugged those questions aside.

'The problem is hers.'

'Isn't it ours?' Ursule asked her.

'How can it be ours?'

'If she's not truthful?'

'Then we go into town. To the shops, or we go to the cinema. It's easy! Or we walk into the woods and get away from her.'

Alina didn't go looking for problems. She balances me perfectly, Ursule thought. Arm-in-arm they would set off along the windy Ballindamm.

Ursule felt younger than the other students at the Hochschule because of her limited experience of the world. She had already seen some raised eyebrows and semaphored smirks. All she wanted was to grow up as quickly as possible.

She thought of herself as having to hurry, forever hurrying after them, busy-busy, just to keep abreast.

Most of all, Ursule envied Alina her unmarked forehead.

Whenever Ursule studied herself in the mirror, she saw two lines rising from the bridge of her nose, like a little knot of worry set there on top of her face. If she folded her brow, horizontal lines went crinkling across it.

Alina would only ever glance in the mirror to check that her hair was tidy, or that her collar lay flat, or her chunky coloured beads were straight on her neck. 'Am I all right like this?' she might ask, not really meaning Ursule to answer. All her young life Alina must have had people confirming for her how presentable she was. She didn't need to bother about failing to match anyone's standards, not when *she* set them.

In her room Ursule would sniff Alina, the traces of her perfume and powder, on her clothes, on her own skin. That stolen intimacy excited her; it felt like contraband. She placed a fragrant sweater beside her in bed, or laid on the pillow a handkerchief which she had lent Alina, and would imagine Alina was lying there beside her in the darkness. She heard her darling's voice, words tumbling over themselves as she enthused about something, and the sound of her laughter, they would be the last things Ursule was conscious of as she sank – reluctantly – into sleep.

They had come to sound more alike, she and Alina.

Alina wasn't surprised. She took it in her stride.

'It's the Trummler voice.'

'What?' Ursule laughed.

It was Marianne Trummler, a pupil of Margreth Gräfin in the 1860s, who had taught Sabine Hebbel.

'It's as if they had gramophone records seventy years ago,' Alina said.

Fräulein Hebbel had been telling her colleagues: two talents in one generation, yes, but in the same year, never. Never before, that is, until now. Those colleagues doubted her, until they had an opportunity to hear both students. Then they had to agree, the young women had exceptional clarity and reach. It was hard for them to judge who might be the better: time would decide that.

Mariel Baxter

She had arrived in Vienna in winter.

Spring finally appeared in the soft green of the leaves. She could taste the fresh air, blown this way from the steppes of Hungary. Everything about this Viennese spring felt new to her, but also oddly familiar, for the good reason that it, as Ursule Kroll reminded her, was the subject of so many lieder. Here she was, in the corner of the world – in its capital city – where the majority of those songs had been written. She had come to the source.

Mariel would find Ben quizzing her about Kroll.

'She doesn't talk about herself,' she told him.

'Have you asked her?'

'Asked her what?'

'I don't know. Things.'

'She's not the kind of person you just ask.'

'Perhaps she thinks you're not interested.'

'I'm not, really,' Mariel admitted.

'But *I* am!'

'I think, to her, it's like a separate life she's had.'

'I wonder why.'

'What d'you mean?'

'I wonder why she won't tell you.'

Sometimes she found herself dwelling on the good things that used to happen.

Boston Sundays. Walking, with David or with girlfriends, down to Quincy Market or the Freedom Trail. A movie at the Brattle Theatre on Harvard Square. The other students in the classes. The glory of a Massachusetts Bay sunset.

But she was thinking less and less about them now.

A message was waiting for Ben, from one of his jazz colleagues on the circuit.

Could he make it to the Holofernes Club tomorrow night? The Cuban band they were expecting wouldn't be arriving till nine, and even without a sound check ten o'clock was the very earliest they'd get on stage. Would he be able to make up a trio for an hour or so, and they'd see what they could get out of the kitty to pay him?

Holofernes was teeming when they got there. It was done up to look like hell, but a very polite version, and Mariel thought the effect was charming.

'A little heavy on the red and orange,' Ben remarked.

'Maybe they'll be the hot new thing,' Mariel said.

Ben laughed at her accidental choice of phrase.

The 'Crazy World of Arthur Brown's' record *Fire* opened the proceedings, and then the trio came on to the tiny stage, and in a couple of minutes had built up quite a head of steam. Mariel was relatively new to jazz. She sat trying to get into it. The rhythm was continually changing – that seemed to be the point – and she felt she was always having to play catch-up.

Ben stayed to hear the Cubans, but Mariel was deafened. Even surreptitiously sticking twists of torn paper napkin into her ears didn't help. The room was sweltering.

Saying she had to be back at Vorholzstrasse, she excused herself. She waved from the door. Ben looked over and held up his thumb. Both thumbs. The evening had turned out trumps for him.

Kroll told her that *Die Schöne Müllerin* wasn't what it purported to be. It wasn't singing the praises of a pretty miller's daughter. The singer was racked with jealousy; he was an obsessive, a fantasist. He had wanted to convince himself his beloved was a blameless soul, lured by the wiles of the world. Like all suicides, he was self-centred, really caring only about himself.

'Did Schubert know all this, Fräulein Kroll?'

'The composers, they wrote music we would be discussing many decades later. The performers and critics,' the tone of Kroll's voice was harsher, 'they think they know its final meaning, but they don't. That was the composers' genius.'

Zoë was going out with Lucien. They looked funny together. Lucien was short and dark, a young version of Charles Aznavour, while Zoë was tall and fair with an English peaches-and-cream complexion and an overbred pedigree look about her.

'You're not surprised?' Mariel asked Ben.

'No,' he said. 'Good luck to them.'

'I think I must be missing something.'

'I figured Lucien must be lonely.'

'You fixed them up, you mean?'

'I guessed', Ben laughed, 'Lucien could do with some help.'

Mariel saw that it was simple, incontrovertible clever geometry: two upper-middles had finally got together.

When they met up afterwards, at the Glockenspiel or any other café where there was a crowd, she could always pull Ben to heel by talking about Kroll.

She felt like Scheherezade. Something trivial or something serious. Something true or something not necessarily false, but elaborated. Scheherezade also dressed up her stories, so Mariel was following in yet another noble tradition.

Usually it was at the Glockenspiel.

Mariel had got to like it best, although it stretched her finances to the limit. The bill would be shared out, and she had to take care that she was never there at mealtimes. Coffee and cake was enough for her lunch or supper; some days lunch had to slug it out with supper. (Americans were reckoned to be a byword for extravagance. Not she. But Americans with her background rarely ventured as far as eastern Austria.)

There wasn't an actual glockenspiel in the café, athough there used to be. The prints on the walls showed ones of all shapes and sizes. They made her think of Mozart, and she heard a sunny soundtrack in her head, aware that that was only half the story with Mozart, some of whose gayest music resulted from the times when his life was darkest and most sombre.

Ben bought her a Chagall bunch of pastel flowers from a street barrow.

'What's this for?'

'Just because.'

'Because why?'

'Does it matter?'

'They must've cost—'

'I *wanted* to buy them.'

'Thank you. They're beautiful.'

But back at Vorholzstrasse, Mariel gave them to Frau Werfel. The thought of having them in her room, only to watch for the first signs of fading, was unbearable to her.

She so wanted to be generous, impulsive, just like the man she knew she loved.

Ursule Kroll

A young composer rolled up at the Fleissners one Sunday and proceeded to hold court. Ursule had already heard something about him from Alina.

The Fleissners had been among the earliest admirers of Otto Litzmann. He called himself a Brutal Romantic. That didn't become a school, but it defined his music well enough. Spiky and voluptuous: Richard Strauss's marzipan and whipped cream, but tartly flavoured with lemons.

For Ursule, listening to a Kulturbund concert on the wireless, the music had seduced and repelled at the same time. A few bars lulled you, then the discords broke through. It wasn't even music as Ursule was used to thinking of music, which consoled or diverted and, at its best, ennobled the experience it was describing.

At the Fleissners' the ebullient young composer didn't have to be asked twice to play something on the piano. Ursule was amused by the look of concentration on Alina's face: that was taking family duty too far!

What Litzmann wrote and called music agitated and disturbed; but for Ursule it lacked the courage of his more brazen contemporaries, because it hid – mocking, cocking a snook – behind the flummery of an older order of things, which was transposed not into pastiche but into kitsch. Litzmann laughed at the mention of Reznicek and

Graener and Unger, and called them old reactionaries who'd had their day.

(But why should any of it matter to *her*, Ursule wondered.)

While others applauded his party pieces, Ursule fidgeted with her cuffs. Being à la mode had its drawbacks. Behind her, a couple discussed him, calling him a Temple Yeled. He was Jewish? Yes, of course.

Litzmann's faintly exotic appearance was explained. He wasn't a pin-up, but – if Mariel was honest – she had seen worse.

She looked over and caught Alina's eye – and smiled. Alina winked back, and in a trice the afternoon brightened immeasurably.

A number of paintings by Schiele hung in one of the galleries at the Kunsthalle.

Alina liked them, she liked modernity. Ursule thought they were too twisted to be enjoyed; they made her want to look away. To her, they were sketches, not completed works, and executed with a shaky hand. The figures were thin and bony, undernourished, limbs mangled, whey-faced, ugly, sorrowful. They were people she wouldn't have wanted to know. If she'd seen them coming, she would have crossed the street. But there they were, set inside a frame, attracting respectful attention from those who thought they knew better.

Alina, niece of the sophisticated Fleissners, was as admiring as anyone. When Ursule asked her to explain to her what was so good about Schiele, Alina talked in terms of 'structure', 'proportion', 'palette'. It was simpler for Ursule just to look, but the same aversion, even repugnance, had her averting her gaze to Alina or to the other visitors in the gallery rooms.

'Everyone's got quite different tastes anyway,' Alina said.

There was more to it than that. Alina had always had access to art, in private houses or in galleries, and to books on the subject. She had a more educated eye. Ursule realised she would always be the provincial by comparison.

The Fleissners had taken them to a recital by Maria Ivogün. As well as coloratura operatic arias she sang some Schubert songs, and Ursule sat listening intently. She wasn't aware that Alina's attention had been wandering until later, when she discussed the songs with her.

'Which did you think was best?' Ursule asked.

'Which did you think?'

'I asked you first!' Ursule laughed back at her.

'I wasn't ... I'm not quite ...'

Fräulein Hebbel was also at the recital. She was more critical of the performance.

'I loved "Im Frühling"', Ursule told her at her next lesson.

'That isn't a young person's song,' Fräulein Hebbel informed her.

'Could I try to learn it?'

'"Der Fluss" is the sort of lied people prefer.' Fräulein Hebbel handed her the sheet music of that song. 'It's a crowd pleaser. It will show off your voice better.'

It was true that when Ivogün sang 'Der Fluss', the entire hall (except for Alina) was rapt. But Ursule had felt that the song had too many effects. She was being asked to admire the great Hungarian's breath control, the sudden surges, the attempt to sound river-like.

'Im Frühling' had depths which Ivogün's river didn't have, and there was a sort of carelessness in its sentiments which Ursule had realised was very artful. Possibly Fräulein Hebbel was correct – experience might be needed to put so *little* weight on the lyrics – but experience was about the knowledge you've gained, and you start acquiring knowledge as soon as you can.

Fräulein Hebbel was determined, however.

'"Der Fluss" suits your voice better. It will last a whole minute longer. It's a show piece.'

One day Ursule saw the ornamental lettering of the title among the music in Alina's case.

'Im Frühling.'

'Are you studying this?'

'What's that?'

'"Im Frühling"?'

Alina made a face.

'It's a wonderful song,' Ursule said.

'Not to sing it isn't.'

Alina sighed and blew out her cheeks.

'Have you lost interest in it?' Ursule asked.

'Don't sound surprised! I never had any.'

'You asked to do it, though?'

'Oh no. No, I said I wanted to learn "Die Junge Nonne".'

Ursule rapidly calculated that Alina had received 'Im Frühling' at least a couple of weeks after Fräulein Hebbel had given 'Der Fluss' to her.

'The old girl said it suits my voice. "People don't always want show pieces," she told me. "They prefer something subtler." But', Alina shrugged, 'I don't know.'

'I don't know either,' Ursule said, not really meaning Alina to hear.

What was Fräulein Hebbel up to?

They had gone away for the day together, the two of them. A holiday from music, on the train.

It got hotter and hotter.

'We should have gone to the sea, to Blankenese,' Alina said. 'But I thought a forest would be cool.'

'It's just fine,' Ursule told her.

She didn't think it mattered where she might have gone with Alina, so long as they were together.

The forest was quiet and still. And very sultry. They came to a pool which was fed by a stream. They sat on the edge, with their feet in the water, before deciding they would try swimming. Ursule stripped to her underwear. Alina didn't stop there, but removed everything. She laughed at her friend's surprise.

'No one will see us! They didn't have swimsuits in classical times.'

Alina was right, there was something ancient-seeming, timeless, about this sylvan spot.

Ursule unhooked her brassiere, then pulled down her pants. It was the most natural feeling in the world, she thought, to be exposed and vulnerable to the elements. No artifice at all, no dissembling.

Alina went ahead and dropped down into the pool. Ursule followed, gasping as she immersed herself in the cool water. The water was clear, and Alina's body was perfectly visible to her as she struck out on her front, then returned swimming on her back.

Ursule saw that her own nipples had hardened, to little blunt bullets. Closer to where the stream ran into the pool, she experienced the rush of flowing water between her legs and opened them wider to enjoy the sensation.

The forest settled round them. The birds resumed their singing. Ursule put her head back and looked up into a cloudless blue sky.

Her pleasure was all the greater for being unplanned. Here she was, closer to her Alina than she had ever been, naked, floating in the water at right angles, with their legs entwined.

Let nothing come between us, she thought. But she also felt that this wasn't enough.

She pretended to lose her balance and reached out for Alina. She put her arms round her, drew her close so that their breasts touched. Alina felt the hardness of Ursule's nipples and looked down, surprised and laughing. Ursule submerged her hands to Alina's waist, as if the current was pulling her down. She dropped her head beneath the water, keeping her eyes open. Holding on to Alina's waist, she let her own legs float to the side, while she drew her head closer to Alina's groin. The hair, as delicate as weed, was showing pink.

Ursule hesitated.

A couple of seconds later Alina's laughing face was beneath the water and in front of hers. They both held out their hands while their legs stretched out behind. Plaiting their fingers together, they turned a circle.

Simultaneously the two of them rose for air, breaking the surface at the same moment. Alina's laughter reached up into the trees.

The whole day was marked by Alina's good humour. Ursule, as happy as she was, envied Alina her capacity for unalloyed joy.

'Please tell me your secret, Alina.'

'There's no secret.'

'No? Really?'

'I'm always like this.'

'Today you're even more so.'

'Ah ...'

That 'Ah'. Ursule lay naked on the rug on the grass, on her front like Alina, watching her friend just inches away. What did Alina mean? She hardly dared to believe what it was she might be thinking.

Alina's eyes were closed.

Ursule reached out, placed her fingertips not where she longed to place them but on the small of Alina's back, just skimming the skin.

My darling, my sweetheart—

Alina opened her eyes.

'Oh, it's you.'

'Of course it's me. Who else would it be?'

'What's the matter?'

'"The matter?"' Ursule repeated.

'I felt your fingers—'

'Oh ...' Ursule spoke quickly, making up a reason. 'There was an insect, I was just brushing it off.'

'You're always so thoughtful.'

Ursule stuck a smile on to her face. In any other situation, the compliment would have delighted her. But at this moment, lying naked with Alina on the grass, it wasn't all she was hoping for.

Ah ...

'We'll burn.'

'What?'

Alina was reaching out for her clothes. By mistake she had got hold of Ursule's brassiere.

'What a joke!'

'Pardon?' Ursule said.

'Let's put on each other's clothes!'

That was how they returned to the city. It was a very strange sensation. For much of the journey Ursule was silent. She was concentrating on not moistening the crotch of Alina's pants. She hoped Alina was leaving traces of herself on her own clothes, so that she would be able to take deep breaths of her afterwards, once she was back in her room, alone, with no need to feel any shame, with the runnel between her legs sodden and burning to her own greedy touch.

Alina didn't catch on. Ursule wasn't sure that even *she* understood. Maria Semmelrogge would have been shocked, she felt, by this Hamburg young woman, with her physical wants. Where had she learned them?

Only a woman, surely, could appreciate what might make another woman feel pleasure. It was unnatural not to be drawn to attractiveness in your own sex – after all you spent so much time looking into the mirror trying to find it in yourself. When you found what would be so personally desirable, but in another person, why should you not celebrate it and want to lay claim to it?

Alina's mind didn't seem to work that way. (Unless she was cleverly bluffing? But duplicity wasn't in her nature.) Ursule was as sorry about her failure to respond as she could be about anything, but – if Alina really suspected nothing – it was also a relief to her. They could continue to be the best of friends, and even if their closeness didn't deepen to anything more intimate, nothing would be lost either.

2008

Time seemed to have no meaning in this apartment.

Had minutes or an hour gone by?

'How long do you mean to be in Vienna?' Kroll asked.

'Until Saturday.'

'Have you an itinerary?'

'No. No, I don't.'

She could have pretended otherwise. *I want to see this, do that.*
Sitting in this apartment, in its tomblike silence, she felt peculiarly
disinclined to the task.

She had come from New York to Vienna in a rush. Up, off and
away. It was disconcerting enough to be back in this city, with all
its associations for her. She had spent all the years since trying to
adjust to the experience.

'Not even the Belvedere?'

Kroll was asking the question with a perfectly straight face. But
why had she mentioned the Belvedere in particular?

'Everyone who comes to Vienna does certain things while they're
here,' Kroll said.

'Maybe they do.'

'You're not everyone?'

Mariel shook her head. Why feign?

Her Vienna existed mostly in her head. Being here was almost incidental. So, just why *had* she come?

'You're very comfortable,' she said, speaking over her other thoughts.

'You approve, do you?'

'Yes.'

Kroll was, of course, goading her, but she wouldn't be provoked.

'Tell me about the opera here in Vienna.'

'Are you interested?'

'Yes,' Mariel said. 'Yes, I'm interested.'

'What do you want me to tell you?'

'Do you go?'

'Not now.'

'*Did* you go?'

'Rarely.'

'They didn't put on anything you wanted to see?'

'Modern singers sound much the same to me. They have so little individuality. They are on the surface of the characters. They don't study properly. A chest voice used for Mozart! Directors and conductors nowadays know no better. Just listen to how it used to be done.'

'The old recordings are the best?'

'Naturally they are. Why are you smiling?'

'Am I?'

'You think recordings today are better?'

Mariel hesitated.

'The technical quality is better,' she said.

'I'm not talking about that.'

'I know you're not. But I suppose *I'*m a modern singer.'

'It was different for you,' Kroll said. 'You had the advantage of studying here.'

'Does that mean I'm exempt from your criticism?'

'I haven't seen you in opera.'

'But maybe you've heard me?'

'You didn't send me any of your records.'

Mariel smiled squeakily, too brightly.

'I – I don't do that.'

'You're too modest?' Kroll asked her.

Mariel forced herself to keep smiling.

'Or you thought I would be displeased?'

'Displeased? How?'

'There are many ways.'

'Sending out records is just a habit I never got into. It – it prevents embarrassment, people feeling they have to say things.'

'What do you think I would have said to you?'

'I have no idea. Perhaps you wouldn't have spoken to me about it at all.'

'We shall never know, shall we?'

The tone was quite equable, Mariel felt, even though they were treading on eggshells.

She sat in the stillness, trying to calculate Kroll's age. She must be – at least ninety. From her appearance Mariel might have guessed eighty or a few years less. But the history of her times defined her. Reference books didn't give a year of birth: that was the prerogative of a very old woman, and one who had become a famous star early on. In 1980 she must have been in her mid-sixties: to Mariel then, Kroll had seemed far enough away from her in age for the specifics not to matter. Now the gap in years was much narrower than when Mariel first knew her.

No, not 'knew'. Mariel had never *known* the woman. How could a jejune twenty-two-year-old have broken through the defences which Ursule Kroll had famously erected against an invasive world?

Ursule Kroll

She and Alina had been up in the top row of the top circle, in the gods, at the Staatsoper. During the interval they were spotted, where they were standing on the mezzanine level looking down at the great and the good of Hamburg.

'We met at the Fleissners, do you remember?'

It was Otto Litzmann.

He was with a small group of dignitaries; the men were in evening dress.

'We're in a box. Come and join us.'

He sought permission from his hosts. They wouldn't have refused him such a simple request as that, and looked over in the girls' direction very agreeably.

Ursule consulted Alina. It had been Alina's idea to come here.

'Why not?'

Ursule was disappointed. Alina was taking the invitation in her stride, and didn't seem put out.

'Come on!' Alina grabbed her arm. 'What's to stop us?'

It felt quite different, sitting as close to the stage as this. Ursule had a sense of being in the line of vision of everyone in the audience. But the others in the box were sublimely unaware; or, at any rate, they seemed quite unfazed by the public's attention.

Their guest was at home with them, even if *his* guests weren't.

Litzmann smiled round at them from his front seat, as if to say, '*This* is the life!' They found themselves included in an invitation to a private reception afterwards. Champagne flowed freely, and the canapés were delicious. Meanwhile Otto Litzmann was approached by this person and that, mostly other Jews. Ursule detected a cooler response from the Hamburg bourgeoise or grandees reduced to accepting others' lavish hospitality. They certainly didn't go out of their way to offer Litzmann praise for music they must have failed, like her, to understand.

He was taking full advantage of his good fortune though. (Singer had commissioned a piece from him, and Rosenstock was going to conduct ...) He basked in the compliments – while his eyes astutely worked the room.

Life in Hamburg changed after that.

Two became three.

Wherever Ursule and Alina went now, Litzmann came too. The first few times Alina had invited him to join them only after the two women had exchanged a look and Ursule had – grudgingly – given Alina the go-ahead. She didn't approve, but she couldn't think of a good reason why not. Once or twice, at the beginning, she had taken Alina aside.

'Don't you like him?' was Alina's response.

'It's not the same as two. Just *us*.'

'Well, I suppose I can take him another time.'

On her own? No, Ursule wasn't going to risk that.

It turned into a matter of course that Litzmann would go with them. Ursule wasn't sure how this had come about. He had a car certainly, and he would arrive punctually at a prearranged time, and who could fault his attention to them both?

She realised later that the two of them, Alina and Litzmann, were taking trips in the car which they didn't tell her about in advance.

'But I never know that he's going to ask me, Ursule. And by then, it's too late, I can't find you.'

Ursule wished she could believe her dearest friend. Whenever she couldn't track down Alina, she knew she must be with Litzmann. She blamed Litzmann. Alina wouldn't have thought of leaving her out deliberately, how could she? They had shared so much. She thought Litzmann must be either thoughtless, and selfish as men were, or jealous.

The conversation now went three ways. Sometimes it seemed to be all between Alina and Litzmann, except when Alina made an effort to bring Ursule in. Alina stopped travelling in the front of the car for a while – Litzmann had thought Ursule would have more room for her legs in the back, if she positioned herself sideways – and they occupied the back seat together. But it wasn't very comfortable like that.

'You try the front seat, Ursule.'

That didn't work either, because it meant Litzmann was talking most of the time to Alina over his right shoulder.

Ursule would have ignored him if she could. But he always had something to say, which would be controversial or even half-amusing in a caustic way, and she might respond in kind. It was *he* who decided where they went. She accompanied them because Alina said it was a chance for 'us two girls' to get out of the city and see places, but more to the point because Ursule didn't want to let the pair of them out of her sight.

Along the banks of the Elbe, Alina would point out a villa in which she wanted to live one day. 'One day ...' She made it sound very far away.

'I'm sure you will,' Litzmann would say, 'if you wish for it hard enough.'

Alina would close her eyes, picturing whichever of the properties she happened to be keenest on at present. Ursule would close her eyes also – wishing it was Litzmann who was far, far away.

'I wouldn't like to think that my lessons are interfering with your pleasure,' Fräulein Hebbel said.

Ursule smiled sweetly.

'My lessons are very important to me.'

'Not as important as your pleasure, I'm sure.'

Ursule couldn't think of a reply quickly enough.

'Pleasure only lasts for that moment,' Fräulein Hebbel said.

Actually quite a lot of moments, Ursule thought, when they're all joined together. But she didn't dare to venture that opinion to Fräulein, and wiped her face clean of the thought.

'Young people always believe they know best.'

'I don't think so, Fräulein Hebbel.'

'You're correcting me, are you?'

The woman smiled. Ursule decided not to do likewise, and to offer a little humility instead.

Otto Litzmann had shown Alina how to drive, and now she was learning English because *he* was learning English.

'Why does he want to speak English?'

'In case he goes to England or America.'

'Why would he go to England or America?'

Alina looked thoughtful.

'To work. To make a living.'

Ursule loved that suddenly preoccupied expression, which would sit so prettily on Alina's face. Unfortunately it often had to do with Otto Litzmann, so that it pained Ursule as well as pleased her.

'Well, I had better learn English too,' Ursule said, and Alina told her she would teach her everything that she'd picked up from her teacher, Otto.

In the car they sometimes only spoke English, to practise. Ursule had to keep up, to be able to interrupt them from the back seat, so that she wasn't forgotten about. She borrowed books in English from the Fleissners, and when she couldn't sleep – for thinking about

Litzmann, and how he had pushed himself between her and Alina without so much as a by-your-leave or hint of remorse – she would pick any of them up and start reading, undeterred if she couldn't get the full sense of one passage but proceeding to the next.

Her English had many flaws. Later she would search out copies of those same books she'd read – when the Fleissners' library had been cast to the four winds – and embark on them again, but slowly and with greater care, and the memories would fly off the page: memories of herself as she used to be, and Alina and the Fleissners, and hardly any – almost none – of that spoiler Otto Litzmann.

A new company was staging a production of *Der Rosenkavalier* in Hamburg. They were looking for the stars of the future.

'The fact is, they can't pay you very well,' Fräulein Hebbel told them. 'But this staging will get attention. They have hired me to assist. When was a woman ever asked?'

Ursule didn't have the nerve to resist.

The first performance caused an uproar. It would have been gratifying to think that their singing was the cause, but the press spoke of the production's 'heightened sensuality', its 'hothouse atmosphere'.

Ursule Kroll sang the Marschallin, and Alina Octavian. Alina found rehearsals hard: it was difficult for her to keep a straight face.

'Don't you think this is so ridiculous? Such bad taste! I won't let my aunt and uncle come.'

Ursule was troubled in different ways. It wasn't easy playing a woman in her middle years, afflicted by time's passing. What bothered her more were the stage movements, choreographed by Fräulein Hebbel to the impassioned music and so strangely intimate in that very public venue: as if these two singers should really have been a man and a woman. (In that case, Ursule felt sure, the theatre would have been closed down, and the management fined for offending public morals.)

These rehearsals, which Alina would laugh over afterwards, came back to rack Ursule's dreams at night. She woke up hot all over, and damp with sweat. The bedding was soaked. She passed her hands everywhere that a lover might. She did things to herself that made her ashamed. She tried to think of the men that she knew, but none of them belonged in this night frenzy. The music pulsed through her head, louder than her blood. Her fingers were wanton. She couldn't help herself. The Marschallin couldn't help herself either. Why not? It's only the way of the world, she had to sing. This is how I am. In the middle of the night, in the darkness of her room, Ursule felt she was more herself than she was at any other time. This was the secret self, which nobody else saw.

Next day, Fräulein Hebbel would be watching her with narrowed eyes: as if she saw the evidence of mental agitation. Stage fright? Anxiety about her lines or performing before an audience? Or was it possible that Fräulein Hebbel saw closer to the truth of the matter?

There was now a shared lesson every week, for Alina and herself. They studied duets. On those days, if Alina happened to be out of the room for some reason and Ursule and Fräulein Hebbel were left by themselves, the silence felt oddly charged, as it wasn't through their ordinary lessons. *Der Rosenkavalier* had upset the balance of everything.

Alina would tell her about Litzmann's difficulties. Somebody had cut him dead, someone else had slandered him, the Kulturbund Opera's commission was in doubt.

Ursule couldn't bring herself to say she was sorry. She supposed that Litzmann helped to bring those problems on himself. Because she only listened, Alina must have thought she was being sympathetic.

'Otto told me there's a Yiddish proverb: "If folk knew what others intended for them, they would kill themselves!"'

Some people invite travails, Ursule felt. Litzmann was one. It was a way of attracting attention. She didn't really sympathise at all. The Jews all stuck together when it came to business, and if things were so bad why was the NSKG still supporting him? He was crying wolf.

She only regretted that Alina was having to worry some of the prettiness out of her face, and her youthfulness, on that man's account. A few little lines had appeared where the skin had been quite unblemished before. Ursule couldn't forgive Litzmann for that.

She didn't even like to refer to him by his name. He, him, his: that was adequate. Maybe if they didn't use his name he would recede, and Alina – just perhaps – would start to forget him.

If only. That crucial conditional infected every other thought in Ursule's head. *If only.*

2008

'Can I come back again?'

'Come back?'

'Come back and see you?'

'I ...'

'Or could we meet somewhere?'

'I don't leave this apartment much.'

'That doesn't matter. We could just – talk.'

'If that is what you want.'

'Only if it isn't inconveniencing you.'

'How would it be? When I do so little.'

'That is your privilege.'

'My "privilege"?'

'To do – just as you wish.'

'Because I'm a ruin?'

'No, I didn't mean that.'

'What did you mean?'

'Because of your reputation.'

Kroll didn't reply to that, but lowered her eyes to her visitor's feet. Mariel suddenly felt self-conscious, as if she was the student again. A $600 pair of boots, Charles Jourdan, and she still felt she failed to pass the test.

And here she was, asking for more of the same treatment?

'Three o'clock.'

'"Three o'clock"?' Mariel repeated.

'Come then.'

'Thank you. Three, that's perfect.'

Kroll offered her a very small, very sceptical smile.

We're exhausted, Mariel realised, both of us.

She moved quickly to the door, before Kroll had a chance to think better of her offer.

'Goodbye, Fräulein.'

That was what she used to say, long ago. But in Vienna time seemed to run to different rules, when nearly thirty years ago seemed no further away than yesterday. If she'd looked in a mirror at this instant, Mariel would have expected to see a naïve but compliant young woman still stuck in her adolescence.

'Till tomorrow,' she said.

From outside on the landing, as Mariel looked back into the apartment, Kroll was already losing definition. She seemed just as she'd been when Mariel arrived, with daylight in the distance behind her, an outline with the details missing.

It was good to be outside.

Mariel was feeling light-headed from her confinement.

She stopped briefly under the trees. The silver-haired man she'd seen earlier, in the green loden coat, was turning the corner of the street ahead of her.

Mariel stood listening to the silence, through the notes of birdsong overhead and other fragments of sound – the unseen passing of a car, the scratching of last autumn's leaves, water gurgling in a culvert, a pair of footsteps somewhere. It was seductive, this zen-like hiatus in the day. Vienna was a city fashioned to be the crucible of history – while *this* felt, very pleasantly, like the evidence of neglect, what had been overlooked. But of course only the well-to-do could afford to enjoy this tranquillity. *They* weren't here by mere accident. They were the ones who had played history, calculating the odds, as if it was a game of roulette.

Suddenly Mariel had the sensation – a sixth sense – of eyes burning into the back of her neck from the apartment window. That was her cue to move on. She was tempted to look over her shoulder, but she'd had enough of looking back for one day.

She wanted to get back into the noise, activity, fractured existence, other lives brushing past her on the city-centre streets, too much happening for her to be able to concentrate on anything in particular, on an April evening with May starting to bloom already, this *now*.

*

Kroll stood at the window watching.

She had a headache.

She wanted now to say 'no'.

If the woman had turned at this moment, she would have signalled to her from the window.

'No, don't come. Don't return here.'

But, as Kroll watched, her visitor began walking. There was no attempt to look back.

Where the man in the green coat who haunted this road had gone a couple of minutes before, round the corner beneath the budding branches, Mariel Baxter followed.

*

All she had to go back to was her hotel room.

She told the taxi driver to take her by the Ringstrasse.

'It costs more to go that way.'

'I'll tell you when I run out of money.'

The man looked alarmed. The Viennese Mariel had gotten to know as a visiting student had never been very strong on humour: or rather – how could humans survive without it? – their sense of humour was very local, very private, they shared it among themselves.

She wasn't really aware of what she was seeing through the windows. In her mind she was still in that apartment. She had done something she'd promised herself she would never do: she had come back. The Ringstrasse, in its portentous stone dignity, wasn't any more convincing to her than a piece of stage trickery, meant to subjugate people and amuse the tourists, while the apartment on Graf-Rhena-Strasse – feeling like a stage set – was the hard, brutal truth of the situation.

They had unfinished business, Mariel Baxter and Ursule Kroll.

*

'Why couldn't she stay in America?' Brigitte asked.

'The world has become very small for the Mariel Baxters.'

'You had a rule.'

'I know.'

'No Americans. She is different?'

Kroll sighed at the question.

'You haven't answered me.'

'No, Brigitte.'

'Well?'

'She was my student.'

'The things you've said about her!'

'The things I've said about everybody.'

Brigitte placed the used china noisily on the tray. There was no point in warning her to be careful, however; she didn't have to be told her job after all this time.

Kroll picked up a cushion to shake it out.

'*I* do that,' Brigitte snapped, and snatched the cushion out of her hands.

*

The taxi stopped at traffic lights.

A girl of about sixteen or seventeen waited obediently for the sign to flash so that she could cross the road. The girl glanced into the car.

Mariel felt embarrassed. Sitting here, she realised she was just the kind of woman she used to *pity*. She had that jaded, isolated look which would have left the Mariel Baxter of twenty-eight years before praying she would never turn into such a person.

*

When Brigitte had gone, Kroll left the apartment in darkness.

It was Sabine Hebbel who had told her that we forget how they lived in Schubert's time. The short days, made as long as possible, and candlelight in the evenings. They rose early, at first light, and greeted the sun. They endured every winter for the joy of greeting spring, for the sight of the first green shoots and buds.

Kroll had never forgotten that. Every time she sang Schubert, or Haydn, or Mozart, she would think of those lives lived by nature's clock. She used to tell her students.

Nowadays novelty was everything. Precedent was boring. You were always looking for a new angle. The past was so long ago.

But really the past is always present, it's never done.

*

This year Mariel would be fifty.

There had been ominously few hints that any birthday events were being planned. Record companies and promoters had a way of using every opportunity. For that you had to be in the public's affection, though, or your name had to have common currency.

Careerwise, Mariel was hanging on in there. Lou Litvinoff had been losing some clients to the Grim Reaper recently, so she was now among the elect who had been with him longest. He still gave her his attention, and pretended it was undivided. She counted her blessings: *shalom uv'rachah*, peace and blessings on the man.

And still she hadn't met Miriam Litvinoff. A photo sat on the desk in his office, taken some time in the 1960s. A Jewish princess: reared on milk and honey, compelling sloe-black eyes, and something about her that hinted at a pampered manner.

Every now and then Mariel had got upwind – or down – of L.L. and smelt sex from him: his afternoon girls. Perhaps that was why he waited on till eight or nine p.m. at the office, making up for lost time before heading down to Washington Square and Mrs L., in her all-day peignoir and open-toed mules.

Nothing had occurred between L.L. and herself. Not even a hint of it. That went against form: if not with him, then definitely with her.

Once she had assumed a man to be married, but he turned out to be a widower forever speaking about his wife in the present tense. Very confusing *that* was.

On stage for rehearsals in Houston (a production of Menotti's *The Medium*), while her fellow singers flashed signals at her with their eyes and even mouthed at her to stop, she brazenly flirted with the director, perfectly aware that his wife was sitting somewhere mid-stalls with their patrons.

Who could say, perhaps the last eighteen months had been a punishment for that?

Or for something worse?

*

Kroll removed the elastic bands and let her address book fall open where it would.

It was a very old friend, made to her specification in Robert Horn's Viennese workshops. The cover was white ostrich skin, now the colour of ivory. The catch had snapped a long time ago, owing to the pressure on the pages of insertions – calling cards, scraps of letter headings with addresses and phone numbers, names jotted down on a shop receipt or the end of cigarette cartons, proper business cards, photographs torn out of newspapers and magazines of people she considered might be worth speaking to.

She had bought other address books to replace it, but in the end she always preferred to go back to this one, knowing where everything was. She couldn't have faced the task of editing the entries. This way she was able to hold on to the names which had been rubbed out (never completely invisible) with an eraser, or scored through with red ink – either because they'd died or because she had taken umbrage – as if they were ghosts tarrying in an old house.

So much of her past was contained in her precious address book. People had gone, buildings and even streets had disappeared, but she retained the memory of them, in the handwriting which she could date to a particular era of her life.

*

Up in her room, Mariel thumbed the buttons on her TV remote.

The screen blinked like an eye, holding the world.

She stopped at CNN. The weather forecast. Tomorrow, the girl on the screen promised brightly as she swept her hand down East Africa, there would be showers in Madagascar.

Dienstag

Tuesday

2008

En route to the hotel's 24-hour breakfast, Mariel picked up the new issue of a music magazine along with her newspaper.

The cover featured Harnoncourt, as well as a new-artist violinist, yet another young Russian. They were as prolific as female tennis players.

Waiting for the waiter to bring her coffee she riffled through the pages. Stopped. Her eyes instantly fixed. It was a full-page ad for the latest soprano on the block, Cara Michaels. Another of those photographs from the fuck-me-in-Versace session, but with even more lip gloss on that pout and more airbrush work on the tanned shoulders (she'd noticed the real-life freckles) and the expanse of flesh down to her globular breasts stuffed into – half *out of* – the sheeny gown.

She looked like a cheap Vegas hooker. That bothered no one, Mariel realised.

She glanced up, did a double-take. A man was looking over at her from his table, clearly curious. She closed the magazine and pushed it into her bag. She swallowed another mouthful of coffee and got up and left, aiming the merest – the vaguest – of smiles in her fellow guest's direction.

*

In the darkness, Kroll realised, she must have brushed against an arrangement of flowers. Every so often a bouquet in cellophane would be delivered to the door, with or without a card to tell her who had sent them. She always had fresh flowers in the apartment.

This morning Brigitte was down on her knees, gathering the petals and complaining sullenly about the stains left by the stamens.

'It's your carpet. If you're going to be so thoughtless.'

'I'm sorry, Brigitte.'

'But it's me who has to clean the carpet. It looks like new. Or it did till you knocked into the flowers.'

'You always say I've ruined the carpet, but you always clean it so nicely.'

'I'm too old for getting down on my knees.'

Brigitte very rarely spoke about her own age or infirmities, only about her employer's.

Kroll was appalled. Brigitte could abuse her as much as she liked, but hearing her bemoan her own state of health was a different matter. What in God's name would she do without Brigitte?

'Can't you look where you're going?'

'I'm sorry—'

'There's plenty more I could be doing.'

'Yes, Brigitte. I realise that.'

Was it possible that Brigitte had tears in her eyes as she pulled herself to her feet? She wouldn't accept help, and shied away from Kroll. Brigitte would brush her hair for her, but she wouldn't have Kroll offer her physical support: that wasn't her place.

'Nothing shows, Brigitte.'

Brigitte didn't speak. She had turned her head away.

'The rug is fine. Thank you, Brigitte.'

Even after so many years, Kroll still feared Brigitte and craved her approval. How many more days would be left to them like this one, with the two of them in their strangely ordered balance?

Mariel Baxter

Ben packed thirty hours into his day. He was tireless.

He was translating and researching, and giving occasional piano lessons, as well as playing his jazz. Ostensibly he was over here to copy-edit for a Viennese art publisher selling books to English-speaking countries.

'The States. But they won't pay US prices. So that's why they get an English guy, because he's cheap.'

He also translated technical material for an engineering company's manuals and brochures, taught English, and conducted musical research on the spot for not one but two harassed media academics, one in New Haven and the other in London, who each employed a team of researchers to do the hack work from which their populist books were artfully constructed. The Yale professor's next exercise had as its subject the influence of German and other European composers on Hollywood. This had allowed Ben to follow several lines of enquiry of his own, and to write some of them up as articles.

'Waste not, want not. Everything gets used in the end.'

He told Mariel there was a lot to be done about the Nazis. Totalitarianism and the Arts. The Furtwängler dilemma: how do you sustain a career under such circumstances? Can you ever *ignore* politics? Is being an artist a case of being complicitous?

'Sometimes there's no answer,' he said. 'But sometimes there is.'

He picked up a copy of '*Du bist die Ruh*' Mariel had placed between them on the park bench. It had Ursule Kroll's initials stamped on the front, an incontrovertible mark of ownership.

'Vienna is filled with the unrepentant. People who have never said sorry. The word's not in their vocabulary.'

He fingered the music reverentially, like a relic.

'Someone would pay good money for this, you know.'

That possibility had never occurred to Mariel.

'They'd want to buy it?'

'Sure.'

'Some sheet music?'

'Straight, no chaser.'

Mariel stared at him.

'You could say you'd lost it, and ...'

'And what?' she asked him.

'And move from that crummy place you're in on the profits.'

'Move where?'

'To somewhere nicer.'

She hesitated, but only for a split second.

'I couldn't.'

'Move?'

'No, I couldn't sell that music.'

'It's okay.' Ben laughed. 'I'm just joking.'

She wondered if he was or not.

Mariel had noticed a stocky woman looking in through the café's rain-spattered window. She wore a belted mackintosh and was sheltered by an umbrella. She stood on the spot, and seemed to be watching them. *Them*, in particular.

Mariel kept an eye trained on her. She couldn't see the woman's face.

Why did she feel the expression would have been disapproving?

Throughout the city, Mariel knew, there were people like that woman, with no fondness for the English-speaking visitors who came here. Ben had told her that Hamburg was just the same or worse, with a bias still against the Jews and fond memories of the Reich.

The onlooker tilted her head, trying to look in through the rain runs on the window. This only encouraged Mariel to play up. She got jokey, she laughed, acted out astonishment or pity or horror or kindliness on her face using exaggerated gestures.

'Who did you say you were?' the girl asked her.

'Mariel.'

'Mariel?'

'Mariel Baxter.'

'It's a bad line.'

Perhaps. But she could hear the voices in the background perfectly well.

'I'm calling from—'

'I'll go look for David.'

The receiver was left to dangle on its cord. It banged against the wall in the hall.

Mariel stood holding Frau Werfel's receiver, counting the seconds. Ten. Twenty. Thirty. She looked at her watch, staring at the stilted motion of the second hand.

She listened to voices, unable to make out what they were saying. Music. A peal of laughter.

Seventy-five seconds. Ninety.

It was the *Saturday Night Fever* soundtrack. David wouldn't even go with her to that movie, he had refused point-blank.

Then the sound of something smashing, a plate or a cup, in the shared kitchen. Another whoop of laughter. A slamming door.

Someone's footsteps. But they carried on past the phone. A man's whistling.

A second salvo from the apartment door. And another sound

to which she pictured a fist hammering on the wall, unblocking an airlock in a water pipe.

She waited until the minute hand reached seven, 6.35 a.m., which meant two minutes had passed. Then she quite calmly put down the receiver.

She didn't know what was going on in Joshua Street, not the first thing, and wondered if she had ever really got into the mind of David Corey.

She called Ben from a payphone in a café.

'The Belvedere,' he suggested. 'Meet you there. At two. Okay?'

'Okay.'

That made everything bearable again.

Ben knew which galleries he wanted to show her. Together they walked through rooms of Klimts and Schieles.

Everywhere Mariel turned, her eyes were greeted by yet another erotic composition.

It was hard to tell with those interlocking couples, if their abandonment wasn't also a kind of frenzied violence. She wasn't actually *persuaded* by those embraces and kisses, just as she wasn't won over when couples performed their lovers' gestures in the streets, in full view. Nevertheless, the paintings left her feeling she had received some sort of electric charge. She seemed to be in a heightened state of arousal. As was the case with Ben, she noticed, accidentally brushing the back of her hand against his crotch as she stepped back. Her hand burned; saliva spurted inside her mouth, her breathing came faster, she realised the colour was rising on her face.

She went outside for some air, telling Ben she would be back. But there was no easy escape. In the gardens, on a walkway, she remembered what Ben had read to her about Klimt and the tree of life, the tree of knowledge; women who turned into trees, who spread their fecundity through nature, offering rebirth and the prospect of paradise.

Or something like that. Loving and dancing and trees. Even the trees were sensual objects in Vienna. Nothing was straightforward.

These tiered gardens, as Ben explained when he came out to find her, alluded to classical legends. The lowest celebrated the four elements, the middle one Parnassus, and the upper Olympus.

They stopped at a stone sphinx. Being a Viennese sphinx, she was sporting two spherical breasts with pointed nipples.

Ben stood fondling one orb.

The sphinx wore a sullen pout.

Ben saw Mariel staring, and laughed, either at the sphinx or at her.

'A girl with a history!'

To Mariel's relief it was agreed that they'd had enough high art for one day. They now set off on foot to Südbahnhof, to get a train back up to town.

'It's only two stops, with a change, to Keplerplatz,' Ben said.

'Where's that?'

'Favoriten. About four blocks from where I live.'

They could have walked from Belvedere to Favoriten. It might have been quicker even. But Mariel guessed that this way *she was being given time to think*. Think about what? About how Ben was helping her on to the train and off, with his arm about her waist, about how he kissed her on Südtiroler Platz platform, about how tightly he held her hand on the last stretch of the journey, about how they missed Keplerplatz because they were kissing again, about how his tongue slipped in and out of her mouth so expertly, about the hardness inside his trousers pressing against her abdomen, about how neither of them was caring they'd missed the stop, about how a bell rang at Reumannplatz to tell them they'd reached the terminus.

It wasn't far to go, Ben told her. And I have Klimt to thank for this, she was reflecting as she seemed to go *skimming* along the street. She thought of another famous artist, of the floating airborne world – Chagall, again – levitating lovers, soaring skywards and cartwheeling above rooftops. She felt weirdly numbed, anaesthetised. It was as if ... as if this street, this ordinary street, had been waiting for her all her life, waiting for this day.

A Sunday. No Kroll. But she had intruded into Mariel's thoughts notwithstanding. Mariel tried to get rid of her, tried to banish her by laughing up into the trees about something Ben had just said. She wouldn't, she *wouldn't*, give Kroll the space.

Ben took a key out of his pocket.

'D'you have the place to yourself?'

'No such luck. The centaur will be at the gate.'

'Frau Knuth?'

'Those battle-axe landladies, they must've all rolled off a production line circa 1925. But I pay my rent, so that's that.'

Mariel smiled at him. She smiled a little nervously, but also as an encouragement to herself. She understood what was going to happen next. *You've had to come all the way from Beacon Hill and David Corey to reach here, but get here you did, you've made it at last.*

'Remember the number?' Ben asked her.

'Forty-six.'

'No hesitation.'

'None at all,' she said.

'Here we are. *Willkommen.*'

'*Bienvenu.*'

'Welcome.'

Ben was assured, speedy, considerate, gentle, and eager to check if he had satisfied her. He knew that she had nothing to compare it with. (She had never gone all the way with David, back in Boston. It was called going to 'South Station', which was the big terminus there, at the end of the line. Instead they would 'get off at Back Bay', the penultimate stop.) Yet she was happy that he asked her; she was so grateful that she found herself crying into his shoulder in bed. He held her closer, and she felt at that moment loved and protected as she'd never been in her adult life.

At some point a floorboard creaked outside the door. And creaked again. They looked over from the narrow bed. Ben mouthed Frau Knuth's name, and something obscene about her. Mariel giggled, and he placed his hand over her mouth. Then, when she wouldn't stop, he put his mouth on top of hers to siphon all the sounds away.

A little later she saw Ben staring at the blood stains seeping across his white sheets.

'Don't be surprised!' she told him.

'I'm not.'

'That's what happens.'

'It's not that.'

'What is it?'

He just smiled at her, very tenderly.

'I'll clean up,' she said. 'I'll steep them in cold water.'

'You really will, won't you?'

'Well, *I* did it.'

'Not exactly unaided.'

'No.'

He gathered her up and it happened all over again. This time she knew what to expect, and she tried to deepen the pleasure for both of them. Sweatily each slithered over the other. Sometimes she was on top, sometimes beneath. Now he got there ahead of her, but only just. He stayed inside her until her last spasms had faded to echoes. She ended up astride him, a hot, soft, sticky melt of contentment.

Nothing in her life so far had been a match for it, to the last quivering nerve ends of her body.

Ursule Kroll

In the early days she and Alina were hired to sing, either singly or sometimes together, at social gatherings. Fräulein Hebbel considered it useful, to them and to herself. Later, the tone of the transactions changed as the two young women set their own tariff of fees and expenses.

One of their patrons was already acquainted with the Fleissners. She was the surviving sister of Ernst Steinicke, the newspaper publisher and philanthropist. Compared with the Niklas-Schwarzenbergers, Jutta Steinicke was nouveau riche, and ostentatious; she was stouter than those inbred guests at the Schloss Esterhofen, and dressed by Schiaparelli herself in Paris. But she was one of life's enthusiasts, which was, Ursule believed, her saving grace. She loved music, almost to excess. At her social gatherings a harpist or a trio would do the hard graft, while a vocalist would become the centre of attraction for a while, during which conversation would almost stop. (Fräulein Steinicke remembered operas in Italy, where the audience in the traditional way talked on through the performance.)

They each performed solo for her. Alina travelled to her home in Baden-Baden, where friends descended every summer, while Ursule took the train to Berlin and sang for her circle there. The two were summoned to a Christmas gathering, intended to take place at another residence on Lake Konstanz, but transferred to the

Charlottenburg townhouse because Fräulein Steinicke had injured her ankle and preferred to be near her doctor. In the event, Alina caught the flu and Ursule went back to Berlin by herself. While chatting with a conductor from Budapest, Ursule discovered that he was planning to stage a piece by Litzmann for one of his more adventurous audiences, and that it would feature a soprano part.

'Perhaps that would suit you, Fräulein Kroll?'

'Oh, I very much doubt it.'

She gathered that Litzmann had been a fixture at the house in Baden-Baden. Alina had made no mention of the fact. They had been happily free of Litzmann of late – he had been in Frankfurt, where Intendant Meissner had taken him under his wing – and Ursule didn't even want to bring up his name. She wished Alina would learn to do without him, and forget him.

'I shall invite you both again to Konstanz.' Fräulein Steinicke was determined the two singers from Hamburg should come south sooner or later. 'You must see Villa Zdenka. It isn't very grand. It's a cosy house.'

To each she sent a courteous letter of thanks, along with photographs of the villa and garden. Ursule laid out hers on the table top in her room, and wondered if Alina was doing the same. She pictured them both there, the sprawling Villa Zdenka conveniently devoid of owner and guests. The gardens sloped down to the shore of the lake, where a launch was shown waiting by a jetty, to carry them – the two of them – to a destination of their choice.

Outside Hamburg's main railway station a man pushed an envelope into Ursule's hand. He hurried past her and off along the Kirchenallee.

The front of the envelope was blank. She waited until she was round the corner before she opened it.

She saw a telephone number. And a message, in small uneven caps. MAN, V. WELL-ENDOWED, LOOKING FOR OPENINGS. It was written on the back of – she turned it over – a black and white photograph. It showed a naked man squatting by a tree, smiling widely, thighs pulled apart to display a giant erection.

Ursule immediately felt sick. A sour taste spirted up from her throat, rolled on to the back of her tongue.

She pushed the photograph back into the envelope and stuffed it into her pocket. Alina had nudged her to look at a Greek vase one day as they were being shown round a museum storeroom of artefacts by a friend of the Fleissners. As a child she had seen rude graffiti, and once a man limped out of a hedge in front of her when she was coming back from school; he had a crying woman in tow, and as he buttoned himself up she'd caught a glimpse of bright red flesh. The animals in the Wendland fields had provided her with her sex education.

She thought she was going to empty the contents of her stomach into the gutter, and had to stop, leaning against a wall. More of the foul taste swirled around in her mouth, but somehow she kept the sickness down. Yellow flares dropped in front of her eyes. Every man she passed that afternoon disgusted her. Now and then she took the envelope out of her pocket and sneaked a look at the photograph. The gap-toothed smile. The pale, thin body. The enormous, blunt-headed tool of his trade, standing up rigid and straight, pointing past his hairy belly at the sky.

At a road crossing she felt a hand on her arm, a man was speaking to her, and she started shouting at him. He looked astonished. She realised several seconds too late he had only been trying to warn her not to step out into the traffic. He pulled down the brim of his hat and hurried away, avoiding the eyes of a couple of women who must have suspected him of quite different intentions.

On the other side of the street, where the sun shone, Ursule realised she had been given the photograph on purpose. It wasn't to entice her, but to lay out the premise of relationships to her. Men sought different things from women. A woman would only find true understanding, affection, love with another woman. Or that was how it was in her case.

She remembered some lines in a book the Countess had given her, to reward her for her honesty, when she found a purse on her way to school which she handed to her father and which he took to the castle. It was a copy of *Tales from the Thousand and One Nights*. Sinbad's adventures carried their own preface.

'Seven voyages I made in all, each a story of such marvel as confounds the reason and fills the soul with wonder.'

There was a story for everyone, she was thinking as she walked with eyes directed at the pavement towards the Ratshausmarkt. Our nature tells us who we are: how we will act, the star to follow, how we will love and who will love us in return.

It was at the same page, page 98, that the book of *Tales* always used to fall open.

'All that befell me had been pre-ordained; and that which the moving hand of Fate has written no mortal power can revoke.'

Mariel Baxter

They belonged to Vienna, she and Ben. They'd had to come here to find each other.

The map of Vienna in her head turned into the contours of Ben's naked body, and vice versa. He showed her corners of the city she couldn't have found by herself. In bed she imagined what lay outside the room. The city might have been created expressly for their pleasure. All the dead composers and poets, all the long-gone philosophers and politicians, they had been means to an end.

To now, to this moment, to their two spirits afloat Chagall-like – somersaulting – over the skyline.

Her voice too, she felt, should have been lighter.

But Kroll seemed to be looking for something else; she was searching to bring out darkness and complexity in her voice, at the very time when Mariel believed that life was resolving itself for her.

Her voice sounded effortlessly, and she couldn't keep it in. She was also conscious, however, of losing track of what she was singing *about*, and of Kroll's instructions to her. She felt she was singing high above the blah blah blah.

Up, up and away.

She found she had left one of her pieces at Ben's, and was going to call by Clarenbachstrasse next morning to pick it up.

At the last minute she decided to phone.

His landlady answered. She had a thick country accent.

'Who?'

'Herr Tompkins.'

'No, who are *you*?'

'I'm Mariel.'

'I don't know you young ones' names. What colour's your hair?'

What a nonsensical question, Mariel thought.

'It's brown. Light brown.'

She heard the woman rapping at the window, and a few moments later Ben was at the other end of the line.

'She's just asked me about my hair.'

'She's mad, I told you.'

'She'll hear you.'

'I expect she'd like to cut it off.'

'What?'

'Your hair. And find a Chinaman.'

'*What*?'

'She wears a wig. Chinaman, yes?'

'It's catching, this.'

'Yes?'

'The madness.'

Kroll asked her how she was settling down.

Personal questions had been few and far between over the past three or four months.

Mariel hesitated. She felt she had to explain her hesitation, which was how she found herself using Ben's name to Kroll.

She hinted, heavily, that theirs was more than the friendship of kindred souls.

For a moment or two she thought Kroll didn't want to hear, looking away and picking up some sheet music. But the woman said nothing, so Mariel continued.

She mentioned Die Gruppe. She told her they met in a café.

'One of our proper Viennese cafés, yes?'

She told her its name, and exactly where it was. Kroll shook her head.

'I don't know where that is.'

She really didn't know? In that case, Mariel felt, I've scored a point: here I am teaching Ursule Kroll something about the geography of this city.

'You have your time once,' Kroll said. 'When it's gone, it's gone. You can never get it back.'

Mariel nodded.

It was true, she wanted to make the most of her time here, both with Kroll and with Ben. Those were the two sides to the coin, she felt. Time did seem more intense here than in Boston: both the solid presence of the past, and also – the opposite in some ways – how quickly she was getting through it. And those songs to learn, and then the freedom of not thinking what to do with Ben and their friends, how they drifted and just let themselves go with the flow.

Arriving at the Glockenspiel one evening it was immediately obvious that Die Gruppe was depleted. There were only five of them. No Zoë, no Karl, no Ilan or Miguel or Helga.

And no Ben.

'Everyone's got better things to do,' Brendan said.

Mariel laughed, but she was disappointed.

Lucien handed her an envelope once she'd sat down.

'Cheer up. Jesus, what am I talking about? We've all been stood up. *O me miserum*!'

He pretended to sob.

Mariel smiled, while tearing open the envelope and pulling out the note inside:

> Something's just come up – as the actress said to the bishop. Off on my White Horse again. They've asked me to make up numbers. Can't say no. Sorry!!! Why not get Lucien to take you to a movie? L. can afford the best seats.

She just couldn't put Ben out of her mind.

She heard his voice even when she was on a crowded tram, or having breakfast at Frau Werfel's with the radio on in the kitchen, or at Schlehengasse 19 when Kroll was giving her instructions. It was especially then, in the afternoons, when she wanted Ben more than ever.

They had agreed, she and Ben, that they would continue with their living arrangements as they were. Or rather, when Mariel had tried to suggest that one or the other move in, Ben had seemed surprised. He told her he didn't want to get in the way of her musical studies, and that he had his boring translation work. Neither struck Mariel as very plausible arguments.

'See what you feel like in a couple of months' time,' he said.

Why wait? And why two months? She could have told him now. She was sure she'd feel exactly the same, or quite possibly more so.

'Flats to rent cost an arm and a leg anyway,' Ben said.

'Yes? If we pool our resources, though—'

'Even if.'

'Really?'

'Let's see.'

And that was how they left it.

Kroll, when speaking about herself, used just her surname: 'Kroll would not have sung it like that'; 'How could they expect me, Kroll, to agree to such a proposal?'; "'Get Kroll,' Tieten insisted, "I want

Kroll for Bayreuth"'; 'Matters were very different when Kroll took over the part'; 'Kroll's Agathe, the critics of *Der Freischütz* used that as their standard.'

To Mariel, the woman sounded almost detached from her own history: a past life which didn't relate to this current one, which might have been someone else's.

With Kroll, Mariel knew to be punctual. She would keep an eye on Kroll's wristwatch, or sneak a glance at her own, to keep track of the time.

When she was with Ben, time didn't matter, it had no structure, no shape or volume. She wasn't looking at the clock; the chiming bells which sounded across that part of the city weren't connected to the hours.

Scheherezade came into Mariel's mind again, spinning tale after tale after tale ...

They would tell each other things about themselves. She elaborated on some of the facts – a little was pure fancy, but most of it was true enough, just muted.

She wasn't able to judge, in Ben's case. She tried to believe him, she wanted to trust him implicitly, but she simply couldn't be sure. She had never visited England, so she hadn't been to London, and knew it only through movies and photographs. When he talked about the woodlands of Sussex, the villages and valleys of Somerset, and the Highlands of Scotland with their wide open moorland, dotted with lakes and pools, she synthesised those places with what she'd seen of her own country: maybe they were nothing alike, but it was the best she could do, trying to blend her world with his.

She never tired of listening to his confident, cultured, slightly clipped voice. She could have listened to him *until*, in one of those expressions of his which transported her from Vienna to an English country lane, *until the cows come home.*

Sometimes Kroll would put on a record of herself singing, and they would both listen.

Mariel marvelled at the beauty of the voice, at its purity and exactness, at its sheer authority. The words were shaped, with perfect adroitness, to the music. There could have been no other language for the sentiments *except* German.

Kroll was also held in silent admiration.

Ben told her he had to go to Munich to meet with a publisher. He was delivering a translation and seeing an earlier manuscript into print.

'Can't I come?'

'They're paying for me, they've booked things.'

'How long are you going for?'

'Ten days.'

'Ten days!'

'You make it sound like a year.'

'It might as well be.'

He shook his head at her.

'You're crazy, Mariel.'

'I can't help that.'

His expression was sympathetic. No, it seemed to be saying, no, I really don't suppose you can.

All the time Ben was away, Mariel wanted him more. She was never done wanting him.

She planned at one point a sign for the front of his door at Clarenbachstrasse. HERE COME DE HONEY MAN. WELCOME HOME!!! Until, that is, she thought of Frau Knuth's reaction, her seismic rumblings.

She endured the lessons at Schlehengasse, just in order to vary her suffering. There would be lots of time to compensate for it later.

She forced herself to narrow her focus to the songs. Once Ben was back, she wouldn't be able to tell him much more about the once-famous Ursule Kroll but she *would* surprise him with some memorised poetry and a few other songs she'd learned.

'I've done what you wanted me to. I've stuck with her. I've put up with her, and you weren't sure if I would, or could. Admit it.'

She would wait for his admission before wrapping her arms round his neck, and in one frenetic night they would make up for all the lost time.

Ursule Kroll

The notice in the newspaper said Bremen. A music society in the city, which liked to think of itself as an arbiter of good taste, had put on a season of subscription concerts celebrating 'The Future of German Music'.

Ursule didn't see how the future could be celebrated when it hadn't happened yet.

Among the names of the patrons dutifully mentioned was Duringer. It was that which had caught her eye as she glanced at the page.

One name led to another – Litzmann – which had elbowed its way into the paragraph beneath, listing the new composers so intent on claiming that future for themselves.

Litzmann!

How could Alina have given herself to him? At first she'd pretended there was nothing in it. For all her vocal expertise, Alina was not a good actress; she couldn't disguise when she was failing to tell the truth, as she was now. Litzmann must have taught her how to lie.

'He's just good fun to be with. He makes me laugh so much. You'll end up just as keen as I am, really.'

Alina didn't seem to mind if she was believable or not. Litzmann had found a way of getting inside her head, infecting it like a tapeworm and twisting how she thought.

It must be some form of sorcery. He had turned that lovely head with tales of his contacts, his friendships, the composers he mixed with – Rathaus, Heiden, Sternberg, Toch. All synagogue boys. He had enchanted her with phoney promises for her career, with his all-pervasive egotism.

His music was vile. 'Decadent chromatism', they were calling it. The knives were out, and quite right too. 'Jewish Bolshevism' was everywhere.

The man's looks alone couldn't explain the hold he had over Alina. Another thirty years on, and his face would have grown jowly, his lips thickened, his nose become more prominent, his crown bald, while his chest and shoulders and back would be overrun with coarse grey hair.

Kabbalah magic, conjured up for his own ends.

She had received a letter from Fräulein Hebbel:

> I have every confidence in you as a singer. However, it is the artiste's lot never to have time stand still. Others will want to wrest that wreath of laurels from your head. Even your closest friend and confidante may harbour secret jealousies. It is wisest to keep one's own counsel.
>
> I can, alas, be no more specific. I know the harsh truth of what I have to say from my own experience.

She read the letter over many times. Her instinct would have been to show it to Alina, but she realised she couldn't do that. Fräulein Hebbel was hinting – no, she was surely warning her – not to trust friendship too much. This was a cut-throat trade, as much so as any other.

The letter was alluded to, very briefly, by Fräulein Hebbel.

'You haven't discussed the contents of my piece of correspondence with anyone?'

Ursule assured Fräulein Hebbel that she had mentioned the letter to nobody. The woman nodded at her compliance, and looked satisfied.

'One day,' she continued, 'when they say the name "Hebbel", they'll add, "She gave her voice to another to use. Sabine Hebbel's lives on in that one."'

Ursule was taken aback. She thought she should be glad to hear it, even though she felt a little guilty for Alina's sake. But the real pleasure seemed to belong to Fräulein Hebbel, so beneficent at this moment in her magnificent condescension.

Litzmann was writing an opera for Hans Meissner. It was based on *Adolphe*, Benjamin Constant's novel of 1816. The cast list was small: a young man, Adolphe, and the woman, an older man's mistress, with whom he allows himself to fall in love as a scientific experiment. The role of Elinore, the woman who later won't let Adolphe go, Litzmann was creating for Alina. Yes, he was writing for her voice – hearing it in his head all the while – but the music made demands she was unused to.

'It will be an amazing achievement,' Alina told her. 'Just think, Ursule. I've helped him to compose this wonderful opera!'

'How do you know it's going to be wonderful?'

'Because Otto is writing it!'

That, to Ursule, wasn't an answer.

'The music is difficult, that's the only problem. Because it's so very clever. Of course he's had to stick in some Volksoper stuff, to keep our masters happy.' Alina made a face, and Ursule was a little shocked. 'But there's enough of Otto left. Schubert is easy by comparison! Even Mozart.'

Alina cleared her throat, and Ursule showed her concern. She had recently noticed Alina's voice straining whenever they were singing together. She had asked her if she was singing too much, with the opera on top of her lessons.

'It's only my time,' Alina said. 'I can make more time.'

Litzmann was damaging Alina's voice, Ursule felt sure. It was a rougher, less precise instrument. There was a loss of sweetness. The subtle modulations were noticeably affected – the degree of softness her voice could reach, for instance.

How could she say this to Alina? Alina didn't appear to hear for herself what was wrong, she was so besotted. It was a kind of insanity. Litzmann came from a golem culture, he must know by osmosis what Ursule had had to mug up on from an encyclopedia, about the angel Raziel's book of secret magic and the Amorites' forbidden black ways. She wanted to put her hands on Alina and shake her until she'd worked the evil charm out of her.

Afterwards, Ursule learned that Fräulein Hebbel had been hinting the very same things to Alina that she'd been hinting to her: your fellow pupil is stealing a march on you, and you should watch out.

Their mouths dropped open, then they started laughing. Privately Ursule felt angry, and she supposed Alina felt just the same.

It was Alina who now came up with a new moniker for the woman, and the nickname stuck, so that in Mariel's mind Fräulein Hebbel would forever be 'the wicked old beldam of Grindelhof'.

2008

Mariel saw Kroll standing at a window in the apartment, holding back the fold of netting. She paused behind a tree to watch. The old woman looked in both directions, up and down the road, then shook her head; where she might once have lost patience, Mariel guessed she was now agitated for a different reason.

Mariel glanced at her watch. She was eleven, twelve minutes late. It wasn't accidental. She had thought to keep her waiting. In the old days Kroll was a stickler for punctuality. Towards the end of her time there (although she hadn't known it would finish so suddenly) Mariel would slow her footsteps on the sidewalk as she drew closer to the building on Schlehengasse. She felt she needed to assert her independence, and this was one way, by delaying the start of the lesson. Kroll's reprisal was to keep her there later and later, and so Mariel's original revolt was shown to be pointless. But being tardy was a gesture, and briefly gave Mariel an advantage; it was worthwhile just to see the displeasure on Kroll's face.

Today, when she rang the bell and the door was opened to her, Kroll smiled vaguely and looked puzzled.

'I couldn't remember if we said today or tomorrow. Excuse me, please, I've just woken up.'

Mariel forgave the small untruth with a smile of her own. If that was what Kroll wanted her to believe ...

Mariel stepped inside and removed her coat and hat and gloves.

Kroll herself took them from her, as she'd done yesterday, and deposited them in the cloakroom with its pine walls and ceiling.

Mariel waited for her, but Kroll indicated that this time she should lead the way through to the drawing room. Passing the kitchen, Mariel saw the door was ajar; Brigitte was busying herself with something and had her back turned to them.

'Go ahead, please,' Kroll instructed her visitor.

In her mind, Mariel hesitated. She sensed a vast airlessness in the apartment, which might have been the accumulation of many years. It was pressing on her chest, making it hard for her to breathe. But her legs, unbidden, carried her through the open half of the double doors, and here she was again: walking scriptless, without a programme or libretto, on to an empty stage.

Mariel Baxter

She felt Ben leaking out of her.

He had burst the condom.

'Christ, I'm sorry!'

She watched him roll it up.

'I must've torn it with my nail or something.'

She felt his warmth, his stickiness. She was thinking of his landlady, eager to inspect the bed linen. That made her smile, then she started to laugh.

'What is it?' He sounded puzzled, and relieved.

Mariel told him.

'Oh, her.'

He got up.

'I'd better go,' he said.

'Why?'

'I've got work to drop off.'

'Can't you stay?'

'I'll be back later. Go ahead and use the bathroom.'

'What?'

'You'd better wash yourself out.'

Mariel lay back on the pillows, watching him dress.

'You okay?' he asked.

'Sure.'

She didn't know what to do. There was no bidet. She sat down on the lavatory, lowered herself into it and pulled the handle. That wasn't the solution. She was filling the tub when there was a knock on the door. It was Frau Knuth. Something about water, hot water.

Was there only hot water in the evenings? What was coming out of the faucet was very tepid.

Mariel turned off the flow. She crouched down, squatting in the bath. Ben's directness had surprised her. This was what the animals did. It was painful, as well as undignified. It didn't matter to her that no one could see her. She imagined Kroll's disgust. Kroll was the furthest away she could think of from this degradation. Maybe Kroll had been correct, the woman's time was being wasted on her: she wasn't a deserving pupil.

She turned the lever to empty the tub. The water ran away, swirling down the plug hole. She was chafed from the friction between her legs. She felt sated by their lovemaking, taken to the limits of herself, too tired to think straight.

More rapping on the door. A shrill voice. The bathroom was for her lodgers, there were rules, everyone must obey the rules.

Mariel unlocked the door. The last of the water in the bath gurgled behind her. She smiled, carefree and innocent, and realised at that same instant, *this is how the singer sings* (thank you, Frau Knuth, for showing me), *she acts, she wills a smile out of nothing, she make-believes – and, ladies and gentlemen, you follow her there.*

Ursule Kroll

Lunch at the Anna Sacher.

In such surroundings the name of Ursule Kroll was always known.

She was aware that Professor Welspricht enjoyed the attention. But since he was paying, she let him savour his brief glory by association.

'Now tell me, how is your new pupil coming along?'

'She has a good voice.'

'As you said to me, Ursule, before she arrived in Vienna.'

The fellow's familiarity grated with her. He was thirty years her junior. At one time such informality wouldn't have been acceptable. But he kept the flame alive, here in Vienna. He had grown up listening to his parents' collection of her records – the wartime Electrola classics, and some of the earlier Telefunken catalogue. She was thankful to him, even if she chose not to make that too obvious.

'Our Vienna air doesn't disagree with her, then?'

'She wants me to give her "technique",' Kroll sniffed. 'We're working on "technique".'

'And does she appreciate what you're teaching her?'

'You must have asked her that yourself.'

'I'm interested to know what Ursule Kroll thinks.'

'She's young.'

'As were you when you began.'

'There's a difference. This is 1980.'

'What difference, exactly?'

'She wants to put on a show. She wants to go through the repertoire, ticking off this, this, this. "I've sung all those."'

The professor waited for her to continue.

'Is she able to sing them?' he asked.

Kroll shrugged.

'She's not old enough?'

'If she's a proper artist,' Kroll answered, 'she can do that. She will become the person in the song.'

'Songs are more difficult than arias,' the professor said.

'Why?'

'You're in a nice, fancy costume, for an aria! Or you can imagine you are.'

Kroll dismissed the remark.

'When you sing lieder,' she said, 'the song is more important than the singer. Nowadays singers only want to draw attention to themselves. When I hear someone, I need to believe what's being sung to me.'

'It will come. We have to give her time.'

'How long? You expect me to wait until she's gracious enough—'

'She has the raw materials, yes? The voice?'

'Ah! The Voice Beautiful.'

Kroll tore a small slice of bread into pieces.

'She *is* grateful.'

'She told you that?' Kroll asked him.

'How could she not be?'

'She said to you, "I am so lucky to have this opportunity"?'

'Not in so many words.'

'No, I thought not.'

Kroll looked round the panelled room. There had always been something just a little cloying about Sacher's taste – those ruched curtains, the potted plants on the window sills – but the surroundings had an air of discretion, of exclusivity, which only the most dedicated and disciplined hoteliers, as here or at the Vier Jahreszeiten in Hamburg, could bring off. It had the feeling of a private dining club, and after studying the company (true-blue *rechtmässigen* Viennese: no tourists, thank God) she felt better disposed even towards the tricky subject of their conversation.

'Let's discuss matters in a year's time, Ursule.'

'Next time I shall take the turbot.'

'And you can tell me the secret of how you turned Miss Baxter into the new—'

He stopped himself just before he said 'Ursule Kroll', but the damage had been done.

Kroll ripped through another slice of bread.

'There is only ever one,' she corrected him curtly.

'Of course. I only meant—'

She wasn't interested in his excuses. He should have known, she told herself, that even a highly expensive lunch such as this one might spin on a pfennig. He had no idea how softly to tread, although dozens here in this city might have warned him.

'There are many more', she informed him, 'who get the small roles, who sing in the chorus.'

'Indeed.'

'Is that what she wants for herself?'

'I don't imagine she—'

'In America,' Kroll interrupted, 'maybe it doesn't matter. You can become famous there because people don't know any better. They don't know where Vienna is, they have no sense of history, of European culture. She makes a nice sound, that is enough for them.'

Kroll could tell that he thought she was being too harsh. For him, being young was an excuse for sloppiness and idlessness. Whereas to her, being young meant you had the vitality and ambition and bravado to do anything at all: nothing would get in your way if you were set on being the best singer, no sacrifice was too great, every moment of time and ounce of energy went into achieving your goal.

No one knows *that*, Professor Welspricht, better than I myself do.

There is only ever one.

Walking along Philharmonikerstrasse after lunch, after they'd taken their leave of each other, Kroll admitted to herself it wasn't the whole truth. Would there have been an Ursule Kroll without Sabine Hebbel? Or without Trummler, who had been Hebbel's teacher? But for the torch to be passed on, the pupil has to learn responsibility, and humility. She had pledged her life, every bit as much as a novitiate to the church does. That was scoffed at now, it was an old-fashioned view, but Kroll clung – tenaciously – to her tenets.

It was that which gave her the confidence to walk through the Burggarten, with strangers' eyes looking twice and scrutinising her, with her history seemingly public knowledge except for what would never – in her lifetime, at least – be divulged.

2008

'What are you looking at?'

'Your paintings.'

'I haven't bought a painting for years.'

'Are these the ones you had at Schlehengasse?'

'I expect so.'

Kroll was letting her see that she thought it was an odd question.
And perhaps it wasn't her place, as a guest, to ask.

'Is that,' Mariel moved closer, 'is that a Klimt?'

She stood in front of it, inches away. She had several books about
Klimt, and here and there about the world she would see his work
displayed in big city collections. Vienna was where he belonged,
and if she'd had time to plan more carefully for this week she would
have fitted in some cultural excursions. But museums and galleries
required stamina, and peace of mind.

'It *is* Klimt?' Her voice was awed. 'Isn't it?'

Another of those luminously complexioned women, wives of
his Viennese patrons, garbed in bejewelled apparel and seeming as
if she would disappear into the riotously patterned background. It
was a smaller painting than the others she'd seen.

'It might be a copy,' Kroll said.

'You don't believe that?'

Kroll didn't speak.

'It's beautiful,' Mariel told her.

The method of representation rather than the woman, who had pleasant but conventional looks. A Jewess, in all likelihood, with a creamy pallor and rouged cheeks.

'You're very fortunate,' Mariel said.

'Am I?'

'I don't remember seeing this.'

'I didn't grant you the run of my apartment, that's why.'

'It must've given you a lot of pleasure over the years.'

Kroll stared at her, as if she was trying to credit the remark.

'I know it would have given me *great* pleasure,' Mariel said.

She knew she was talking too much. She sounded naïve and inexperienced and gauche. In other circumstances, people got tongue-tied talking to *her*. At least she would hear them out, or try to assist them. That wasn't Kroll's way. Being gauche didn't excuse anyone.

Ursule Kroll hadn't softened. And yet—

And yet she had allowed Mariel to call on her here. She hadn't refused to see her again. She was giving her her time. She was having her privacy invaded. Someone – an American – was standing right in front of her prized Klimt making inane remarks.

'I wonder what story your painting has to tell.'

Mariel Baxter

Kroll wanted her pupil from Boston to understand, she kept insisting, that now she was part of a tradition.

She was in the royal line of descent which went back to a simple apartment at No. 6 Kettenbrückengasse, where Schubert once lived. Brahms and Richard Strauss had made their indirect contributions to that accumulation of knowledge.

So Kroll was never done reminding her.

Mariel felt caught in a trap. She didn't want to think of all the singers who had gone before Kroll. She wanted to learn some handy tricks of the trade, but even more she wanted to sound *like herself.*

Europe had way too much history, she thought some days, when she was left longing for the shiny and new. Too much survived, and she felt there was a strong case for ephemerality. Why look backwards all the time, when circumstances were quite different then: when women didn't have the vote, and children were seen and not heard, and men were like gods in their homes. That was then, and even if there was so much of it, why imagine the past to be *better* than what we have now?

She would speak to Dr Brokmeier if she saw him on her way up to the fourth floor. It was strange how often he emerged from his surgery door. She might have suspected he didn't have any patients, but Brigitte had been telling Kroll about them one day when Mariel walked in on the conversation and killed it.

He liked to practise his English, he told her. If he also liked talking to girls, that wasn't Mariel's concern. Nor was it that he wore a wedding ring.

It *was* love, this, what she had with Ben.

She had no doubts.

She was only half herself.

Just as flowers needed water to stay alive, she needed to feel wanted. She needed to have someone to receive all *her* affection, to whom she wouldn't be afraid to confess anything.

What else could this thing be but love?

Most of the songs ever written were about this mysterious emanation of the heart.

She had been admitted to the pantheon of the blessed.

Kroll was giving her more work.

Ben was up to his eyes, he said, in overdue translations. He was also taking every jazz job he could get.

In her pocket diary, where she jotted down her homework tasks for Schlehengasse, Mariel kept a note of how many times she'd been to bed with Ben at Frau Knuth's.

Ten. Eleven. Twelve.

When she was with Ben, she would close her eyes and think of those Klimt women, elegance personified. She'd reach out and clasp the back of his neck, pull him inside her glittering gold negligee. Or, without shame but still dreaming of Klimt, she would lie back and lift her legs; like Danae, between her thighs a shower of bounty would fall – a spree of gold coins, and his precious spermatozoa. (No more accidents occurred. Ben knew to be more careful and had changed the brand of condom he used.)

Mariel lay afterwards looking up at the ceiling, and saw not its cracked plaster but sparkling jewels, priceless and mesmerising: the play of light, indigo and ruby and emerald, reflected from the panel of stained glass in the window.

She forgot how this affair had started, and couldn't imagine it ever having an end. But what she *didn't* do was think about it: she just lived it out, from one moment of simple sentient being to the next.

The lesson had overrun and Mariel got to the *bahnhof* late. She saw the train moving out of the station with Ben standing looking out of the back window.

Had he spotted her?

She took the following train. It was leaving the next station when she saw that Ben was on the platform, waiting for her to get off. At the next station she disembarked, to wait for the following train. He didn't get off that one. She decided he must have stayed on at the previous station, waiting for her to return. Mariel jumped on to a train going in the opposite direction to take her back. She arrived, just in time to see Ben in the rear carriage—

She stood waving, but she didn't know if he'd seen her.

She sat on a bench and cried, which was how he found her. She threw her arms round his neck. Every frustration she'd felt for the past days and weeks forced its way to the surface and sought expression now. She sobbed into his shoulder.

'I'm sorry, Ben!'

'Cry away.'

'I'm so sorry!'

'No, that's what I'm here for.'

'I – thought – I'd lost you.'

'There, there.'

'I – love – you.'

'It's okay now.'

Sobs still shook her.

'I – I *love* you, Ben.'
'Quiet now, hush.'
Miles, as ever, had the last word.
'Sshhh. Peaceful.'

Ursule Kroll

'And Frau Fleissner does have Jewish blood.'

Fräulein Hebbel offered the remark casually, as an aside: or seemingly so.

Ursule looked up from her music.

'You will have realised, of course.'

No. No. Alina had said nothing about it.

'From her aunt's side, I believe. They're not wholly German.'

Ursule didn't speak. She saw what Fräulein Hebbel was thinking: how ignorant this girl is.

'Some of the Jews flaunt themselves. One would never mistake them, anyway. Others keep it hidden. One can only speculate as to why they feel they need to.'

Ursule guessed that the words had been rehearsed. This was a revelation the woman had been planning for some time.

'Not that it should make any great difference. But these songs are rooted in the landscape of our country. The trees and rivers, the soil. They're German to the core. Now – where were we? – ah, yes, "Gretchen"–'

My heart is heavy,
My composure has fled,
And I shall never,
Never find it again.

Ursule felt, oddly, that she couldn't ask Alina outright.

In the streets they passed very obvious Jews – rabbis and scholars, tradesmen and their wives, rich merchants in their cars, pedlars with the soles hanging off their boots – and Alina didn't bat an eyelid.

At the Fleissners' Ursule was more vigilant. She sensed that her scrutiny was observed in turn: not by Frau Fleissner, but by her genial husband. She felt a little false. She was the one ill at ease, not Frau Fleissner. Looked at in this new light, the woman did betray herself: her jewellery was just a little too garish, wasn't it?; her hands were manicured, nails polished; her hair, close-to, had an evenly tawny hue of the bottled sort. She trilled with laughter at the witticisms of her guests, who – for all Ursule could tell – weren't of thoroughbred stock either.

This didn't seem fair. To confuse people's expectations. It wasn't fair to lead a double life. Ursule thought of those lizards which change colour according to their surroundings; they disguise themselves and go unnoticed, but suddenly lash out with a tongue or a claw.

Hamburg didn't thrive as it did on the concept of fairness or just desserts. Everyone else seemed to have understood that, and it was only now at this late stage that little Maria Semmelrogge from the back of beyond was finally catching up.

She thought she could smell Alina's breath, just momentarily, a sourness to it.

It was the first time it had ever happened. Alina, she knew, was punctilious about cleaning her teeth. She knew all the professional advantages of a bright smile.

Having noticed it once, and then – after an interval – a second time, Ursule couldn't not be attentive. She worked out that her breath soured whenever Otto Litzmann was around, or a day or two afterwards.

She couldn't stop looking at Alina's mouth. It was a little wider than her own: with fuller, more generous, sensuous lips. She loved Alina's mouth. Alina would bring it so close to her, to whisper something, and shivers ran through her. Sometimes Alina had kissed her affectionately, not on the lips but on her cheek. Nothing would have given Ursule more pleasure than for their lips to meet, to melt, fuse.

Mouths didn't stale from too much kissing. Their kisses should have been pure and sweet: perfumed things.

Would Litzmann have been content with just kisses? Ursule doubted it. He was impatient, always in a hurry, needing to impose his will. Kisses? No. Too slow, too egalitarian, too cliched, too humdrum. Litzmann liked to shock, as he imagined; even when he didn't have an audience, in his head he was affronting the bourgeoisie.

Alina was so smitten, he only had to tell her to open her lips and, next thing, he would be thrusting his—

Ursule couldn't bear to finish the thought. It made her want to retch.

Sabine Hebbel had sung for Richard Strauss and Pfitzner. She had known Brahms's nephew, who had many of his uncle's manuscripts, and who had given Mahler's *Rückert Lieder* their premiere in Paris. Hebbel's *Dichterliebe* was judged the best of its day. Her speciality, however, was Schubert. She had studied with Marianne Trummler, who was taught by Schubert's own pupil, Margreth Gräfin.

Hamburg, where she was born, seemed to her the most Germanic of all cities. It was a port, but strangers were treated as strangers and sent on their way, which was how she and her friends were content to see the world ordered.

Into the apartment block had come a new neighbour. Frau Zechbauer started to complain about the sound of singing seeping down through the upstairs floorboards, and the reverberations caused by the piano, which she claimed set the plates in her china cabinet rattling. (Ursule noticed that Fräulein Hebbel, when she was playing, made less use of the soft pedal now and more of the sustaining one.) The building had begun its life as a large house for a single family, which probably meant that sound-proofing had been less of a priority than in a structure divided into apartments. The neighbour, therefore, may have had a legitimate cause for complaint.

But Fräulein Hebbel thought the woman was being entirely unreasonable. She told her other neighbours, both in the building and nearby on the street, that the complainant – who was 'hounding her mercilessly' – was a lunatic. She ought to have been locked away in an asylum, hidden behind high walls. Instead she was here, plaguing decent God-fearing citizens with her small-minded grievances, her spiteful grudges.

Fräulein Hebbel took on more pupils who wanted to sing in a small choir. She allowed some of the piano students from the Hochschule to use her Bösendorfer.

One day Ursule returned to the apartment, for sheet music she'd left behind, and found only Fräulein Hebbel there. She was standing in the music room with her back to her; she had pulled back the rug and was slamming the heel of her shoe repeatedly against the floorboard like a demented flamenco dancer.

Fräulein Hebbel continued harrying the woman, remorselessly, unable to forgive her for daring to criticise someone so eminent in the city as herself. The neighbour could eventually put up with it no longer, but before she was in a position to move – perhaps unable to reason anything out any more – she stepped into a bath she had mistakenly filled with scalding water, fell over from the shock, and burned most of her body in the process.

Ursule wondered what any of the misfortunes in Apartment H had to do with Schubert's Goethe songs, which she was currently studying. Upstairs they took the lieder line by line, savouring every subtlety in the music and the words, worked together so seamlessly by the composer. Frau Zechbauer, meanwhile, was being treated for her burns in hospital, while provision was made for her removal to a secure institution, where she would be kept under lock and key to prevent her doing herself any further harm.

Fräulein Hebbel expended her energies now, poring over the songs, and Ursule felt she should be grateful, however it was that this closer focus had come about. She also sensed a little chill go through her now, several times in the course of every lesson, realising the malevolence and cruelty of which her august teacher was capable.

Litzmann's music churned Ursule's stomach.

She could digest the recent work of Strauss and Korngold: their melancholy was wholesome by comparison. Litzmann's compositions had a modern dressing, but only a little way beneath they turned soft and sickly sweet. It was a nauseous mixture: the sentiment of the rich for lost privileges, and the self-pity of the Jews at their vicissitudes.

His first reviewers included some of his cronies, so of course he got a falsely good press. Other critics didn't want to seem out of step. He was praised to the skies. How could anyone pretend to be modest at such a reception, Ursule wondered, especially when their heavy eyelids wouldn't open properly and their mouth was so shapely and full, the features of a man so perfectly self-assured and bolstered by arrogance?

His music put great demands on the performer, not just the listener: which was how she knew him to be completely heartless.

2008

This year, by rights, the posters should have announced that Mariel Baxter would be singing Arabella at the Met, reprising a role from the late 1980s. Strictly she was too old now for the role, but the director had always promised her she would sing it for him. Ten years ago McClanahan had first tried to get it on in New York. It had taken him this long to bring it off.

And now she'd had to pull out.

'Unavoidable personal circumstances.'

Some were saying her nerve had failed her.

One of the recordings she used to listen to was Ursule Kroll's, conducted by Clemens Krauss.

Mariel mentioned it now.

'Forty-two,' Kroll said, without any hesitation.

'The one you sang for Hitler?'

'The Führer, yes.'

'He must have been impressed.'

'His instinct was sometimes very good.'

'Good for Ursule Kroll?'

Kroll ignored the barb.

'He knew a fine production when he heard one.'

Mariel wasn't going to commit herself.

'I sang for the music's sake,' Kroll said.

It sounded like an oft-practised argument to Mariel.

'Art', Kroll told her, 'is superior to everything.'

'To politics?'

'Yes. Politics is forgotten.'

'Superior to morality?'

'One age's morality is not another's.'

'You wouldn't give them what they wanted?' Mariel asked her.

'Who?'

'The Allies.'

Kroll winced contemptuously at the word, at her memories of the experience.

'You didn't do what they asked you to do?'

'No.'

'You refused – for your country's sake?'

'Yes, of course.'

'A patriot?'

'Yes.'

'What's the difference between a patriot and a nationalist?'

Kroll dismissed the question with a wave of the hand. She didn't care to discuss a petty matter of semantics.

'You were a heroine?' Mariel asked her.

'I leave that to *you* to decide, Miss Baxter.'

Mariel Baxter

It happened again, with a harmless enough enquiry from Kroll.

'We shall continue, shall we?'

Mariel hesitated.

'Yes,' she said.

'Very well.'

It was already a few minutes past six o'clock. There was an informal but established routine that those of Die Gruppe who could or wanted to would rendezvous at the Glockenspiel at about six. That was when their evenings, planned or unplanned, began.

In the apartment, meanwhile, they were carrying on.

Ten, twenty minutes. Half an hour.

Mariel tried to concentrate. 'Des Mädchens Klage' was a complex song, and of course they needed the time.

... name the cure for a broken heart, After the joy of sweet love has vanished.

She realised she was in good voice, as Kroll too must have done, so it made sense, for that reason, not to stop.

Kroll was pointedly not looking at the clock.

They continued for a further twenty minutes, and it was almost seven o'clock when Mariel stepped out on to the landing.

'It was the best thing to do, no?'

That was the first time Kroll had thanked her for something. And, as events turned out, it was also the last.

Mariel ran downstairs. Dr Brokmeier two floors beneath was coming out of his consulting rooms, locking the door behind him. He smiled and nodded at her.

When she got to the Glockenspiel, Zoë was just leaving.

'I got held up with my lesson,' Mariel explained. 'Sorry, sorry.'

'Ben's had to go off and hand in an article to that proofreader.'

Which one? There were several proofreaders. Zoë didn't know. 'Maybe he'll come back.'

'Did he say he might?' Mariel asked her.

'I didn't hear. You know what it's like, trying to make out anything people say in this place.'

It wasn't *that* difficult to hear, Mariel thought as she sat at the end of the table. But it was always busier earlier on, admittedly, with people catching up on everyone else's news.

That evening she managed to avoid the waiter's eye, and finished someone's untouched glass of water.

She hung on, but Ben didn't come back.

'Were you expecting him to be here?' Karl asked her.

'I was late.'

'And now he's vamoosed.'

'Oh well,' Mariel smiled bravely, 'hey.'

She smiled at her little performance as she gathered up her things. It was now that she realised how much her evenings with the others at the Glockenspiel had come to mean to her.

She went to find Ben at his apartment. It was all she could think of to do.

Into the building, past the concierge watching TV. Upstairs. She rang the doorbell once. Twice. Three times. Four.

He wasn't there. She couldn't *make* him be there, even by the force of her will.

Help me, Miles.

Not this time.

'Gone, gone, gone.'

Nothing could be worse. Mariel felt she couldn't get any lower than this, literally, as she slid down the wall, crumpling into a heap.

She ended up in the record shop on Katrin-gässchen.

An LP was playing through the speakers. The soprano voice was singing Schubert. 'An die Sonne'. There was a light sizzle on the original recording, 1930s vintage maybe. And the voice, *that* voice, could only be Kroll's.

Mariel stood listening. She loved that particular lied.

Tomas was watching her from the counter as she listened.

Mariel smiled.

'That must be her in her prime,' she said.

'Who?'

Who else?

'Kroll,' Mariel said.

'Kroll? No.'

'It's not?'

'It sounds like her.'

Mariel was confused.

'Who is it, then?'

'Giebisch.'

'Giebisch?'

'Alina Giebisch.'

Mariel shook her head.

'You haven't heard of her?'

'No.'

'People have forgotten her. Alina Giebisch.'

She did sound very like Kroll. Had she set out to imitate her?

'Was she a pupil?'

'Giebisch? No. She died just when Kroll was—'

With his hand and arm the man imitated a plane's ascent into the air.

The song finished. An audience, many of them no longer alive, applauded. The first bars of introduction from the piano announced—

Mariel got to it an instant before the words, 'Mignons Gesang'.

Tomas explained that most people wouldn't have been able to tell them apart, only the aficionados.

The Deutsche Grammophon record sleeve was a 1950s facsimile of the original 1930s shellac disc. There was no photograph.

The owner searched in the racks to find one.

The face was pretty and wholesome. She was laughing, unlike Kroll in *her* photographs.

'That's an earlier one.'

He looked for one from later in her career.

It was contained in a German book about musical life during the Deutsches Reich. Giebisch was more sedate in that, as if more aware of her status as a star singer at Weimar and Stuttgart. Even in black and white, she had learned the tricks of make-up, and her darker, geometrically cut hair and elongated eyes gave her the exotic appeal of Salome – or possibly a Judith, finding herself trapped inside Duke Bluebeard's Castle.

These days Zoë had a distracted look. She seemed to be somewhere else.

She would catch Mariel's glances and smile across the table at her, and Mariel would wonder what private trouble she was having to keep to herself.

Mariel smiled back, meaning only to offer good cheer.

Be brave. It'll pass. Zoë would take on that lost look again, as if she was trying to work out – trying to remember – how to be carefree.

Or—

Sometimes she felt that Zoë was meaning to warn her about something – suddenly those big eyes – before she looked away, stared down at the table top, and her nerve failed her.

Mariel was going to ask Kroll about Alina Giebisch. She had every intention of asking her. It wasn't awkwardness that prevented her, but irritation: feeling that Kroll was nitpicking, and spinning out the lesson.

She *would have* asked, and handed on her response to Ben afterwards.

But these were proving difficult days at Schlehengasse. She couldn't please Kroll at all. So she was damned if she was going to show any special interest in her career, or in her contemporaries' careers either.

Ursule Kroll

If Aunt Hanna Fleissner was Jewish, she didn't resemble the Jewesses whose caricatures appeared in the daily papers. She had grey-green eyes, pale skin and fair hair. Would anyone have known she wasn't indigenous? Only a very slight hesitation with strangers, and then the obsequious civility, hinted at any complexity. Uncle Georg, tall and elegant, was from an old Hamburg family: it was his short, portly wife who laughed at that expression, causing her loving husband to laugh along with her, asking him – since he was the one who had spoken the words – 'Aren't *all* families old?' Uncle Georg went red in the face, realising it was a foolish thing to have said, and while most people wouldn't have noticed – except to be impressed – here in Hamburg they were among the intelligentsia who enjoyed playing with words and their meanings, as if conversation were an addictive game.

She would return, as ever, to a room on Garberstrasse, in one of the boarding houses which the Hochschule used.

There were six other women students living there.

The hallway and staircase smelt of soap and eau de toilette and hair lacquer and nail varnish and their sexual desperation.

Marta was the louche member of the Hochschule septet, and liked to kick up her heels in the hottest night spots. Her friend Lili, who was a dancer, failed to show up one evening, and Marta needed to find a replacement.

That was how Ursule met Richard Hirsch. Marta told her Rick was Lili's squeeze.

'Won't Lili mind?'

'She called to say she's sprained her ankle. She said we're not to think about her. So we won't!'

In the course of the evening, at a club which Marta hadn't been to before, who did they see but Lili: she was up on her feet and out on the floor, dancing with an agility Ursule could only dream of. Marta was furious, but Rick thought it was a big joke.

'Hey, I'm being angry for *your* benefit,' Marta shot back, heading for the door.

'I guess we don't know Lili.'

'Quite right. We don't.'

'She certainly knows how to enjoy herself.'

And so did Rick. He was a salesman by trade and gave Ursule the slick talk, and somehow – short of being sober, certainly – she ended up in bed with him in a hotel in Sant Pauli.

At least, being a practical man, he protected them both.

The operation was over almost as soon as it had begun. Ursule lay waiting for rapture that didn't come.

Rick rolled off her, leaving her with a dull throbbing sensation inside. He placed the evidence of their encounter on the bedside table, in a saucer. He lay back on the pillows with a lit cigarette, and started to laugh about Lili's miraculous return to good health.

Ursule said she would walk home. Dawn made the city unfamiliar to her. Near the river it smelt of salt and tar and faraway places. Nobody seemed threatening to her, because she scarcely even noticed them. She felt she was carrying around a vast disappointment inside her.

More than ever, she envied Christine Duringer her accomplishment on the stable straw. More than ever she sorrowed over the loss of Alina to that *Yid* predator. She remembered the man outside the station thrusting an envelope into her hand, and wondered why he'd singled her out: did she advertise her dissatisfaction to the world, as he advertised the thrusting tool of his trade?

Well, she'd done it. It had given her no pleasure. Here was confirmation of her instinct that she wasn't meant to respond to a man – to his mind *or* his body – as she was to a woman. Something very important had been clarified for her, and her dejection started to lift as the streets filled with light, as the day in its invincible and miraculous way began to take shape.

The future – a notion Ursule had once been sceptical of – had arrived. Too many people were telling her that for it not to be so.

Great things were expected of Ursule Kroll and Alina Giebisch. In the RTK state exams they had shared top marks and each qualified '*summa cum laude*'. They had both been issued with membership cards of the Hamburg Gauleitung, which equipped them to be professional singers.

Their major achievement, Ursule felt, was to have survived Sabine Hebbel.

She had done what she could to turn them into rivals. Whenever Ursule had dropped a hint that she knew quite well what her tactics were, the woman just shrugged. That's how it is, it's the way of the world. She wasn't offering any defence or apologies. I'm a teacher. I do what I must to get results.

Everything Ursule knew about singing she owed to Fräulein Hebbel. She couldn't unlearn it. Those who heard them said they could tell that she and Alina had been coached by the same person. You might distinguish between their voices, because nature creates everyone's a little differently, but it wasn't straightforward. Their vocal mannerisms were quite similar, and even in tone and timbre they had increasingly come to resemble each other.

'And now you will go out into the world, young lady, and this music will continue to live. You will play a part in its history. That is a great responsibility. You will be required to make choices, and I pray that they are correct choices.'

'I just want', Ursule intended to sound modest, 'to make a decent living for myself, I'm not dreaming of—'

'The correct choice for the *music*,' Fräulein Hebbel corrected her sharply. She wasn't talking about the financial rewards. How could the question be misconstrued in that way?

Ursule smiled, chastened for the moment, like a good apostle.

Sometimes those who booked them became confused about who was who.

Ursule Kroll. Alina Giebisch. (Sometimes they were even called Alina Kroll and Ursule Giebisch.)

Alina thought it was very funny.

'We should try to be each other for a while.'

Memories of their day in the forest by the pool flashed into Ursule's mind.

'Then *we* would get confused,' Ursule laughed along.

There was no shortage of offers of work. They could have sung every day of the week, but Fräulein Hebbel had warned them both (separately) about the dangers of overdoing it. (In her usual manner she had made her advice sound like a secret imparted *to you alone*.)

Some of the engagements proved to be mistakes – ineptly publicised recitals, in unheated halls, to small audiences – but Kroll learned to put that down to experience. Exacting critics such as Zimmermann and Paul Ehlers, on 'ZfM', heard much to be enthusiastic about in young Ursule Kroll.

On postcards, Alina summed up the places where she was performing in very few words, breathlessly – Augsburg was a real noses-in-the-air sort of place – and preferably with a pun: Passau was '(possibly) passable'.

She never forgot to send her friend a card whenever she went to a new city, or even to one where she'd been before. Ursule felt remembered, a presence in Alina's thoughts, and reciprocated in kind.

Germany had so many dozens of cities that Alina's movements and her own hardly coincided at all.

Kroll extracted herself from one manager, ignoring his threats, and hired another, Hans Jessen. The venues got bigger, the publicity was much improved, the audiences grew. One of Jessen's assistants broke away and set up on his own; Kroll went with him. Anton Teschermacher, who was to become even more successful than Jessen, strongly recommended she woo the wireless audience.

He said that was the most important twenty-six-letter word in the language: *Reichsrundfunkgesellschaft*. Hadn't Goebbels himself called radio 'the eighth wonder of the modern world'?

Teschermacher got to work on the administrators and string-pullers at Reichssender Berlin, Leipzig and Munich. He found someone who had director Hadamovsky's ear.

'Always get to the top man.'

Kroll was as keen as Teschermacher on using the popular methods of communication. He managed to land her a film role, which involved more singing than acting – she played a young opera singer on the rise. She then recorded three songs for another film, but those were withheld and only released on disc later. (Teschermacher had refused to have his client's voice dubbed over an actress's.) Screen acting wasn't Kroll's forte, as Teschermacher pointed out to her, but when Riefenstahl used her recording of 'Schmerzen' from Wagner's *Wesendonk Lieder* as a separate track on a film, Kroll received attention for it while (Teschermacher argued in his silver-tongued way) preserving her mystique. (Once *that* had gone, he claimed, it was irretrievable.)

More postcards.

From Mainz. From Darmstadt. From Mannheim. From Worms.

Their length depended on how much time Alina could spare, and whether she had Otto Litzmann with her or not.

Mariel Baxter

'I rang with a message,' Ben was telling her.

'Rang where?'

'La Kroll's residence.'

'What?'

'Didn't you get it?'

'No.'

'I spoke to the housekeeper.'

'How did you know where to call?'

Ben pointed to where she'd jotted down the number, inside the back cover of the manuscript pad. Mariel had told him the trouble she'd had to get hold of the number.

'It was to tell you to come to the De France.'

'I didn't get it.'

'She made me repeat the message, so I just presumed.'

'No.'

'We were going to a movie.'

'No, I didn't get the message.'

Brigitte had come in with a tray (coffee for Kroll, and a herbal tea as requested – the bane of Brigitte's day – for Mariel). She'd said something to Kroll. Had Kroll just forgotten to tell her?

When the music was so involving to her, wasn't that understandable?

Yes. But if Mariel had learned anything, it was that Kroll was unpredictable.

Of course, if they hadn't had to depend on messages—

But that too was part of the ethos of Die Gruppe. Notes were always being retrieved from pockets or bags and then handed over, or left in someone's charge to be given to the person they were intended for.

Zoë may have been the originator. She had spoken of cycling round the Cambridge colleges, picking up and delivering. Notes there were placed in individual pigeon holes inside the porters' lodges, and it was a reflex to check for your own every time you went by, peering in or reaching a hand up to the cubbyhole. Mariel pictured it, and could feel nostalgic for a way of life she hadn't experienced.

This was as close as she had come to it.

She hadn't heard of any misplaced messages at the Glockenspiel, which made her all the more irritated that Ben's communication to Schlehengasse hadn't been passed on to her.

'A lied contains as much drama as an opera. Except that it's in the singer's mind. I can be sincere and I can be deluded, both at the same time.'

Kroll had been more complimentary about her singing today, and Mariel had responded. When Mariel mentioned Zemlinsky, Kroll had said, yes, very well, if that was what she wanted, and if she worked at her 'Thekla' this afternoon. *Next* time.

'Zemlinsky is *Jugendstil*. In Vienna he sounds different. If you sing him anywhere else—'

The Viennese also loved their Schubert, Mariel realised, but sometimes it was all just too comfortable. Sentimental, even. Zemlinsky wrote splintered music, you couldn't easily tell where the melody might be leading you.

Kroll was summoned to the telephone. Normally she had Brigitte tell callers to ring back.

Mariel was left to walk round the music room. She stopped at a framed photograph of Kroll in her prime. At Salzburg, as the Countess in *Figaro*: the very picture of aristocratic hauteur and self-command.

'She's beautiful, isn't she?'

Mariel spun round, heart up in her throat.

Brigitte was standing just behind her. Mariel felt she'd been caught out. She stood trying to get her breath back, looking past Brigitte. The woman was standing so close that she could feel her hot breath, see the tiny burst blood vesssels on her nose, the goosefat on her thick neck.

'They all said she was the very best,' Brigitte told her.

'If anyone rings for me—'

'What?'

'If anyone tries to leave a message – I'm expecting a message – could you please let me know?'

Brigitte took a step or two back.

'I work for *her*.'

'Yes, I know.'

'I think you need a secretary, young lady.'

Brigitte's smile was sneering.

'Sometimes we run on late in here. And—'

'Someone will call?'

'Yes.' Mariel made herself taller. 'They've called before.'

She watched Brigitte's face for a reaction.

'Another day,' Mariel went on, 'but I wasn't told that anyone rang.'

'I recognise Fräulein Kroll's friends.'

'No one tried to leave a message for *me*?'

'I can't remember. We get wrong numbers. And people will try to pester her: it's my job to get rid of them.'

Brigitte wasn't going to admit to any fault on her part.

'If an Englishman rings—'

'An "Englishman"?' For Brigitte the word seemed to have a bitter taste to it.

'Otherwise – I don't know where I'm to go afterwards, you see.'

Plans with Die Gruppe were kept fluid, which created difficulties.

'And your evening is more important than your afternoon?'

'No.' Mariel didn't consider it Brigitte's place to ask, but she wanted to be quite definite on the point. 'No, not at all.'

At a sound they both turned round: Kroll's heels stabbing on the parquet blocks out in the hall.

The lesson resumed.

As Mariel was leaving the apartment, Brigitte – unfastening the belt of her mackintosh – appeared from the kitchen.

'The Steps at half past seven.'

The Steps? Out on the street, Mariel stood at a tram stop trying to work out how to get there. Brigitte had said something else. 'Millöcker', it must have been. It was Ben who had pointed out the house where the once famous operetta composer Karl Millöcker was born, before he dared her to race him up to the top of the Fillgrader Steps. That was very close to – Mariel traced the route on the tramcar map with her index finger – Gumpendorfer Strasse.

She waited at the Fillgrader Steps for nearly an hour. Two or three men walked past several times, the same ones, and a woman who looked as if she was out early on the game glowered at her. It had been a long, hard afternoon. And now this. Mariel found herself getting more and more irritable, and her period was nearly a week late, and now it was starting to rain. She had no umbrella, so she had to shelter in a doorway.

Eventually, after an hour and twenty minutes, she left. She could go and leave a note at Ben's, to ask him what the hell went wrong. But wasn't that his business to tell her?

The next day she discovered what had gone wrong. He hadn't said Millöcker, but Molker. As in Molker Stieg. The little lane with steps, up onto the fortifications. 'Remember, I was going to take you. I showed you on the map. It's near Café Haag.'

She couldn't be sure that Brigitte had said 'Millöcker', not 'Molker'. She'd still been irked by their earlier conversation, and had wanted to get away from her gloomy hovering presence and out of the apartment as quickly as possible. In that case, the fault was her own, which she couldn't bear to admit to herself.

'It's okay,' Ben said. 'I was still in time to get to the White Horse for my gig.'

'I'm really sorry.'

'No harm done.'

Mariel picked up the receiver on the phone and dialled the number of the White Horse Inn.

'Is Ben Tompkins there? Can I speak to him, please?'

'Why should he be here?'

'I thought I'd find him—'

'Can you speak a little louder?'

'He's been playing a lot for you?'

'Ben Tompkins? When?'

'Recently.'

'Not since a month ago.'

'A month?'

'Yes.'

'You're sure?'

'A month. Is four weeks. Yes?'

'Yes. But—'

Mariel had a headache.

'Before that, though?' she asked.

'Before?'

'Before a month ago?'

'A few times, yes. Since last year.'

'How many?'

'Three, four.'

Of course he had spoken of other bookings, other places where he played. But the name 'White Horse Inn' was always one which Mariel picked up on, which sounded so picturesque to her, from the Benatzky and Stolz operetta, from the movie. A couple of times per week, it had seemed to her.

'There must be some misunderstanding,' the man said down the line.

Ursule Kroll

Young voices appealed to the new masters of the country: young voices which alluded to the past, perhaps, but which sounded fresh and irrepressible.

If the singer came with an attractive face, so much the better.

In terms of politics, Kroll claimed to be unexceptional. She was quoted in an early interview in *Allgemeine Musikzeitung* as saying she 'respected order' and felt 'deep loyalty to the country of her birth', which were to prove impeccable credentials.

Nothing stood in the way of a brilliant future.

Only Alina was any kind of match for her. And of course, as the press understood, they were very close friends.

Unfortunately Alina and I don't see as much of each other as we would like. I hadn't appreciated just how large this homeland of ours is. We both have such busy lives now. So many cities, so many concert halls!

Conrad Niklas-Schwarzenberger was standing behind a bouquet of white roses.

'Remember me, Maria?'

Tall, blue-eyed and flaxen-haired. Perhaps at a second glance his brow was a little less clear, and his jawline not so firm as it had been.

Mexico and wherever else had weathered his skin, but the effect was attractive: as he probably knew for himself.

Kroll took the bouquet from him and buried her nose in the cornucopia of roses.

'They smell heavenly,' she said.

He had booked a table at the Adlon. He showed her to his car. A driver jumped out of his seat and opened the door.

'How did you know I'd say yes?'

'I didn't. But I hoped.'

'Where is your wife?'

'In Essen. With our daughter.'

'You're a father?'

'An absent one.'

During the drive to Unter den Linden he had been vague about his movements since Mexico, and Kroll had realised he was going to give away little.

'But you're here,' she said.

'With *you*. Yes.'

The hotel was the most select in Berlin, and Kroll felt awkward at first. But her companion took her arm and led her to the table.

'I have to thank you,' she said.

'You haven't eaten yet.'

'Not about supper. Why I'm singing, I mean.'

'You had the talent.'

'Getting to Hamburg.'

'You did all the rest yourself.'

He complimented her again on what he'd just been listening to. The evening had been a Schubertiade, and she was one of half a dozen young singers on stage. No one compared, he told her, none came close.

She hadn't performed with the others before, she said. A couple of them had wanted to hog the limelight.

'Wasn't Alina Giebisch due to sing too?'

'She had to withdraw. We'd have sung a duet.'

'She's your friend.'

'How d'you know that?'

'Ah ha!'

He also knew about Litzmann. That was why they ended up talking about him.

As Kroll was giving him her side of the story, a fussily dressed woman stopped at their table.

'No armband?' she tut-tutted.

Kroll's companion got to his feet. He reached into his pocket and showed her the swastika.

'Doesn't suit the décor,' he said.

The woman took several seconds to smile.

'Perhaps they should think of changing the décor,' she said.

'What a good idea, Frau Goebbels.'

Frau Goebbels shook hands with Kroll. She had heard her sing only the other day on the radio.

'We were very impressed.'

'Thank you,' Kroll beamed.

'I've interrupted you both. You were deep in conversation.'

'I'm glad we sorted out the matter,' the Esterhofen heir said, tapping his pocket with the armband back inside.

The florid-faced woman smiled briefly before moving on.

The Count-in-waiting sat down.

'Where were we? Litzmann—'

Why was she telling him so much about the man, Kroll wondered. Because she'd had no one else to tell. About Litzmann's friends and associates, the indiscreet things he'd said to Alina which she had teased out of her, the way he'd cut in on their friendship, the toll he'd taken on Alina's voice.

'Alina said she couldn't get a train from Bamberg to Berlin on time. I'm not so sure she felt she could sing Schubert.'

At one point Kroll found his hand on top of hers. She left hers where it was.

What might be coming next?

After dinner, when they'd left the table, he was called away to the phone.

She waited for him in the hall.

She heard a name being spoken at the concierge's desk – Duringer – and a shock went through her. A shop had delivered an order, and it was to be sent upstairs to the lady guest.

Kroll was still upset when her host returned.

She had remembered an appointment, she told him, she couldn't stay.

'That's a pity.'

'Is it? I'm taking a train to Stuttgart tonight.'

'Do you never stop?'

'I have a career to make. As best I can.'

'You explain my own situation exactly, Maria. Ursule—'

'Yes. Ursule.'

He took out a notebook and wrote down some names and telephone numbers. He tore out the page and handed it to her.

'You may want to keep this.'

Magda Goebbels appeared from the orangery. She noticed them both across the lobby; she waited until Conrad had taken the armband out of his pocket and attached it to his suit jacket sleeve.

Kroll found herself straightening it for him. Beneath the good flannel, the muscles in his arm were flexing.

'There!'

The redoubtable woman nodded over, smiled, then continued on her way.

'Speer, *he* understands music. He's the sophisticate among them.'

'I'll remember,' Kroll said.

She looked at the piece of paper. The script was in caps, as if he was disguising his handwriting.

'If there's something else you recall – or anything develops which you think might interest any of those gentlemen—'

'Who are they?'

'Our security. They protect us from the wrong sorts of people.'

Kroll didn't say anything. She had her own clear idea of who society needed to be protected from. The blood of the German people must be cleansed of impurities.

She put the names into her bag.

For a moment or two she asked herself if she wasn't having second thoughts about him. Then she pictured the hat boxes being sent upstairs, 'for Frau Duringer', to be signed for by her maid.

'Goodbye,' she said.

He took her hand and kissed it.

'I should have liked you to stay longer, you know.'

'I don't doubt it. But I have to go.'

'Really?'

She snapped the clasp on her bag shut.

She stood taking in the grandeur of the Adlon's lobby, fixing it in her mind.

'We all do now as we're bid, Maria.'

'Ursule,' she corrected him. Her final word.

On the most recent card, Alina said *Adolphe* was nearing completion, and that it would be 'Otto's great achievement', everyone 'out there' would be talking about it.

'Out there' was underlined.

Did she mean Germany, or the world beyond?

On the previous card, she had mentioned meeting Jutta Steinicke, who had come to one of their recitals. The very last postcard was franked 8 November 1938, Tuttlingen. Could Alina possibly be heading to the villa they always used to talk about visiting together from Hamburg, just the two of them? Kroll remembered it still, very clearly, from the photographs. She and Alina had promised Fräulein Steinicke, and themselves, that they would go.

Villa Zdenka. Shangri-La.

Kroll kissed the signature, then laid the postcard down beside the telephone.

Three days after she received the postcard, Kroll heard the news.

She heard, like the rest of the country, on a radio news bulletin.

Alina Giebisch was dead.

She had been driving, alone, at night, in the remote east of the country. She was negotiating the road through a forest in the Oberpfalz. Her car had hit a tree, spun across the road and careened down an embankment before bursting into flames.

All that could be hoped, announced a representative of her booking agent clearly lost for words, was that the driver died on impact, before the conflagration.

No one could have doubted Ursule Kroll's shock.

Teschermacher merely said that now she had the field to herself.

'I wish I didn't. I would give anything in the world—'

Kroll couldn't bring herself to discuss her feelings about it, even with Teschermacher, from whom she had kept back so little.

She merely asked him to step up her schedule.

'More? You want *more*?'

'Whatever you ask me to do, Anton, I shall never say no.'

After Kristallnacht.

Thirty thousand Jews had been deported. Otto Litzmann's name wasn't among them.

Kroll's silence on the subject of her best friend was put down to terrible frustration and anger, even despair.

They would never truly appreciate how deep those feelings went.

Two, three years into the war, Kroll would simply say, 'How can it be that even Otto Litzmann is spoken of now more often than Alina Giebisch? How, in God's name—?'

Kroll had been to hear Maestro Richard Strauss conducting, and it was from him that she learned to delay her arrival at the theatre for a recital. Even though she might have been rehearsing there earlier, for two or three hours or longer, she didn't appear until as late as a minute before the performance was due to begin.

Excitement would be at fever pitch.

She would be dressed and made-up, ready to step on to the stage once she had removed her cloak or fur.

The lights in the auditorium would have been dimmed in readiness. The audience would be sitting there in darkness, silent, while she delayed her appearance on the spotlit stage for another couple of minutes. Tension was ratched up yet again.

Then, from the wings, the sound of her heels slowly approaching on the boards. Her hand would brush the folds of parted curtain from behind. The first glimpse of the hem of her gown, a shoe. And there she was.

Applause would break out.

All that relief and anticipation, it travelled in waves round the theatre. She would stand waiting for the clamour to subside, and continue standing there almost motionless, until the very last pair of hands had stopped clapping, until there was complete silence in the building.

She would signal with her eyes to the accompanist.

Then the recital proper would begin.

Kroll would sing many times in Hamburg.

She hated going back there. She only went because, if she hadn't, her public would have wondered why – and her rivals would have become curious.

Hamburg always required an enormous effort of will. She sang in halls where once she and Alina used to stand or (if they were flush) sit listening to the likes of Ursuleac or Jeritza. She only ever sang for one person, for someone not there, *for Alina*. Even Fräulein Hebbel, now bedridden, wasn't a consideration during a recital at the Staatsoper or the Musikhalle.

Whenever Kroll went to Hamburg she would visit the house in Grindelhof, as a duty. The old witch watched her through hooded eyes, through Trummler's eyes, or Gräfin's. Fräulein Hebbel offered no real response, and Kroll guessed that pride and envy cancelled each other out. Little was said. Kroll was in dread of hearing *that* name spoken, the absent one's, but it never was. So long as neither of them mentioned Alina, Kroll found it hard even to look in the direction of the bed. Instead she focused on the flowers she'd brought with her, or on one of the framed programmes on the bedroom wall, or on the view through the window of Rotherbaum's rooftops. Anything but be drawn back into the past, even though it was the past which had summoned her.

Why *did* she come? A superstition maybe. Some of the best press she had received came from Hamburg, which treated her as one of their own; from Hamburg reports would always travel south. She stuck to her routine for no better reason than consistency.

But increasingly Fräulein Hebbel's vertiginous silences disturbed Kroll, until it became impossible for her to return to the house. Somehow, in spite of that, her run of luck continued to hold. She sent Fräulein Hebbel roses or lilies instead, and a card of profuse apology, and so she realised that she would never have to be in the woman's presence again, not looking at her, hearing the frightening layers of stillness in the room – and the most chilling of all, the one which held Alina Giebisch's name mute, as if it was encased in preserving ice.

2008

Kroll mentioned some interviews she'd seen over the years.

'I didn't know you kept up,' Mariel said.

'You sound surprised.'

'I am a little. Yes.'

Surprised, and possibly flattered.

'In Vienna we like to think we're informed. Just like you people in New York.'

'I'm sure you are.'

The remark fell flat, and had a condescending ring.

'You don't talk about Vienna. Did you ever talk about Vienna?'

'How do you mean "talk about" it?'

'I mean, mention that you studied here.'

'I can't remember everything I've said.'

'Naturally not.' Kroll watched her slyly from her chair. 'They would have been able to tell, of course. Your more intelligent critics.'

'"Tell"?'

'From *how* you sang. In the Viennese way.'

'I – I expect so.'

'Even if you didn't want to discuss your apprenticeship.'

'It wasn't that I didn't want to discuss it.'

'No?'

'No.' The word didn't sound very definite. 'There were other things to discuss.'

'Your busy life and so forth?'

'It's about promoting yourself.'

'Is it?'

'Well, Litvinoff's told me something about—'

'You blame them for bad advice?'

'Not "bad", no. That's just how it is.'

'I see.'

Her tone must have seemed mocking.

'"I don't hold with this business of traditions,"' Kroll said.

'Pardon me?'

'I'm quoting.'

'Quoting who?'

'Quoting you.'

'Did I say that?'

'"We make our own tradition. My voice is my own."'

'Are you sure?'

'Yes. Yes, of course I am.'

'I don't remember.'

'Your *New York Times*. 1991.'

'I can't remember the details of conversations seventeen years ago.'

'No?'

'I don't file them away.'

'What about nearly thirty years ago? Twenty-eight, isn't it, since we last spoke?'

Mariel twisted her mouth.

'If you don't remember, if you forget, if you don't want to keep the details – didn't you say? – then why have you come back here? Why are you in Vienna, Ms Baxter?'

It was a perfectly legitimate question, but Mariel wasn't sure enough of the answer to offer one.

Mariel Baxter

People said the 'Old World', but coming from the 'New' Mariel had had no idea what to expect.

It was like – like looking down into an ancient well. Forget any pretty-pretty picture of a wishing well. Think of it as dark, and stinking, and bottomless. Everything there was turned on its head. The disc of inky reflected sky seemed mile away.

The stone walls dripped. Up to the surface, from the weed-clogged depths, came whispers and sighs.

The well was the source, but to this American in the fall of 1980 the spring had been poisoned.

Mariel suddenly stopped singing.

'What is the matter?'

She reached out and closed the music on the stand.

'What is the matter, young lady?'

Mariel didn't know what the matter was.

Ben was in Munich, maybe that was enough. They hadn't had sex since her call to the White Horse Inn. There was a curse on them now.

'Well—?'

She hadn't planned to stop singing. But she realised she couldn't go on with this charade.

'Continue,' Kroll requested.

Mariel shook her head.

'Sing, please. Sing to me.'

She removed the music from the stand.

'Are you unwell?' Kroll asked.

Mariel shook her head again.

'Why don't you sing?'

Mariel turned towards the door.

'Stay where you are!' The voice was lashing out at her. 'Don't leave this room, Miss Baxter.'

Mariel realised she had no choice but to leave.

'I feel sorry for you,' she said to the woman.

Kroll immediately paled.

'Say that again.'

'I pity you.'

'What?' Kroll scoffed at her. 'I don't need your pity!'

'If all you can do is make people unhappy—'

'You understand nothing. Nothing.'

Kroll's face was now reddening with anger. But Mariel had started to give her the unvarnished truth.

'You must be really miserable yourself.'

'Have you finished, Miss?'

'And cruel as well.'

'Enough!'

'You can't tell me what to think.'

Mariel realised that she couldn't undo any of the past half minute. What she might have tried to write more carefully, in a farewell letter, she had said in this blunt and brutal form. It went to the very heart of the matter.

She had expressed herself. She didn't even want to see the effect her words had had. The truth was as far as she could go. She didn't need to say any more. By turning her back, she was telling Kroll that she wouldn't be tainted by her spiteful, loveless life. Perhaps 'pity' hadn't been the correct term to use. 'Disdain' maybe, or 'contempt'.

It was too late to change any of it. All the real damage had been done, not by her but by Kroll.

She pulled the front door shut behind her with a bang. The din echoed in the stairwell. She walked downstairs. She saw, emerging from the back of the hall where she had been speaking to one of the lawyer's lowly menials, Brigitte. Brigitte, surprised, glanced at her watch. The lesson wasn't due to stop for another half an hour. If she didn't have her little reconnaissance trips, or couldn't make a noise with her housework, time went slowly; she didn't have an ear for that kind of music, even though she had been coming to the apartment since Kroll moved in.

Mariel walked past her, without explaining, and out on to the street. She carried on walking, astounded by her own coolness. She didn't turn round, didn't look back. It was the hardest thing she'd had to do since getting on the train out of Benton SC by herself.

Unplanned, but inevitable. Along the intermittent line in the dead centre of the shaded sidewalk, wavering to neither right nor left, following a course which had been mapped for her since the paving stones were laid and tender saplings staked alongside.

One foot and then the other.

She was ready to drop, her knees felt as if they were going to give way beneath her. Tears were blurring her vision.

One foot and then the other.

The voice, that *thing*. In church, while the junior choir shuffled their feet, little old ladies would weep to hear Maybelle Baxter.

'Now I know what an angel sounds like,' the pastor told his congregation.

Her parents, and her sister and brother, looked on, amazed and embarrassed. When she opened her mouth, out came a voice which seemed to have nothing to do with her. She didn't own it, but it lived inside her.

At school she was asked to sing for any special visitor who came. Anyone who might be thinking of giving a donation was treated to a performance. Some of her fellow students were jealous, while others hung about her so that a little of her glory would be reflected on to them.

She hadn't known she was musical, let alone a prodigy, until other people told her that, so she guessed she must be. 'It's a crime to waste a God-given talent' was said to her several times, which showed her how thin the line between praise and disapproval really was. It was nicer to be smiled at, and complimented, and given fifty or one hundred dollar prizes at singing competitions, and a hi-fi, and a five-day Amtrak pass (which took her and her mother to Charleston, where they heard Frederica von Stade in recital), and half a closetful of new clothes from a mail order catalogue, all because she'd opened her mouth and let the voice sound from it, rising high (nearly as high as Rita Streich's on the first LP she ever bought), and as pure and refreshing (Professor Taylor told her parents) as Absaroka spring water.

She realised that, all along, she had only ever been a spectator looking in. The members of Die Gruppe had a worldliness and sophistication she didn't share. It had amused her to think the spirit of Mary McCarthy's era lived on, but the charm proved to be as exclusive – excluding – now as it must have been back then.

The others were cleverer, savvier, more hard-headed. They'd already had lives detached from their families, or they were brought up flitting between two parents, or had a step-parent. They didn't come from somewhere as small and insignificant as Benton, and they didn't have a father trading in white goods, and a mother who took whatever small-time secretarial work she could find to 'give her an interest', and a sister who merely aspired to being a prom queen and a younger brother who would have been a surfer if they'd lived by the sea or a skier if they'd lived near mountains and who seemed to sum up the dissatisfaction of the family by letting down tyres with his buddies and sneaking into movie houses to see adult-rated films.

She kept her background to herself. She didn't wish to be judged by that. It didn't stop her trying to find out about the histories of the others, though. Perhaps there were quite a few lies told, but lies are truths of a sort.

She wanted to ask Ben about the White Horse Inn, but couldn't bring herself to do so. She felt guilty, as if she'd done something wrong. She had betrayed his confidence in her, when she had no evidence that he had actually betrayed *her*.

They might have been mistaken, at the White Horse Inn, but she doubted it.

And then she realised, what should have been so patently clear to her all along, that they were bound to tell him someone had rung up, a girl with an American accent, keen to learn about dates he would be playing and when – very definitely, the week and the day – he'd played at the Inn last.

Ursule Kroll

'War work', Teschermacher called it.

Kroll sang three recitals in the first year of the war, one for each of the services, not at the front but at their bases. She included some Weimar nightclub songs by Hollaender and Nelson, and even Kolb, imagining there might be a stampede for the doors if she didn't. Perhaps because the performances were being recorded for radio, for Deutschlandsender, the audiences stayed eerily mute while she sang, and then would erupt into wild applause.

Hinkel, Goebbels' appointee, was highly approving, and came to 'favourable terms' with Teschermacher over future appearances for the military. (Each would involve three days' work, for thirty-five thousand marks apiece.)

Other radio highlights included the Mozart series for Grossdeutscher Rundfunk and Michael Raucheisen's exhaustive lieder tapings.

Kroll went through half a dozen accompanists. The last two, alternating tours between them, became her regulars; with them the relationship on stage was entirely compatible, and in Rudolf Weigel's case almost telepathic, as if they were thinking with one mind.

The schedule was demanding, but she trained herself to be physically fit – and vocally rested between performances – and so up to any task. No impromptu singing on request, no losing her temper with colleagues and letting rip, no extempore acts of derring-do (as with certain other singers) such as late night skiing or skinny-dipping in private pools not monitored for cleanliness.

It wasn't *all* exemplary rectitude. Temptation regularly presented itself at the stage door, bearing bouquets and gifts of French perfume. But, compared with some others, her private life was disciplined, observing stringent rules she imposed on herself. (At the back of her mind were those guests at the Schloss Esterhofen, straight-backed and unerringly proper, with modest appetites and calm digestive systems, the match of those regulated and undemonstrative exteriors and unlined faces. As ideal to her as – as marble statues: ever reposeful, and oh so cool to the touch.)

Ursule Kroll had never needed to compromise her dignity by giving interviews. Publicity had been very favourable in the national dailies and music journals. The Party had ensured that assigned pressmen covered her travels; the ablest photographers in the country were at their beck and call.

Many of the photographs happened to contain, somewhere in the background, a swastika.

Her accountant informed her that she'd been granted the maximum percentage of relief on income tax; even as an 'interpretative' artiste, she would be on a par with the most favoured 'creative' ones, as if there was no distinction between the two.

Every time might be the last that a particular piece of music was sung. Bombs might rain down on the hall at any moment. Or the sky might open as she and the audience were making their way home.

Kroll put everything she had into those performances. Her listeners came from far and wide, braving great danger to fill the houses high. The German language sounded, as foreigners never understood, especially beautiful when she was shaping the words.

The music came from her heart, that was clear. Sometimes the loudest applause was an audience's stricken silence afterwards.

The studio photographers were able to eliminate the worry lines and the creases across her forehead. They left her features smooth and pristine, calm and untroubled.

Clever lighting gave her high cheekbones, a sharply defined jawline, and a classically shaped mouth and nose. There was something sculpted about the effect, and just a little lifeless. She was an image of aristocratic Aryan pedigree. Nobody would believe this woman had any self-doubts, that she didn't precisely know her place and purpose in life.

She became the owner of several cars, including a Hispano-Suiza, although she preferred to be photographed in her Maybach open-topped tourer. Her luggage was custom-built for her, as was the Windsors', by Prada in Milan. She wore Mainbocher and Balenciaga, and Vionnet shoes: the latest designs would be despatched to her, and special terms offered. (When Hartmann took her to the Paris Opera for his *Die Walküre* in 1943, she set aside time to scour the Right Bank showrooms.) Horst photographed her many times, including at his villa in Capri.

She became friendly with some of the press photographers, tipping them off as to when she would be in the mountains or by the sea, and disclosing her precise whereabouts.

Her diary was filled, quite literally: a big page-a-day social inventory, with the daytime and evening demarcated every half hour. A secretary kept her appointments listed, a maid and dresser packed for her, her chauffeur drove her, her various pianists were on call, while all the time Anton Teschermacher – installed in some pomp at Dahlem – arranged where she should sing, and for how much (or, at Berlin birthday parties, for how little: *if* she could be allowed use of her own personal railway carriage for the purpose) and – by and large – *what* she sang.

There was hardly even time to think, and – if the truth be told – that suited her very well indeed.

One day a car collected her and they took the road north-west out of Berlin towards Spandau.

The officer who was accompanying her didn't speak, except when Kroll addressed him. Perhaps it was her reputation which had him tongue-tied? Occasionally she would forget that the awe she used to feel for others was now turned on herself.

They arrived at their destination. Gates opened, papers were checked, her identity was confirmed and they were waved through.

The building looked like an aircraft hanger.

Conrad Niklas-Schwarzenberger, in Waffen-SS uniform, was waiting for her. He clicked his heels and kissed her hand, in the Prussian style. That was how guests at the Schloss used to be treated.

After an amiable exchange of greetings, he conducted her into the first of the storerooms. At the back were packing cases, stacked on shelves. In front of them, on racks, were hung paintings. From her Hamburg education with Alina, she recognised Flemish, Impressionists, Watteau (or possibly Fragonard), Matisse, Friedrich, a Tintoretto maybe.

'You must tell me what you would like.'

She didn't ask him to repeat what he'd just said. He spoke clearly, and she had heard quite well. But she struggled for something to say.

There was a second room of paintings beyond.

'Renoir is very popular. I can't offer you any worthwhile Renoirs, I'm afraid.'

'No, not Renoir.'

'I thought not.'

She stopped in front of a society woman's portrait.

'Klimt?' she ventured.

'His middle period. You like Klimt?'

She hesitated. 'Some of them, yes.'

'Shall I mark that one?' He had taken out a little notebook, with gilt-edged pages inside a crocodile skin-cover. A tiny pencil on a cord was held poised above a blank page.

The painting's provenance hadn't been mentioned.

'It *is* very fine,' she said.

'I shall have it put aside for you.'

She didn't tell him not to. That might have proved a damning detail in the future, but by then – even now, at the height of her fame, did she have an inkling? – she would have learned to wipe her memory and her conscience (almost) clean.

They went outside. Lieutenant Niklas-Schwarzenberger took off his peaked cap and ran a hand through his hair. He produced a cigarette case. Kroll took one and he proffered a light.

They stood by themselves.

The names of Litzmann and Giebisch still hadn't been spoken. Did he know? He *must* have heard.

'We used to get days like this in Wendland,' he said. 'The same blue sky. A fine northern sky.'

'You go back?'

'Sometimes.'

'Your wife is in Berlin?'

'She prefers Essen. Her old haunts.'

'Ah.'

'That's where her friends are. It's all politics in Berlin, she says.'

'Is she correct?'

He shrugged. 'If I want a career, it's where I have to be.'

'And if you get to see masterpieces like those, that helps?'

'Indeed.'

'A private show. An Aladdin's cave.'

Still no mention. There wasn't time to say anything, and so she didn't, and neither did he.

In the distance Kroll's car was waiting, with another security car drawn up behind.

'Perhaps we'll meet again?' He cleared his throat. 'I do hope so.'

She smiled.

What *could* she say? So much to explain, and only ordinary words to say it with.

'I often play your recordings. They're a comfort to me.'

'I'm glad,' she told him, quite truthfully, but surprised nevertheless.

A couple of hundred yards away, the driver got back into the Mercedes and began his slow approach.

'There's always a timetable,' the Lieutenant said. 'If nothing else, we're very good timekeepers.'

Kroll smiled again, and again she didn't know how to reply.

'Well, they get the trains working properly. Isn't that always the justification?'

'Is it?'

Her admirer's eyes moved off her. He seemed to sense that it was *his* lookout, to take care what he said.

He laughed.

'Without us, Fräulein Semmelrogge, how do you think your private carriage would reach its destination?'

'I have no idea,' she said, laughing along with him.

'They'll be perfectly punctual, I assure you. To the very minute, departing and arriving. And if not, heads will roll.'

Mariel Baxter

The lesson dragged on. Eventually Mariel let Kroll see her glancing at her watch. But that had no effect at all. If Kroll saw, she ignored it.

Kroll couldn't have *forgotten* about the time.

They laboured over tiny details of interpretation, which Mariel felt were unimportant.

This is quite deliberate, Mariel thought. She's keeping me here as punishment for abusing her, for saying what I said to her. It's payback time.

Mariel was annoyed, but she also knew she had no choice.

Perhaps if she used the Durchhausen, that warren of back passages, she could still cover the ground in time.

But when she got to the theatre, the doors were closed to her. They wouldn't admit her unless she stood downstairs at the back. His first free evening since he got back to Vienna and Ben had gotten them a couple of seats in the first balcony.

She argued with them but it was hopeless. She gave up.

'That old bitch! Spiteful old *bitch*!' Mariel didn't care who heard her.

She ended up in the record shop on Katrin-gässchen.

Tomas had found another record by Alina Giebisch. He put it on for her.

'Richard Strauss?' Mariel asked, after only two or three seconds of piano accompaniment.

The Alina Giebisch version of 'Ruhe, meine Seele!' was very similar to Kroll's own. Breathing, timing, intonation – where accents fell. It was uncanny.

Tomas reckoned he could account for it.

'Teachers in those days kicked their asses.'

'Just in those days?' Mariel asked him.

'Kicked the shit out of them.'

It was much how she would have attempted to sing the song herself, Mariel felt, but without Giebisch's confidence and the silky sheen to her voice.

She returned to the theatre. The audience was spilling out on to the sidewalk. From the opposite side of the street she finally caught sight of him. Ben. He was talking with—

—Zoë.

Mariel's eyes fixed in their sockets.

Ben briefly turned and looked round. Was he trying to find her? But it was dark, and there were too many people between them by now. He couldn't see her. She didn't think to lift her arm and wave, or to try shouting across. By the time she raised her arm it was too late. He and Zoë had already left, they were walking away. He was pushing Zoë's bicycle for her.

She stared after them.

Come back, come back!

She felt helpless to do anything about it.

Turn round, won't you? Turn round and you'll see me. Look again!

She lost them in the crowd. Cars were crawling along the street, and the crowd was parting to let them through.

I'm sorry, Ben. She wouldn't let me leave. She knew I wanted to get away. It's as if it's an insult to mention the time to her.

Mariel had her words ready for him.

From the sidewalk outside the entrance to his building she heard the concierge's voice. No chance of her getting past the door.

She stood out on the street, trying to see what was happening. The woman was complaining loudly to one of the residents, pointing to a pile of someone's cardboard boxes awaiting collection. And as if that wasn't enough –

'A bicycle!'

Mariel recognised it.

Those distinctive red mudguards and wicker basket. Zoë's bicycle.

She closed her eyes and turned round, started walking away.

Goodbye, Ben.

Goodbye. Goodbye. Goodbye.

It was still warm, unseasonably warm, and she walked about the city for hours, steering herself by the stars. In the darkness the flowers and even the foliage had an intensity of perfume that wasn't there during the day.

Kroll's words went round and round inside her head. When they wrote those songs we sing, they could only see by moonlight, or if a lantern lit their way. Every minute of the dark brought them closer to dawn, and the green ray that preceded it.

Mariel lay on a bench beneath a tree. She watched as clouds passed across the moon, then revealed it, then concealed it again. She fell asleep in that strange state of abandonment, listening to the slow breathing of the plants and trees, the competing rhythms of decay and regeneration around her.

Et in Arcadia ego.

Next morning she had lost her voice.

Stress, dampness – whatever was to blame, it had happened.

She tried drinking very hot milky chocolate in a Konditorei. She gargled with it. There wasn't time for steam inhalation.

She couldn't disguise her condition from Kroll. Kroll made no comment, but continued to coax her to sing. The woman tried to mould a voice from her with her hands – sinewy, strong hands – placing them on her diaphragm, on her ribcage. At a certain point those hands grazed Mariel's breasts. It occurred again, and swallowed what voice Mariel had.

'Application. Self-discipline. That is what *I* was taught. Without those, you are wasting your time. You are wasting *my* time. The time is here and then it's gone, nothing! I guard my time. You throw yours away, yes?'

'No.'

'It seems like that to me.'

'You've always tried to make things difficult for us.'

'For who?'

'Me and Ben.'

Kroll made a noise with her mouth, to indicate her impatience.

'You put up all those obstacles,' Mariel continued, 'and you imagine I didn't see them?'

Kroll shook her head at her, not to disagree but to try to move them past the subject.

'Was that what you intended to do all along?' Mariel asked her.

'Do what?'

'Break us up?'

'Nothing that wouldn't happen anyway. I don't involve myself with—'

'We were bound to break up, you mean?'

'I didn't say that. I might have been saying the very opposite.'

'Which is?'

Mariel was getting muddled. Kroll seemed bent on tripping her up, setting her up for a fall.

'You have to learn,' Kroll said.

Mariel stared at her. Why else was she here?

'To sing,' Mariel said.

'And for you to sing well,' Kroll spoke plainly, 'you have to learn what suffering is. All the great composers knew that. We, the interpreters, we also need to understand.'

'You don't believe me, I think,' Mariel said, 'but I've read about the composers, their lives—'

'I'm not talking about reading. I'm not talking about books.'

Mariel couldn't follow.

'I think you are on the outside of what you sing,' Kroll told her. 'You say the words, but you don't mean them. You don't *know* what they mean.'

'So – so how do I get to know? Tell me. Learn more German?'

Kroll shook her head.

'You give yourself to the music. You give yourself to life. And then—'

'And then?'

'It all becomes clear.'

'What becomes clear?'

'The pain that's in the songs. It's the composer's pain, and it's the pain of those who listen to you sing. And it's *our* pain.'

'Ours?'

'The singers. We understand by our own example.'

Mariel finally comprehended.

'You wanted – you want *me* to suffer, is that it?'

Kroll didn't deign to reply to such a crude question.

'That's what you're saying to me?'

Now, for Mariel, everything fell into place. Kroll's philosophy was laid bare. It amounted to a perversion of life, of someone else's life. Her's *and* Ben's. Kroll had played with them, from some sick compulsion to prove – prove *what*? – that suffering ennobled?

No, suffering just brought you down to zero, it took you through the floor, it made you feel like shit. What could anyone do with that?

'You wanted me to be like the composers or something?'

Kroll only raised one arc of eyebrow, as if to mock the ambition.

'They were depressives,' Mariel told her, 'some of them.'

'But here in Vienna, you know that is only half the story.'

'How?'

'The ego drove them on. They were determined. They would endure. At last, yes, they triumphed over their sorrows.'

Mariel stared at Kroll, she tried staring her into the wall.

But Kroll wouldn't be intimidated by a twenty-two-year-old *naïf*.

'You think you loved that man.'

'Who?'

'Your Englishman.'

'I—' The breath tightened in Mariel's chest. They were talking in the past tense. 'Of course – of course I do.'

'No, you didn't really.'

'What – what're you talking about?'

'You wanted to be loved, and so you convinced yourself.'

Mariel couldn't speak now for anger and incredulity.

'You thought he was in love with you.'

'He was. He – he is.'

'With men, it's a matter of lust.'

'No!'

Kroll carried on regardless.

'Or else it's duplicity. To prove something, or get revenge. Lots of reasons. They know a woman will only believe what she wants to believe.'

Mariel stood shaking her head.

'*He* never loved you, young lady.'

A moment later Mariel had leaned sideways onto the desk top. She grabbed the paper knife and felt the warm smooth ivory of the handle in her palm. She turned it, pointing the steel blade at Kroll, who was two or three yards away.

The sudden movements had stopped Kroll in her tracks. She was standing quite still now, eyes focused not on the knife but on Mariel's face. Mariel wanted to look away, but found that she couldn't. She was angry for herself, and for Ben, and because of everything that Kroll was doing. She was a stranger in this city, in this apartment. She came here to study songs about a winter landscape, or a mill by a trout stream, or a lemon grove, and all of them were only imaginary.

Pictures, ideas, not real. Music was the most insubstantial of the arts, immediately turning to ether; a split second after it was made, it was gone.

Nothing at this moment was connecting: the thoughts in Mariel's head, the presence of her body.

But somehow ... Somehow Kroll's eyes were undeceiving her of so much. She was just conscious that her fingers were loosening, and that her hold on the hand of the knife was weakening.

There was a soft muffled sound as the tumbling knife hit the floor. Mariel closed her eyes, saw Kroll behind her eyelids. She opened her eyes again and looked down. The knife was lying on the rug. Kroll stretched out her arm, retrieved it, then stepped back, placing the instrument out of harm's reach, while Mariel continued to look at the pattern on the rug.

Mariel could feel her heart banging against her ribs. Yellow-green spots were floating in front of her eyes. Her stomach had shrunk to a squashy ball. She had a bad taste in her mouth; she felt like she was going to be sick.

'That is enough for today, I think,' Kroll said. 'You look tired, I shall have a taxi come.'

'No.' Mariel, relieved, could hardly speak. She wasn't able to afford a cab fare.

'I shall pay for the taxi,' Kroll said, reading her mind once again. 'You need to rest for a little while. Give me a call tomorrow and tell me when you want to come back.'

Did Kroll think she was simply going to swallow her pride and forget everything that had been said, everything that had happened?

Mariel was too exhausted for any more. She allowed Kroll to take her to the door, hand placed firmly on her elbow as a support. Her legs felt ready to buckle beneath her. Kroll pressed the button for the elevator, which she had never used before.

'Tell me tomorrow, my dear,' she said through the spaces as the steel cage's gate clattered shut.

Ursule Kroll

'The paper knife, where is it?'

Brigitte pointed at the desk. 'The paper knife is always on the desk.'

'I'm sorry,' Kroll said. 'I—'

'Where is it?'

'"Where is it?"'

Brigitte waited.

'The girl ...' Kroll began.

'The girl knows not to touch things. You forgot to put it back on the desk, and now you blame the girl.'

'No, that's not right.'

'You forget what you've done with things.'

'No, Brigitte. Really.'

'It's not on the desk.'

'Here it is.'

Brigitte took the knife from her. She examined it, turning it this way and that as if it might be a fake. Because it hadn't been on the desk, it was immediately an object of suspicion.

'You move things. That's crafty. It's to confuse me. You're confused. You only annoy me when you do that.'

'It wasn't deliberate.'

'What'll you be like when you're really old?'

'I don't want to think of that.'

'My auntie was only in her fifties. She never put things back. It used to drive us berserk. Half our time we spent looking for what we couldn't find.'

'I'm sorry, Brigitte. Truly I am.'

'If I worked for someone else, they would know better.'

'Yes, Brigitte.'

'They wouldn't tease me. Test my patience as you do.'

'It won't happen again.'

'Promise me, then.'

'I promise you.'

'Again.'

'I promise you, Brigitte.'

Mariel Baxter

Mariel put off calling the next day. By the afternoon she had the strength of mind to decide she wouldn't ring Kroll at all.

Instead she went walking, first of all to Clarenbachstrasse. She didn't intend stopping, which was just as well because the bicycle with the red mudguards was back in the hallway, leaning against the wall and turned in a different direction from last time, confirming that its owner was back 'in situ'.

Upper-middle and lower-middle. Perfectly compatible after all.

So, that was that.

She crossed the street and carried on walking. She couldn't think of anywhere to go: only to the little record store.

Tomas nodded over and smiled – seemed to be smiling sympathetically – as she entered. Odd, she thought, how this shop was starting to feel like a refuge from the world. Tomas held up an LP cover.

'Look what I've found!'

It was a compilation of previously lost 78s by a noted conductor of the 1930s called Reiff.

'Where've the motherfuckers been hiding *this*?' Tomas laughed.

Reiff had recorded sometimes in Hamburg, where he persuaded

Kroll and Giebisch to sing a couple of duets. (There may have been more, so the sleeve notes hinted.)

Mariel said she wanted to hear the second act aria from *Hänsel und Gretel*. They stood listening.

Kroll sounded boyish – this Hänsel was a little self-important, but not as sure as his bluster suggested – while Gretel's delivery was lighter, but at the same time this Gretel managed to be more knowing than her brother, alert to others' faults.

Mariel was able to detect these readings of the characters from just a couple of hearings. The music still managed to be sumptuously sweet and melting. It was hard to imagine the duet better or more lovingly sung. You believed that these two wanderers into the wood were siblings, with blood thicker than water.

2008

'You can't forgive me,' Kroll said. 'Can you?'

'Forgive you? For what?'

'Because I was correct.'

Mariel stared at the wall.

'The truth', Kroll said, 'was very hard.'

'*You* should know.'

'What do you mean by that, exactly?'

Mariel switched her eyes from an oil landscape to Kroll.

'You were just a bystander, were you?'

'A bystander?' Kroll repeated, as if the term was unknown to her.

'Someone who just stands and watches.'

'Watches what?'

'The events of their time,' Mariel said. 'History unfolding.'

Kroll hesitated.

'My life was very busy then. I couldn't involve myself with every—'

'No, no,' Mariel shook her head. 'No, I can't let you get away with that.'

Kroll attempted one of those regal stares Mariel was familiar with. She wasn't going to allow her, and deflected it by looking away, back to the wall. The painting showed a scene devoid of human intruders: a forest of towering fir trees, with a path winding off into the blue-green shadows.

'But you were always *aware*.'

'Was I?'

'You told me that, didn't you? You said I had to be aware.'

'Of nature. Of the seasons. Today, in the city—'

'Aware of my own failings. And to know how to control them. Not to let my heart rule my head.'

'Is that what I told you?'

Mariel looked back at Kroll.

'Of course it is. Don't you remember?'

'If that is what *you* remember— '

'You think I'm making it up, do you?'

'I don't have any opinion on the subject.'

It was true: Kroll was being oddly compliant, as if bowing to necessity. Now and then the old Kroll would show through. But she was older now.

A door closed somewhere. Brigitte. Always Brigitte was there. Movements in the other rooms, doors quietly opening and closing, pressure on the floorboards in the hall just outside the room they were in.

'Not tomorrow,' Kroll said.

'No?'

'I live very quietly.'

'The day after?'

'If you wish,' Kroll replied.

'Do *you* wish?'

'No one asks me that question any more.'

'I'll come, shall I?'

'So many questions.'

'Yes,' Mariel said. 'I'll come back.'

Kroll nodded gravely: as if she knew there was no avoiding it.

'Why is she here?'

'I don't know, Brigitte.'

'Why now?'

Kroll shook her head.

'You don't want her here?'

'She asked to come.'

'From America?'

'Yes.'

'And you let her?'

Kroll sighed.

'Yes.'

Brigitte, with her mackintosh hanging open, was blocking the doorway into the hall, and Kroll couldn't get out of the room.

'She wants something. They always want something. She hasn't told you what it's about?'

'No.'

Brigitte's expression was leery.

'You answer without looking at me.'

Kroll directed her eyes towards her.

'I don't know what you want me to say to you, Brigitte.'

'The truth.'

Kroll smiled sadly, and her reply was silent. *Oh, the truth, that is very complicated. You know that as well as I do.*

'I'll tell her to go.' The woman's voice had softened. 'Shall I?'

'No, Brigitte.'

'I'll tell her you're tired, you don't see visitors.'

'She knows that very well.'

'I'll say you need to rest.'

'It isn't as simple as that.'

'What're you talking about?' The tone was as brusque as before. 'You're old, you can't decide these things for yourself.'

Kroll sighed again.

'It doesn't really matter what I think. She's here.'

'Next time I won't let her past the front door.'

'It makes no difference. She's in the apartment, she won't leave.'

'She's at her hotel, you crazy woman.'

'I mean, she's got in. Whatever you do can make no difference. She's been in that chair, she played the piano. She's in the curtains now, in the shadows, all around—'

'Stop it. I won't hear any more.'

'We can't change anything.'

'Stop talking!'

Brigitte pushed her hands into the older woman's chest. Kroll lost her balance, slumped sideways, but was able to just hold on to the door jamb.

Brigitte had turned away. Kroll crouched, as if she was waiting for something else to happen. The door into the kitchen was slammed, and she realised that this was an end to it for the moment.

*

From the taxi Mariel saw a road sign for Favoriten.

The sight of that name, on a tram's destination board, used to make her blood race.

She was in half a mind to ask the driver to take her there. But no, she'd had enough wringing of emotional withers for one day.

She stared out of the side window. More than glass, she felt, separated her from the bustle on the streets.

She was in transit, still returning from twenty-eight years ago, not here and not there but in between, somewhere and nowhere.

*

Kroll stood looking from the window of the dining room. From here she could see halfway along the road.

He was there again. The man in green, a long loden coat and loden hat.

He was waiting under the trees, on the opposite pavement. Close by was a street lamp. The pool of light stopped just short of his shoes, but lit up enough of his face for her to recognise, even at this distance, that it was the same man.

She hadn't asked Brigitte who he was, his name or what business he had in these parts. Brigitte knew most things. But this one time, Kroll chose not to ask her.

She had her own suspicions, however. About his identity, and just why he was here.

Mittwoch

Wednesday

2008

'Maybe she won't come back.'

'I don't know, Brigitte.'

'We can hope.'

Kroll didn't reply. Brigitte was standing in front of her, however, waiting for a response. The daily breakfast tray, finished with, was a dead weight, but Brigitte stood her ground in the doorway of the bedroom.

'I can't tell you anything,' Kroll said from the little table she sat at every morning.

'Eh?'

'Nothing.'

'Tomorrow? Or the next day?'

Kroll didn't dare admit what the arrangement was.

'I'm no wiser than you, Brigitte.'

'If you say so.'

Oh, Kroll knew that tone of voice very well. It had taken decades of maturing. It was the aural equivalent of the pointing index finger. But she hadn't invited the American here. All she was guilty of was not saying 'no'.

*

A whole day.

How was she going to pass the time?

When Mariel went back upstairs, her room was being cleaned. The girl offered to come back later.

'No, I'll go out for some air. Take your time.'

Mariel stood on the street corner, trying to orientate herself.

North, south, which?

She stood turning like a weather vane in a gale.

As it was, she didn't get further than another couple of blocks before she was distracted.

She was passing a big record store, on Mariahilferstrasse. She stopped, walked backwards a few steps, and went in.

She searched the CD racks for her recordings among 'Female Singers'. The BAXTER section was as large as any. Maybe BARTOLI just above contained more. BONNEY and FLEMING and GRAHAM about the same. She cast an eye over JO, Sumi and OTTER, Anne Sofie von, then, by way of FRITTOLI, back to GENS and DESSAY.

This was what it came down to. Counting CD cases. She realised she could be spotted, but no one would have expected it of her, so they'd think, no, it couldn't be *her*. Not in a downtown music store in Vienna.

She moved on, to DVDs. 'Opera', 'Recitals'. Gheorghiu had eight, Callas more than anyone. She didn't see her own *I Sing A Tapestry*. Perhaps they'd sold out? More likely American songs didn't travel well. The recital had been her suggestion, and the film shot in the composers' neck of the woods, but she had sensed less than twenty-four carat commitment from the honchos on Madison Avenue.

She was just about to leave when she turned and saw the poster, *that* poster, with the girl oozing out of her Donatella dress. Mariel's friends knew to call her She Who Will Be Nameless. Hennaed hair with extensions, silicon implants, a nip here and a tuck there, collagen-injected lips to give her that sexy pout, and a voice which – God knows – she didn't deserve.

Here in Mitteleuropa. According to marketing, they hadn't

gotten beyond trying her out in the States. Maybe they thought of this as a low-key experiment she wouldn't find out about. They began with some outlandish idea they could promote their 'product' in Midwestern shopping malls. Other young stars had burned bright and waned, and with luck this one would blaze to earth also. But the others hadn't got Dieter Spengler against a stairwell wall, following the big sales conference in Delaware; Cara Michaels had, and she lost no time in going down on her knees to prove the suction quality of those surgically enhanced lips of hers.

*

No, Kroll didn't really want her here. Not today or any other day. The Amerikanerin.

Brigitte was right, it was stressful. She was simply trying to protect her employer, and Kroll felt that she shouldn't have been so hard on her.

Hard on Brigitte? My God! Kroll half-smiled at her reflection in the dressing-table mirror.

Today should be a holiday. But the past was already knocking at the window, heaving on the front door, clambering down the chimney.

Mariel Baxter

It was the only place Mariel could think to go, back to Schlehen-gasse.

If Kroll was surprised to see her back again, she didn't show it.

Nothing was said: about the incident with the knife (no longer left out on the desk), nor about her recent erratic behaviour.

It was as if they were starting over again.

It was a time for second chances. For both of them.

The lessons would now be as they should have been all along.

Mariel was ready to immerse herself in the songs. Every time she opened the pages of sheet music she felt she was escaping to somewhere better.

The disciplinary process began before she went out in the mornings.

Mariel stood in front of the mirror in her room, making her final adjustments prior to leaving. She only had to think of Ursule Kroll, and lo and behold her face grew sterner. She had tied her hair back, which gave an impression of purposefulness – and severity.

Kroll's words went through her head.

You have to give everything to the music, young woman. You need to give your heart and soul.

'Mariel Baxter. Mariel Baxter. Mariel Baxter.'

She spoke the words back to herself, in the glass, the cold glass.

Through most of her girlhood, she answered to Mae. At school she was Maybelle on the register. Maybelle-Clare.

When she received her application form for music school, she decided what she had actually known all along, that Maybelle-Clare didn't suit her. It wouldn't look right on the page. She had thought of Margot instead, and seen the spelling Margaux. But at the last minute, she wrote down Mariel. (Marielle? No. Two letters too long, a drag on people's patience.) Baxter was easy, because that was her mother's name, and so it wasn't a deception. Not that Mariel was: it was only how she saw herself really, or rather it was how she *heard* herself.

She didn't return to the Glockenspiel.

That was behind her now. Over.

Something about Die Gruppe.

All of them, Mariel realised, were incomplete. Some were probably damaged, others were inately dissatisfied. They had stuck together, without moving beyond the social confines they'd set themselves. No one local was drafted in, and there were no defections.

Mariel felt she'd been drawn to Die Gruppe as spare matter might be pulled into a vortex, not appreciating that vortices consume.

There were no messages for her at Schlehengasse, or at Frau Werfel's either, and Mariel didn't enquire.

She became what Kroll wanted her to be: a model student.

She arrived on the dot, and she didn't get twitchy if they overran. She had nowhere else to go anyway.

Even on the morning when she woke up feeling lousy, she went and got the tram. Kroll had Brigitte make her some lemon tea with honey.

On the second day of feeling unwell, she had to drag herself in from Penzing. She vomited two streets away from Schlehengasse, but she had cleaned herself up by the time she reached the apartment's doorbell. Oddly, quite inexplicably, that afternoon she sang like a siren who could have charmed a shipful of heroes to their watery graves.

Ursule Kroll

In 1943 Brigitte had been working in a hotel in Tegernsee. She was a chambermaid.

Kroll was taking a vacation, on her way home from Berchtesgaden, where she had been invited to sing at the Berghof on the great man's fifty-fourth birthday.

One day Kroll returned to the suite to find the contents of her trunk being subjected to careful examination.

'Please don't tell on me, madam,' the girl pleaded. 'Please.'

'Why should I not report you?'

'I can't afford to lose my position, madam.'

'Why is that?'

'My mother's bedridden. And my sister has just lost her husband, his ship was torpedoed by the British.'

'Why should I believe you?'

'If you ask anyone here who knows me—'

Probably it was true. Kroll normally clammed up at hard luck stories. Her career had elevated her beyond the mundane, and it was a habit she was happy not to break.

The maid wasn't pretty. She wasn't quite plain either. She had a full, ripe figure. Kroll had glanced at her as she went about her work, from the front or from behind, as she stooped or bent over.

She had a boyfriend, who – Kroll guessed – might be stringing her along. And vice versa. Kroll took the opportunity to quiz her, while keeping the girl on tenterhooks for a couple of days as to whether or not she would inform the management.

Her name was Brigitte Brank. It was nice for her to come to the hotel, she said, to get away from home.

'What is my ambition in life?' She repeated Kroll's question. 'I can't say, madam.'

'Everyone has hopes and dreams.'

'*Only* hopes and dreams, madam. Not many get the chance.'

'Tell me.'

Why was she listening for her answer?

'Tell me,' Kroll said again.

Something humdrum about a cottage by the sea. How predictable it was. When Kroll beat her down, the girl spoke of – not the sea – but getting a job in the city. A housekeeper's job, if she could, in some fine establishment.

'Not a cottage?'

'That's just for me.'

'And your boyfriend? Husband?'

'I don't know—' The girl struggled. Her eyes swivelled towards Kroll, then away again.

'Not the mountains anyway?' Kroll waved towards the window and the view of white Alpine peaks.

'This is seasonal work, madam. I'll go back to our local commercial hotel in the winter.'

'Do you like it there?'

'I don't like or dislike it, madam.'

'Tell me the truth.'

'Then, so help me God, I wouldn't care if I never saw the place again.'

*

'Or "Im Frühling" perhaps?' the student has asked her teacher.

While she stands waiting for a response, Kroll is singing through the lines in her head.

See, the spring colours already peep out from the buds and flowers. Not all the flowers are the same to me; I like best to pluck them from the same stems as she did.

Alina Giebisch used to include 'Im Frühling' in her repertoire. But she sang it sparingly, and where she possibly could she dropped it. Critics had been very favourably impressed; Giebisch, however, was unusual in that she didn't set out to please them, and the fact that they expected her to include the song seemed – to her – to be one very good reason why she shouldn't do so.

Kroll had looked on. She wanted to sing 'Im Frühling', but felt that she couldn't. Although Alina was performing it as seldom as she could, that lied remained hers, to her (mildly disappointed) audiences and to Kroll.

Afterwards, when Alina's name was already starting to be forgotten, Kroll wanted to include it in her concert programming. She sang it to honour the Führer at a rally in Düsseldorf, with Maestro Böhm himself accompanying her, and that august occasion helped to confer ownership of the song. She continued to perform it during those war years. She didn't overuse it. The song was one she meant to be special.

Critics were divided as to whose version was the better: Alina Giebisch's or Ursule Kroll's. The matter was argued hotly. To Kroll, it didn't matter. The debate was unseemly; the Schubert-o-philes were surely the only people concerned, and their interest was unbalanced. It was the song which had fascinated Kroll because, as Fräulein Hebbel said, she could have shown off to better effect with others.

Kroll felt herself becoming protective of the song: for the song's sake, for Alina's sake, and for her own sake too. She recorded it twice. Some songs she would try to interpret differently, and perhaps with that one she could have gone on refining. However, she knew she had taken it far enough away from Alina's rendition, and from von der Osten's earlier one, to have it bear her own stamp.

There was nothing more she wished to do with it. She didn't want to ever become tired of singing it, and so she decided to stop. Inside the rooms of her own apartment, and inside her head, she sang it, but not in public, not ever again.

Now—

Now the American girl is asking her.

'No. Not "Im Frühling". Others would be better for your voice. They would show it to a better advantage. Crowd pleasers.'

Kroll nudged that one aside on top of the piano lid, bringing other titles to the fore.

The girl didn't speak of it again. She seemed grateful for what her teacher was offering her instead.

They had recovered an equilibrium of sorts.

Kroll heard something new in the voice. What the girl was singing was brushed with sadness, as by an angel's wing: sadness even in the songs which celebrated life and spoke of joy.

The result was, thus far, quite satisfactory. Kroll offered encouragement, believing that it was only as much as was due.

While the sky stayed gunmetal grey outside, and the Viennese afternoons gloomy, they were both cheered by quiet progress.

Maybe, just maybe, the American would amount to something after all. If she persevered. If she knuckled down. If she cleared her mind of what – who – didn't deserve to be there.

'We shall try something new now.'

Richard Strauss. In proper season. Opus 68, the *Brentano Lieder*. Number 5, 'Amor'.

> *By the fire sat the child*
> *Cupid, Cupid and was blind;*
> *with his little wings he fans*

the flames and smiles;
fan, smile, wily child!

Kroll explained about the early nineteenth-century German poet Clemens Brentano – and Strauss's writing the songs in 1918 for Elisabeth Schumann – and about having heard Schumann sing them in Hamburg.

But somehow, as Kroll also instructed her, she was to imagine that she was singing the song for the first time, as if she was only now bringing it fresh before the world.

Singing them through first, Kroll then handed the lines to her pupil. She listened.

Yes, she could hear Ursule Kroll, and Sabine Hebbel, but she was also hearing Mariel Baxter. She was hearing Elisabeth Schumann, and Pauline de Ahna, Strauss's wife.

Time was flowing as a flood through the room on this grey, monochrome afternoon.

Kroll was thinking of the text of *Der Rosenkavalier*. 'Music is a holy art.'

On the fringes of the afternoon, somewhere, putti and hobgoblins were gathering. But Kroll shut her mind to everything but the music.

Mariel Baxter

Mariel returned to Schlehengasse 19, but climbed only to the second floor. She knocked on the door of the doctor's consulting rooms. Without delay the door opened and a smiling woman invited her to come in.

'You would like to talk to Dr Brokmeier?'

'I think so.'

'That would be best.'

He looked only a little surprised when she walked into the reception room.

'Please come through, won't you?'

Mariel hesitated. She had no idea how she was going to pay for this.

Dr Brokmeier seemed to assess the situation very quickly.

'Don't worry about anything. You are here as my guest.'

Mariel smiled as best she could, then followed him into the inner sanctum. It was all being made so straightforward, so effortless for her.

'Please sit down, young lady. Now, why don't you tell me a little bit about yourself?'

Stepping out on to the street, Mariel immediately slammed into fresh air. All her nerve ends seemed to be on the surface and exposed. She had tears in her eyes. Her legs felt like rubber.

She concentrated on just getting round the corner. She dropped on to a bench, wiping her tears with her fingers, not caring what anyone thought. The street was made up of crazy, jagged angles.

Vienna, the future, life, everything, was collapsing in on top of her.

An hour later she was sitting in a café. She was staring at the wall, at a poster, curling at its corners, of a faded Istanbul.

Why Istanbul?

It was a perfectly run-of-the-mill café, the first one she had come to when she realised she couldn't walk any further.

They brought her coffee instead of a chocolate, but she didn't think to send it back. She was only thinking about one thing.

She felt so ashamed. She had turned the atmosphere in Dr Brokmeier's consulting room, the niceness and friendliness, on its head. Whatever she tried to tell him about herself came out skewed. She sounded cheap and whorish. She thought she needed to be honest first and foremost, but nothing she said could present her in a favourable light.

She already knew, in her blood and bones, that she was pregnant.

'Yes,' she said, as the doctor confirmed what she already knew. 'Yes, I see.'

She sat stupidly in front of him, offering no response. She had a sensation of wearing another person's face, or a mask. Her brain was numbed.

On the way downstairs, out of the corner of her eye, she caught sight of Brigitte.

'Did you forget, then?'

'Pardon me?'

'The lesson.'

'I – I ...'

Mariel nodded and walked past, out on to the street.

The sun was shining when she left Vienna.

It was the wrong weather, but the wrongness meant it was right, because everything now was inverted, reversed. It should have been grey and overcast, but *of course* the clouds had cleared, the sun was out and the future was bright.

If you believed in the future, that was.

Mariel watched from the back of the cab.

Bitches Brew, she remembered. Ben's favourite Miles Davis album.

The sun shone down long streets and reflected off the façades of buildings, it dazzled in windows, smithereened into hundreds and thousands of suns. The city had a loveliness and a lightness she hadn't been conscious of before. It was only now that she understood what its fascination was: the mixture of impressive grandeur and its *dreamlike* quality, somewhere already known from sleep or woolgathering.

The buildings of the Ringstrasse should have been looming over her, making her feel helpless, hopeless. Instead they had a charming appropriateness: they could only be as they were, emblems of Austria's soaring intellectual ambitions and a sovereign sweet tooth for confectionery and froth.

She had the address of a hostel in Paris. She'd been given it by Ilan. His sister had stayed there. It used to accommodate women journalists, in the days of high morals and delicate sensibilities. Now it took in mainly professional women from overseas, working for short-term spells in the city, who wanted a same-sex environment.

'I'm not professional.'

'Music *will* be your profession.'

Mariel smiled wanly.

Ilan had written down the street and the phone number, and the name of his sister's friend who was in charge.

She also had Lucien's address, near the Avenue Foch. When she rang the bell and the door was opened to her, she found she was speaking to a very handsome young man who wasn't Lucien. He called through 'Lucien!' and Lucien appeared from the shower with a towel wrapped round his waist.

Mariel wasn't in the mood to be shocked by what Lucien got up to in Paris. She just needed to talk to *someone*.

She and Lucien sat down to discuss things after his handsome companion had been sent on his way.

'Have you told Ben?'

'No. Promise me you won't tell him.'

'Okay. I promise.'

Silence.

Mariel hadn't appreciated how much Lucien's nose was like a boxer's. His eyes were too wide-set, but their expression was kindly.

'D'you trust me, Mariel?'

She sat stirring her coffee.

'Yes,' she said, needing to believe it. 'Yes, I trust you.'

They went out for lunch, to restaurant where Lucien was a regular.

Lucien thought she should have the baby and put it up for adoption.

'I mean', he apologised, 'him or her.'

'No, better stick to "it".'

Easier like that.

'What d'you say, Mariel?'

She wasn't sure. Was that the solution?

Lucien saw how she was hesitating.

'It's up to you,' he told her.

'Yes.'

'Ben can't help?'

'I never asked him.'

Everything in Paris was winding down for Christmas. But people still had sex, and mistakes got made and needed to be dealt with. This was a year-round trade.

The air of good cheer, even if it was forced, made her feel worse than ever. Lunch parties reeled out of bistros in the late afternoon. Nativity scenes were set up in shop windows and at street corners. The big department stores stayed open into the evening. The only sad-looking person she saw in the whole of Paris was the one staring right back at her out of the plate-glass windows on the shopping streets.

Lucien offered to pay. So that she could be 'fixed', if that was really what she wanted.

'It's called an abortion, Lucien.'

'Yes, I know.'

What did it matter what the business was called?

She felt lulled by her surroundings. She could put up with her room at the hostel when she was able to avail herself by day of Lucien's parents' comforts in the 16th Arrondissement. The plush carpets and heavy drapes which muffled unwanted sounds, the over-stuffed and plumped-up opulence.

But it wasn't real to her. Nor, for that matter, was Lucien's ready supply of funds, although he would have given her whatever she asked for so that they could be rid of the problem and go dancing at Le Palace, rubbing shoulders with Marisa Berenson and Maria Schneider, maybe even Yves and Loulou. Mariel felt grateful, but she didn't want to be prey to softer sentiments at the moment. She needed to be hard, resistant.

She decided not to accept his money. She didn't tell him she wasn't taking it. She asked an Australian girl at the hostel she'd got talking to, who gave her an address out past Bastille. She said they did the job at a competitive rate, a friend of hers had gone there: it wasn't The Ritz, but what the fuck.

'If you'll pardon my French.'

And they laughed.

No, it wasn't The Ritz.

The girl in the front room might have been Turkish (from Istanbul?), and French seemed as problematic to her as English.

In her mind's eye Mariel had pictured white walls, white uniforms, silence. Lucien's money could have bought her nice surroundings, and service and discretion, and maybe something like peace of mind. She had none of those now. There were plaster cracks on the walls, covered over by movie posters. Linoleum on the floors. The seepage of sounds: radio blather somewhere, a washing machine or a tumble drier, and a persistent squeaking she couldn't explain, until the Turkish girl stood up and Mariel noticed she was wearing new-looking sneakers.

The doctor was in a hurry. Mariel guessed he was just back from a late lunch. Later she would tell herself that she had smelled drink on his breath, before she went under the chloroform. Later she would tell herself that she'd been able to feel pain, that they hadn't used enough gas. (Inefficiency? Cost-cutting?) Guilt might have been twisting its knife into her, delighting in her agonies; but the hunch persisted that she'd been too close to the surface of consciousness and that they'd dealt with her too roughly.

They scraped and scraped and scraped.

If guardian spirits were hovering above her, they were those of Sylvia Plath and Marilyn Monroe.

When she came to, it was to hear voices speaking urgently over her head. Back and forth, Mariel tracked the words, to and fro, although she couldn't get their sense. She grabbed on to them – flying fish they were like – clung on, which was how she raised herself into the air, into here and now, the actual.

She was up on her feet, being supported on both sides.

She felt shaky, drained of energy. Trying clumsily to move forward, she was aware of a numbness between her legs and at the tops of her thighs. She stumbled, and the arms held her upright.

She was taken to another room and placed in a faux leather armchair. There was a rip in one arm, where someone might have clawed at it; the slash had been covered with two bits of sticky tape. Tea in a green enamel pot ('Elephant', the label on the tea bag said) was brought to her, and she fidgeted with the cross of grubby tape. A door banged loudly. She could still hear the washing machine. A song was playing on the invisible radio.

Songs were still being sung, and washing machines churning, people were going about their lives, and she wondered what they did with the mess, if the slop got taken away in a pail or a plastic bag, and if it went out with the rest of the garbage, and where was it now, in a trash-can already? *Oh my God*! On the way here, on the bus, they'd passed a cemetery; she'd seen a winged angel blowing a trumpet, forgetting it was stone, and sounding jubilant, as if summoning the dead to a party. In death as in life, some got to celebrate while others didn't. *Oh Christ God*!

They sent for a taxi to collect her.

The Turkish girl took her arm till they were at the door. Then she was on her own. Perhaps the neighbours didn't like to be reminded of what went on inside the house.

The fresh air went straight to her head. She felt dizzy, she had to cling to the outside wall for several seconds to regain her balance.

The surly driver waited with his engine ticking over. He watched her, but made no offer to help. He was to say nothing to her on the journey across the city. He seemed to be in a hurry to get somewhere else. He jumped lights, rode up on the curb at a couple of corners.

As Mariel looked out of the window, trying not to cry, her brow knocked against the glass several times. She didn't know how she could feel more lonely, more unhappy than she did now.

Every time she saw a child, or a mother with a baby in a pushchair, she closed her eyes and waited for a few seconds before opening them again. Soon enough there was bound to be another child, or another mother pushing another baby. It was endless. A parade of normal people who appeared to be on top of their lives – and even if they weren't really, they were compared to *her*.

Her eyes blurred. The buildings wobbled, started to melt. It wasn't raining, but everything was turning to water, running headlong for the Seine.

Lucien and his friend Patrick had arranged to meet her. When she didn't show up, they came to the hostel for her. They had a hire car and driver waiting at the door and wouldn't take '*non*' for an answer.

Lucien's choice was a shiny American bar on the Avenue Franklin D. Roosevelt. It was a sophisticated Right Bank notion of Americana: red leather, polished chrome and steel, recessed lighting, Sarah Vaughan turned down very low. It was lovely, and Mariel felt so ridiculously grateful she had tears in her eyes again.

'Do you forgive me?' she asked in a paper-thin voice.

They must have seen she wasn't up to it. She wasn't hungry, but she did drink the brandy cocktail, and the second one, which Lucien ordered for her.

'Best pick-me-up in the world, Mariel, in my opinion. Nothing ever seems so bad.'

She was beyond brandy, she felt. She was still numb inside. It was as if she'd been chloroformed internally. Not far behind it, she realised, she was in a lot of pain.

She drank up.

Lucien told Patrick he would see her home. They walked along the drying lamplit streets *à deux*. She felt exhausted, quite drunk, but also invigorated by the rush of night air. On the Pont Neuf she stopped. She could hear the music of *La Traviata*. Her grief, she thought, was no match for Violetta's. Here, perhaps, *she* had stood.

(No, it wasn't true that Violetta had never existed. She was as real as any of this: *more* real, because she had endured, because Mariel was thinking about her right now.) Violetta was the expression of herself, and of every woman who felt she hadn't lived up to life.

The Seine flowed between the arches beneath them, so darkly and alluringly. Mariel was aware of Lucien's hand tightening on her arm, with a surprising resolve and strength. She closed her eyes. A carriage passed along the night street behind her, hooves sounded on cobblestones.

She found she was singing.

'Sempre libera degg'io'.

One day Kroll had played her one of her recordings from long ago, made at the start of her career in Aachen. She was singing that aria, where Violetta is at her most temperamental and irresponsible. The music rose and rose to a thrilling E flat. Mariel saw how fascinated Kroll was to hear her young voice, criticising herself as if she was listening to a pupil.

While she was singing on the bridge like this, Mariel felt life was bearable. It was – as Johann Strauss had called one of his waltzes – the music of the spheres. It was transfigured night. A perfect sickle moon rode high. Chagall's liberated spirits went flying through the air. She would have flown after them, borne high by the music, but Lucien held her arm firmly in his grip.

Still singing, Mariel turned and watched him in the lamplight's glow. He was astonished by her. She would have taken him with her if she could, across the starry sky. In fact, she would never see him again: nineteen months later he would be knocked down and killed while dashing across a busy street, in pursuit of some impossible ideal Adonis. Life – or death – is almost poetic in its cruelties.

For the moment, though, even at the end of the worst day of her life, here everything rhymed, everything chimed, and you might have thought that reckless beauty owned the world.

The next day she found a postcard of the bridge and bought it. She sat down on a bench in the street, crossing her legs to make a little improvised desk for herself, and thought about what to write.

The name first, *Fräulein Ursule Kroll* (no *Professorin*, no *Doktorin*, and God help them no *Kammersängerin*), followed by the address, *Schlehengasse 19*.

She turned the card over. The bridge looked like ... exactly like a bridge. How could she sum up her sensations of yesterday, and the surge of euphoria coming from she didn't know where?

She didn't have the vocabulary for it. The experience had come and gone. She couldn't remember now why she had felt so elated, unless it was supposed to have been denied to her, and so she had been determined to have it and enjoy it. Why else?

She uncrossed her legs. More cramps in her abdomen. She had no good reason to be writing to the woman. What did she owe her? Nothing, nothing at all.

Into her cupped hand she caught the tiny pieces as she tore up the postcard.

Ursule Kroll

The Führer was charm personified.

He bowed to her. He took her hand in his.

He had seen *Arabella* six times already, he told her, but *her* portrayal was the finest of all.

A flunkey presented her with a bouquet of white orchids. Kroll's delight was quite genuine.

The Führer made her feel beautiful, and desirable. She felt the radiance of his power. For those moments she was dwelling on Olympus, among the gods. It was a sensation even more exhilarating than being on stage, soaring above the orchestra and hitting your top note.

She realised as she was experiencing it that this was the greatest moment of her life. Nothing could ever be so perfect again.

A photograph of the occasion was sent to her, in a heavy solid silver frame.

It was dedicated to her.

Und du wirst mein Gebeiterin sein.

The intimate second person singular. The words were a subtle alteration of von Hofmannsthal's in the *Arabella* score. 'And you will be my mistress.'

And signed, *With profound admiration, A.H.*

It became, at that instant of reading his message, her most treasured possession, which would remain dearest to her all her life.

Mariel Baxter

On the plane she looked past the woman next to her, out of the window, at the sun-silvered English Channel beneath them.

A year had gone by.

She had learned so much, and so little.

She would never know enough about German lieder.

She had discovered how to love, and then how to hate.

She had carried another life about inside her, before she murdered it.

Defending that prosaic passage of water beneath the aircraft's wing had helped to determine the fate of the modern world. Hope and glory.

I wish I had a camera right now, the woman in the window seat said.

Mariel smiled before leaning back and closing her eyes. After just a few seconds she felt her smile slackening. Somewhere on the plane a baby was crying.

Ursule Kroll

Ursule Kroll's final recitals, so it transpired, were in Munich, then on Austrian soil.

She was in Salzburg when the war ended. Imminent appearances in Germany were suddenly being cancelled, and she found herself seeing in the new age as a resident of Vienna.

The landscape of Vienna, especially after daylight, was lunar.

Kroll went out walking, taking care which streets she hazarded on to. The ground was unstable in some, while the danger was from fellow Viennese in others. Broken buildings assumed fantastic shapes against a vividly coloured sky, purple or yellow or red. She skirted the mountains of rubble, trying to remember from visits long ago what had been in their place.

An empire lay at her feet. Blue moonlight shrank palaces and slums alike to details on a chiaroscuro frieze. Animated figures scrambled up from beneath the ground; others, returning, quickly burrowed themselves back into their foxholes.

Sometimes she heard only her own two feet sounding on the cobbles. Occasionally she nearly stepped on a sleeping person, sexless, huddled beneath a coat or a piece of sacking. The dogs mostly went into the stockpots, and only the nimblest and luckiest cats held on to a ninth life.

She wasn't as afraid as her friends thought she ought to be, out by herself after dark. She saw hunchbacks, men with no legs, wild children; a plaster shop mannequin sticking up out of brickwork grinned at her, while Kroll dispensed her own smiles in the direction of those she presumed to be ghosts, wraiths in the clothes of a different era.

She rented an apartment close to the Hofburg. Accommodation on such a grand scale cost next to nothing, even with so many people homeless. (It felt safer to some to remain out of doors, sleeping under the sky.)

They were the first-floor rooms of stately premises on a street of palaces. The back of the building had taken a hit from German artillery shells, and consequently the structure had lost its confidence. Bits of masonry continued to crumble and fall off, on the front aspect also. Kroll felt she was trying to save the whole edifice from lapsing into irredeemable melancholy.

The Prada luggage, twenty-six pieces in all, stayed largely unpacked. She had her possessions still in Berlin, including her paintings, moved very discreetly to a secure depository, which also held some of Hitler's inner circle's private treasures and mementoes. The Kroll container-loads were in choice company, the most illustrious she could have hoped for.

Correspondence reached her, as much by good luck as anything else. (Once upon a time the trains had run, and the post had been unfailingly efficient.)

The fan letters cheered her, even when they seemed too earnest, and some quite deranged. Most of the other mail was dispiriting. Music was in hibernation. Confirmation of one cancellation followed another; contracts were null and void, and there wasn't a thing she or the ailing Teschermacher could do about it.

By day people huddled at street corners. They sat next to one another on boxes or stones or on kerbs, not speaking, slumped over in sleep or with their heads in their hands.

Elsewhere, groups huddled round fires. Kroll smelled cooking, although God knew what it was. Clothes were washed in any water that could be found, and fixed to wherever they might get some wind, so they'd dry.

Mutilated men, demobbed, were a common sight. They pitched forward on crutches, with dummy legs or arms strapped to their shoulders or back. Once proud voices begged for small change, and muttered thanks no louder than a whisper, if at all. (But why should they acknowledge this casual charity of strangers?)

People continued to distrust being indoors, and lived outside, among the ruins. Without money to spend, they bartered or stole. Those who weren't cowed looked dazed or simply indifferent.

Another letter, requesting her presence in Berlin, *at your earliest convenience.*

She knew what it concerned. It could *only* be about one thing.

She placed the letter in an empty drawer in the escritoire. She walked about the rooms in her palace quarters, adjusting to the furnishings she had acquired with the premises, imagining back to life the Habsburg spirits who had preceded her.

The letter nagged at her, from the drawer of a desk grand enough for signing and ratifying a national treaty.

She saw herself, uncertainly, in misty mirrors. Life was a dream.

Berlin. The old Reichskulturkammer Headquarters.

She who holds the Martial Order of Merit enters the room slowly. Timing is all. The men in their different uniforms stare at her.

She hands her gloves to one of them, who doesn't know what to do with these kid sheaths of extraordinary fineness, made bespoke for her in Madrid.

'Ursule Kroll—?'

The voice is American. He speaks her name as a question. She glares at him, as she waits for someone to pull out a chair for her.

The chair legs scrape on the floor.

Kroll seats herself without being asked.

They have the papers ready and waiting for her to sign.

The idiot who spoke a few moments ago explains what is written on them. It amounts to, firstly, an admission of NSDAP membership; and, then, agreeing to a statement of regret for past actions.

Yes, she had Party membership, or else how could she have sung? Why should she regret and apologise for what she was doing merely as a good German?

The term 'good German' affords them some amusement. But Kroll sits unsmiling and stony-faced. She has prepared herself to be inscrutable, but finds she is, instead, angry.

The papers are placed in front of her. You sign on this one here, here, here.

She sits back in the chair.

'You propose to resurrect your career, Miss Kroll?'

'"Resurrect" it?'

'Begin again.'

'My career never finished,' she replies witheringly.

'This is 1946.'

'People will always remember. They will play my recordings.'

They stare back at her.

'And on these pages, where I've indicated—'

The American has hairy wrists and stubby fingers, and she hates him with a passion.

She turns and motions to the aide who pushed in her chair. The reverse process takes place, allowing her to rise to her feet.

She holds out her hand, without looking, until the gloves are returned to her.

'I take it you wish some time to think about the matter, Miss Kroll?'

'There isn't anything to think about.'

'But if you intend to sing again—'

'You're asking me to put my name to what has no meaning for me.'

'Doesn't that make it easier?'

She wasn't going to apologise to these insolent bastards. It was they who ought to be apologising to her, for the indignity of the proceedings. The Germans had humiliated themselves already by capitulating: wasn't that enough?

She was waiting for someone to open the door. A young adjutant realised, and jumped to attention.

'Glancy—!' his commander warned him.

But he had opened the door for her anyway, and nothing – nothing any of them could do – was going to stop her from walking out.

They came after her.

You will probably have reconsidered this issue in the interim, and thought better of your earlier decision—

The hell she had.

If you would care to make an appointment, to call by when it might be most suitable to you—

She didn't respond to the letter.

They tried again. This time their tone was less polite, less conciliatory.

It would certainly be in your own best interests to address the question of—

Her eyes scanned the lines of print. They spoke to her as if she was a chorus singer. Imbeciles! One of them had indicated that he knew her recordings quite well, and he alone had seemed unsurprised when she got up out of her chair and made for the door.

This letter was the work of Stubby Fingers, she felt. He of the thick hairy wrists. A revolting specimen. His grubby fingerprints were all over this. He wanted to rub her nose in it. But she wasn't going to be demeaned.

She understood what non-compliance entailed. It meant that her glory days were behind her. But she had been marked out to be a woman of her times, from the hour she was born. Her future now was dim. Her achievements might be behind her. So be it.

She had believed what she told them that afternoon when she deigned to face them, in the old Reich's Chamber of Culture building, even though she had been speaking entirely off the cuff.

A great singer survives. The voice is remembered for as long as an audience has the power of recall. The songs are somehow wrapped, not lost, in the ether – and are preserved. They exist outside the reductions and curtailments of ordinary time.

Life is short, and art endures.

Ursule Kroll's obscurity in the late 1940s and 1950s wasn't total eclipse.

She recorded, for smaller companies than she was used to. She gave stage recitals here and there, but not in the major cities. When interviews might have benefited her, only a very rare one was forthcoming. There weren't any radio performances until 1951, and they were slipped unobtrusively into the programming.

Her diehard admirers could at least say of her: what an example she is. A star to the last, she's given it her all, and has never stopped singing.

Kroll didn't mention Alina Giebisch, and the name very seldom came up in people's conversation with her. If it did, it happened inadvertently and Kroll would say as little as she could get away with. It was understood that true stars were happiest discussing only themselves.

Kroll's rivals, the ones who had gone to make their peace with the Occupiers ('Done their shoddy deals,' according to Kroll) were occasionally referred to by her, but unfavourably, sneerily. One, a favourite with the Scandinavian royal families, was remembered for her soubrette-on-the-make ambitions and her petulance (kicking a foot through stage scenery in a fit of pique).

2008

Somehow Mariel got through the day.

The stores and boutiques. A walk round the Albertina to see the Dürer graphics. Coffee and an almond pastry at Café Hawelka. A swim in the hotel pool, followed by a massage. Avoiding the trailing eyes of another guest, an American businessman, in the cocktail bar. TV upstairs in her room, an in-house movie, *The Page Turner*.

> To: *Lou Litvinoff*
> cc:
> Subject: Guess What
>
> Hi Lou, Calm down. Cool it. Chill. POSITIVITY!
> Next week I'll explain if I can. I promise.
> Vienna? Ach! (Lou shakes his head.)
> *Le'hayim*, to life!
> M xx

She deliberated over whether she should call Kroll, finally deciding yes – yes, she would.

She rang early evening, from her hotel bedroom.

Brigitte answered.

'This is Mariel Baxter.'

The woman inhaled sharply, said nothing.

'Would it be possible to speak to Fräulein Kroll?'

The receiver was placed, noisily, on the table top, while Brigitte went off to deliver the message.

'Hello?' Finally Kroll's voice sounded into the mouthpiece. 'I wasn't expecting to hear from you.'

'Tomorrow is still all right for you?'

'Tomorrow afternoon?'

'Yes,' Mariel said.

'But that is what we agreed.'

'Yes, it was. I was just checking.'

Mariel found herself blabbing.

'These cellphones, they're a great temptation. Something occurs to you, and if you don't want to text – it remembers the numbers, so you don't need to go looking. There's no excuse, you feel, for not making sure – or just saying hello.'

'Life used to be simpler. And quieter. Telephones were for important matters. Even for *you*, I think.'

'I'm sorry—?'

'You didn't always communicate so freely, Mariel Baxter.'

'No?'

'You didn't get in touch with me,' Kroll said.

'When?'

'When you came to me, to learn the unwritten secrets.'

Mariel was silent.

'When you decided you'd had enough. When you packed your bags and left. You didn't contact me.'

'No. No, I didn't.'

'Nothing. No warning.'

Mariel stared in front of her, at the bedroom wall.

'I didn't know where you'd gone,' Kroll said.

'Did you enquire?'

'Naturally.'

'Not even Brigitte knew?'

'Brigitte?'

'Little escapes *her* notice.'

'You left Vienna.'

'I needed to get away.'

'Couldn't the matter have been sorted out here?'

'I thought you'd be glad to see the back of me.'

'Why?'

'"Why?"' Mariel repeated. 'Isn't that obvious?'

'I had put a lot of time into teaching you.'

'So I was saving you wasting any more of it.'

'You were making good progress.'

'I was?' Mariel couldn't disguise her surprise.

'Of course,' Kroll said. 'I wouldn't have continued if you hadn't been.'

Silence.

Mariel wondered if this was the moment for a confession about events in Paris. She decided it wasn't. Some secrets she was determined to hold on to, for as long as she could.

'Just think,' Kroll said, in a manner that seemed to be taunting her, 'how extraordinary a singer you might have become if you had stayed.'

Ursule Kroll

Brigitte had made coffee for them both with the expensive Landtmann grounds, and brought a pastry for each of them from Demel Konditorei.

'What is this in aid of?'

Brigitte ignored the implied criticism of her indulgence.

'It isn't a birthday,' Kroll said.

She sat down where Brigitte told her to sit.

'So what are we celebrating?' Kroll asked again.

'I've been speaking to my friend Frau Müller.'

'Who?'

'In the building. On the stairs.'

'Which one is she?'

'Dr Brokmeier's receptionist.'

'And—?'

Brigitte poured coffee from the pot, into Kroll's cup first.

'And you might be surprised, some of the bits and pieces she comes out with.'

'How can I be if you don't tell me?'

'Is the coffee to your satisfaction?'

'It tastes very good, Brigitte. As expensive coffee should.'

'The pastries are on me.'

A Mohnstrudel roulade of poppy seeds and raisins for herself, and a chocolate Marmorgugelhupf for Kroll.

'Why have you been throwing your money about?'

'I'm in a good mood,' Brigitte said. 'I'm filled with festive cheer.'

'Christmas?' Kroll asked sceptically.

'No.'

'We're celebrating something else?'

'You could say that.'

'I can't say anything, Brigitte, until you tell me.'

'Are you sitting comfortably? Storytellers always ask that.'

'Dining chairs are to aid deportment, they're not for comfort.'

'Don't go spoiling things.'

'Very well, I won't.'

'I'll start again. Are you sitting comfortably?'

'If you want me to say so – yes.'

'Good. Then I'll begin.'

Mariel Baxter

Beginner's luck?

Certainly she had an easy start to her career.

A soprano pulled out of *Figaro* at short notice and Mariel stepped in, surviving on a few hours of sleep every night for a week so that she knew Susanna's role inside out. It happened again the following season with *Leonore*. Meanwhile, a famous accompanist had a run-in with a temperamental Slav soprano, and heard from someone who had heard Mariel Baxter sing at a Tanglewood class—

Happenstance, good fortune. Good timing. She was the right person in the right place at the right moment. She had studied abroad, and critics pointed out that she had a restraint and air of command on stage she probably hadn't learned on home soil.

Yes, okay. She got lucky.

But she'd had to help that luck befall her.

She'd had to deal with her sister sopranos, by fair means and foul.

It began, her then agent Mirah Spiro claimed, with elbowing them out of the way when you took your curtain call, to get your time in the full beam of the lights.

From her first days, as one of the trio of Damen in a Boston Lyric Opera *Magic Flute* as a student, she had known about wearing a padded bra and pulling down your decolletage to make the most of yourself. Sure, some knowledge about contracts and options and commercial blackmail was useful. The details of *how* you went about it – La Spiro maintained it was a principle as old as time, since mankind hauled himself out of the slough – were always justified by the end result.

And there was the down side. The awful depths she plumbed.

She had stabbing pains in her abdomen which kept her awake at night. They were worse when she was lying down.

She had to get up out of bed. She studied songs and scores from the page. It was too silent in the building to start singing. She sang inside her head, trying to dull the spasms of pain in her uterus.

She missed one period. There was a fitful one after that. They hadn't said anything about this happening.

On a bus one day she started to bleed between her legs. The blood was dark, like offal blood on a butcher's slab.

She couldn't afford the discretion of an uptown clinic.

The woman gynaecologist informed her bluntly that, no, she wouldn't be able to have children. They'd done a bad job.

'Paris, you said?'

(She must have thought Paris, money, what are you doing in a big city hospital like this? Even hookers go to the clinics.)

The specialist said she was sorry (oh yes?) to have to tell her, but sometimes medicine doesn't know enough to put things right.

A light knock on the door.

'I'll be through in a minute.'

Mariel was stunned.

'There's nothing you can do?'

'You can get a second opinion, if you like.'

The doctor would prescribe her some drugs. Time would do the rest. If there was a recurrence of pain after six months, bad pain, she was to come back. But the clever money was on them not needing to operate. She might think of alternative sexual activity in the meantime, okay?

Mariel went down to the Hudson Walkway and – it might have been the salt wind in her eyes, or maybe it was the pity she was feeling for herself – she started to cry and couldn't stop. It was the quiet sort of weeping, not out of control, and she wasn't even sure that the passers-by would notice.

But she had as much unhappiness as a river to pour out of her.

In the United States they really only like success stories.

Mariel Baxter gave them one.

For the next decade and longer, everything seemed to go her way.

Success manufactured charisma. Charisma, you could believe, was a force of nature. She attracted offers without having to try. The skill lay in choosing what to do and what not to do.

No one among the younger stars was her equal in the great Germanic roles.

Another agent-impressario in New York had her on his books; she employed *him*, Lou Litvinoff, it wasn't the usual case of his deigning to represent her. She expected results, and if she felt she'd had to do the hard work in any deal, she argued for a reduced percentage and usually got it.

Her voice wasn't universally praised: some thought it hooty, others found her too literal and mannered, a few detected strains and a lack of precision here and there.

Between the two – the hoped-for and the possible – Mariel followed her career and made her name. The lieder she had learned with Kroll were the bedrock. Kroll had helped to give her a voice – Mariel learned from her how to carry a line, she knew how to hold breath and expel slowly – which suited certain songs, as if they were destined to be hers.

Years later she still felt that Kroll was sometimes standing by her side, expecting nothing less from her than her very best.

Whenever anyone asked, in the early days at any rate, if they specifically brought up Kroll's name, yes, Mariel would mention her. If they didn't, which was more often the case, then she wouldn't speak of her.

Why encumber herself with a past beyond the past, which didn't feature on her American CV? She had worked so hard (only *she* knew how hard), why should she split the credit with anyone else? She deserved better than shared billing.

And so the name of her last teacher worked its way off the print in interviews and profiles.

How could you acknowledge every single person who had assisted you along the way?

When she collected her first Grammy award, for her live Carnegie Hall debut, she had her acceptance speech of spontaneous pleasure very well rehearsed. 'I would like to take this opportunity to thank everyone – *everyone* – who helped to make this possible. They know who they are.'

She had kept in motion for twenty-eight years.

She had never stopped working. Even on her vacations she spent time practising new roles, both in and outside the German tradition. (They weren't really vacations. She called them 'my travels'.)

Those who were critical, the snipers, claimed that she wasn't selective enough about what she took on.

She did a rough count in 1989. Upward of eight hundred thousand miles. It included, in that year alone, four trips to Japan and a separate long-haul to Sydney, six forays to Europe, and some dates in South America. She flew the length and breadth of North America, and took a couple of those so-called vacations (studying for *Die Frau Ohne Schatten* and *The Rake's Progress*) in the Caribbean.

Looking back on 1989, she would see that she was already at the peak of her career. However hard she might try to disguise from herself the truth of the matter, there was only one way to go after that.

Ursule Kroll

Kroll stopped teaching.

She never taught again.

Probably it wouldn't fall to her to find a finer voice than the American's. Young singers now didn't want long apprenticeships; they were in a great hurry to get wherever it was they wanted to go, thinking you could do a little study with this person and then a little work with that.

This most recent experience had worn her out. She felt she'd been used and betrayed. She had given the best part of herself to someone who seemed to believe she had no more to learn.

She blamed herself for taking the girl on. Others had been too persuasive; she had allowed them, and ought to have known better. There would be no risk of her ever making the same mistake again.

Theodor von Törring invited her to lunch, at the Drei Husaren, and another day she was taken by Christoph Gohr to the Ambassador, and on both occasions she discussed her finances. Each party got to hear that she'd been talking to the other, which set them in competition – just as she had planned – vying to come up with the surest portfolio of investments for making money. She went to von Törring for some, and to his younger rival Gohr for others – taking a risk or two along the way – and found herself comfortably able to make a move from the centre of town to Hietzing, where the *haute bourgeoisie* rubbed shoulders (only figuratively) with the true patricians, and where her reputation lived on.

After the war Ursule Kroll had become a heroine to many.

She was guest-of-honour at dinner parties. She was invited to lead the dance at balls, while the company applauded.

She criss-crossed Germany. At the height of her fame, she'd had a private carriage put at her disposal for getting to those unmissable performances for their leaders. Now she travelled Pullman class, or took a wagon-lit; at the station she would be collected in her host's car, or in a family barouche drawn by horses.

Or she flew, at her host's expense, and had her departures and arrivals on the airfield recorded by the new breed of society photographer, feral as alley cats.

At those functions she attended, even at the Hotel Kempinski's reopening in Berlin, she wouldn't sing: that was her one condition. (Sometimes she *did* sing, at a small party, but only ever spontaneously, on the spur of the moment, because the fancy took her.) It was her stage allure which was in demand, her iconic Germanness. She understood this quite well. She had been the Berliners' darling, and given the ultimate sanction as the Führer's favourite lieder singer. (Yes, he requested her recordings, and yes, she signed them for him.)

Die Meistersingerin.

An immortal.

Lunch at the Savoy.

Nothing was the same, but some things had changed less. The hotel had retained its exclusive air. The Adlon suffered bomb damage and had been demolished back in '45; the Savoy, on the ever elegant Fasanenstrasse, carried the torch.

Conrad, Count Niklas-Schwarzenberger was wearing a dark

double-breasted suit. Like several of his army cronies, he had aligned himself with the Christian Democrats. He was one of the new rising stars, with Adenauer's ear.

Kroll was wearing a Dior two-piece, beneath a blue mink coat. Heads were turning as she walked in. The Count sprang to his feet, clicking his heels as he used to do for important guests at the castle. Behind the pince-nez, his eyes were wide.

As they walked into the restaurant, Kroll realised that they could have been mistaken for a couple. They looked good together.

The atmosphere was hushed, muffled. She sensed that everyone in the room was bound by the past. They were the survivors. (She saw news of their arrival pass from one table to the next.)

Over their breast of veal, her host discussed a future career for her. He could arrange this, arrange that, pull strings here, there, whatever had to be done.

The wine, an Austrian Weissburgunder, was as fine as any she'd had during the war. The vintage was 1937. Kroll allowed it to course through her: the vineyard sunshine of ten years ago seemed to be warming her on this mid-autumn day. A woman at a table looked over, smiling at her, and mimed applause. Kroll graciously acknowledged her, listening meanwhile to an auditorium ringing to its rafters.

Upstairs she let the Count have his way. She stood against a wall with her dress hitched up. That was his style. Like the good Catholic he was, he withdrew in the nick of time, but catching her skirt and shoes with dollops of semen. Almost better if he'd done it inside her. She went off to the bathroom and sponged briskly.

Leaving the hotel, a flashbulb went off just in front of her face, and for a couple of seconds she was blinded. She recognised the cuplrit when her eyes cleared. A photographer called Nagel. He hung about outside restaurants and stage-doors, only a minor irritant until now, selling his pictures to magazines very ready to buy.

The taxi driver said he hadn't seen the flash go off. Photographers and drivers were usually as thick as thieves, and she was surprised, but she didn't think any more about it.

Once upon a time, yes, she had thought her heart beat in time to that man's. When he had kissed her in his car, she would have done anything he might have asked her to, without a moment's hesitation.

But in her mind she had never really separated those feelings – whatever they were – from her curiosity about Christine Duringer. When she remembered the kiss, she remembered herself thinking that his lips must also have kissed *her* like this. When she remembered discovering them both in the stables, in the throes of lust, she was seeing again that expression of rapture on Christine Duringer's face, and envying not her but her ravisher, that he knew how to give her such intense pleasure.

The Niklas-Schwarzenberger family had always been a presence in her life, from which the Semmelrogges kept their most respectful distance. The Duringer woman was a new specimen to her: very probably she had been a *demi-mondaine* when she met the banker she would marry, and when she found herself a widow she merely reverted to type. She'd been the Odette de Crécy of Bremen.

Kroll had often wondered what happened to her. It occurred to her to ask as they were lunching at the Savoy, but somehow the right moment never arose. (Or just possibly she didn't want to give herself away like that.)

The woman Conrad Niklas-Schwarzenberger eyed across the table was a carefully contrived creation. They half-acknowledged this: after all (they'd laughed together) she was still Maria Semmelrogge to him. He was aware that she had male admirers. But he didn't know – probably hadn't even guessed – about her Sapphic other.

Other? Couldn't she even be truthful to herself?

She didn't even see the names of those chambermaids, chorus singers, secretaries, cigarette girls, shop assistants, waitresses and usherettes who had given themselves so gladly to the cause as she turned the pages of her address book. They were working women, ready and willing to supplement their income in a small way. Compared with them, *relationships* – with wives, with society hostesses – became too complicated. She tried to choose working class women, preferably younger than herself, who wouldn't have any expectations. Occasionally she had been proved wrong, but as a rule of thumb it held true: they were content with a modest gratuity, a gift or two, and the experience of having been Ursule Kroll's lover for a short spell. For her part, she would become obsessed and trail them, which mostly they found flattering if not a little alarming. It wasn't a case of wearing down their resistance, because she only selected those who gave off the signals she was tuned to pick up on. (If they did resist, they were only pretending. Her instincts with women were foolproof.)

And so she had politely steered them round these obstacles over lunch. Too successfully, maybe. Afterwards, upstairs in the bedroom, she was picking up from where they had left off at Esterhofen. No Christine Duringer now, but she wasn't far from Kroll's thoughts.

At lunch he hadn't brought up the name in conversation either. What happened against the bedroom wall was a kind of celebration: she had got him in the end.

And yet—

Why were the pictures in her head of Christine Duringer as clear as they'd been in the days long ago when she used to wake up, flooded with a sense of despair that this woman was the real obstacle between Maria Semmelrogge and happiness?

A few days later, at her serviced apartment in Berlin, she received an anonymous package in the post.

FOR YOUR SPECIAL ATTENTION.

Inside were three photographs. Not black and white, but full colour.

One showed a villa and its garden, with a blue lake and distant snowy mountains visible in the background.

Fräulein Steinicke's property at Bodensee, Lake Konstanz.

The second showed chained gates, with a sign fastened to them: NO ADMITTANCE BY ORDER.

The third photograph had been taken in a bathroom. The white pedestal of a basin – the scrolled corner of a white bath – and a green-and-white tiled floor. Blood lay in a pool on the floor, and had splashed on to the pedestal and the end of the bath.

Kroll let the photographs fall on to the table, and dropped – stumbled – on to a chair. She had no idea afterwards how much time had passed while she sat just staring at the photographs, at the whorls of wood on the table's polished surface.

The photographs must have come from Nagel. He would have got her address from the taxi driver.

There was no message. The pictures spoke for themselves.

She asked for used banknotes from the bank teller, and before she mailed them she counted them three, four times so that that dog turd, Nagel, couldn't come back to her and claim he'd been swindled.

She was angry with herself, and despondent.

All that she wanted was to have nothing more to do with him.

Berlin had drawn her back.

Vienna bore its wounds too openly, and she hoped that, if a miracle was going to happen, Berlin was a likelier place to find angels than smoky, smashed-up Vienna. Or was it the northerner in her who had made the decision for her?

Her furniture remained in storage. Others now would never reclaim their possessions, but she was only biding her time. She had planned to live on the surface of events for a while, and to decide later where to settle and root herself. She simply hadn't anticipated that what she did and didn't do would be dictated by someone like Nagel, the sort of gnat that hangs round a cow's backside.

She tried to divert her thoughts. She sent them off in pursuit of Conrad Niklas-Schwarzenberger. But at some point, with the man clear in her sights, those thoughts would come to a standstill, a dead stop.

It was like turning a page in a book and finding that it was the last page with print on it. The remaining ones were blank.

She wanted to read on, but the book's pages were empty.

Mariel Baxter

In 1990 she arranged lunch at the Savoy Hotel during a stop-over in London. The River Room. A table at the window.

What bothered her chiefly was that Ben wouldn't meet the restaurant dress code. He arrived wearing a green corduroy suit and rust-coloured shirt, along with a tie and proper lace-up shoes. They let him in.

She had spent so long in the Ladies beforehand that the concierge had to ask her if she was feeling quite well. She was nervous. She was more apprehensive than before any performance.

He was still handsome, still sexy, but he was ten years older now. He looked his – what? – thirty-eight years. Now that she'd seen him again, she wasn't in freefall as she'd feared, heart leaping and stomach flipping over.

Over an aperitif before lunch he was polite rather than effusive. What else could she have expected? They got through the 'It's been a long time' routine, and he even tried a humorously posh accent.

'*Brief Encounter*,' he explained. 'The film. Trevor Howard and Celia Johnson.'

'Ah.'

There were still English references she didn't get, even though some magazines back home spoke of her as 'Europeanised' or 'Anglicised'.

He asked her about her new programme of concerts. She asked him about the jazz scene in London, and where he liked playing.

'I've got some dates at the Pizza on the Park. A quartet.'

'Uh huh,' she said, nodding. 'Still "Pfrancing"?'

'What?'

'Miles Davis,' she reminded him.

'Oh. Yes.' He gave a dutiful little laugh. 'Still playing to the "Freddie Freeloaders".'

'That's good.'

He sat fidgeting with his swizzle stick. He seemed distracted.

'*Isn't* it good?' she asked him.

'Yes. Oh yes.'

He pulled himself more upright in the chair, clearing his throat to speak.

'I guess you want to talk about the book, though.'

She had mentioned it on the phone. It was why they were here. She had heard he was touting a manuscript, about music-making in the Third Reich, round the London literary agents.

'It doesn't seem to have much to do with what you play yourself,' she said.

'The Germans couldn't decide about jazz. Too modern, too alien.'

'Yes?'

'That was the official line.'

'They had lots of nightclubs, though.'

He smiled, as if he'd caught her out making an apologist's defence.

'The young wanted it. Goebbels had to go halfway. They had jazz: yes and no.'

'You're still interested anyway?' she asked.

'In German jazz?'

'In – in *all* their music?'

'The classical, you mean?'

'Yes. Classical.'

'I had the information. I thought I'd do something about it. That's the thing about jazz, you get to play it at night, so you've got the daytime to fill with other things.'

'A bit like singing?'

'*You*'ve got to rehearse. We just do it off the tops of our heads.'

'What?'

'We just hope for the best, you see. It's all very accidental.'

He remembered that remark she'd once made at a tram stop, which had had him laughing in mock or possibly real horror.

'Your memory's too good,' she said.

'For a man of my age?'

How much else did he remember? She had assumed that he would have moved so far beyond it by now, too much else would have intervened, or that he would have *wanted* to forget.

Their table was ready.

He noticed her glancing at her watch.

'I said I'd be back at two-thirty,' she told him. 'Accompanists are slave-drivers.'

'Even to you?'

She waited until the main course.

'I don't want you to publish it.'

'Why not?'

'All that's better left where it is.'

'Where's that, Mariel?'

'In the past.'

She wasn't sure why she was asking him not to publish the manuscript. He had let her see the sections which mentioned Kroll.

'You want to spare her?'

'Yes. Yes, I suppose I do.'

No. No, she knew as she was saying it that that wasn't the reason.

'The oxygen of publicity', they called it. Whatever was written kept Kroll's reputation current. People's interest could be whetted. Mariel's instinct was that it wouldn't be helpful to *her*. It alarmed her that the name 'Mariel Baxter' might be tarnished by any such association. Nazis were still the bogeymen. None of those careers had been salvaged, even now. America wasn't yet ready to forgive.

'Kroll asked you?'

'Certainly not.' She softened her voice. 'I've had no contact with Kroll.'

'So what am I to do? All the research that went into it.'

'I know, I appreciate that.'

'It's all been for nothing, you mean?'

'I've been to see the publicity people at the record company I'm with.'

She had spoken to their head of European operations.

'They'll give you privileged access to their roster of performers,' she told him, repeating what was written in their reply. 'They'll agree to your working freelance. Although they would prefer you deal with the high-profile publications. You can have exclusive interviews, and preview records.'

'But?'

'But what?'

'But I have to be – not unfavourable?'

'They believe someone of your intelligence will provide a fair and balanced view. Of whatever it is.'

'I won't bollock them?'

'They would like you to liaise with their department.'

'Write the stuff they want to get put about?'

'Come on, Ben. You know they just want to get their message across. But everyone thinks they have to be snide.'

'About you too?'

'So far I've been lucky. It'll happen. That's how it is.'

'So why will the editors go for my material?'

'Because no one else will be available to interview those people, or get behind the scenes. You can go to recordings.'

'I don't have a free rein, though?'

She hesitated.

'Everything has a cost, Ben.'

'You've already asked me not to publish the book.'

'You'd be earning much more than an author.'

'Money talks?'

'This is an industry. We both know that.'

She let him think about it for the next ten or fifteen minutes, over coffee. She had to get back across the river, to the Festival Hall, for her rehearsal.

'Well,' he sighed, 'there *is* a lot of time in between gigs.'

'I've seen things you've written.'

'Yeah?'

'Some of them.'

'And?'

'They're very good.'

'Hard to get my stuff onto the bestseller lists.'

'Now you can.'

His eyes were ranging across the items on the pale pink linen cloth, the crockery and the table silver and the flowers.

'Do I have any alternative?' he asked.

'Yes, of course you do. You just don't agree. Say no and walk away.'

'And if I *do* agree?'

'Then you get your access forthwith.'

'And the book?'

'It doesn't appear.'

'Ever?'

'Ever.'

'Okay.'

'What?' she said.

'Okay.'

She tried to temper the relief in her voice. 'You mean yes?'

'Well, you Americans say okay all the time, don't you?'

'If you tell me we do.'

'They used to say you trained in Vienna. Not any more, I've noticed.'

'They've just forgotten.'

'Yeah?'

'Well, you know what journos are like!' she laughed.

In ninety minutes they hadn't, incredibly, mentioned Die Gruppe. Nor Zoë, who Mariel imagined was safely married by now to some older man, a diplomatic high-flier. She hadn't put Ben on the spot by asking him, 'Did you ever see *Les Liaisons Dangereuses*?', because in all probability his and Zoë's behaviour had been a lot less sinister than that of the Vicomte and Marquise. She could think of Die Gruppe as the last gasp of hippiedom: passing around and sharing, all for one and one for all, and if there was something else kinkier in the mix, it seemed a long way from the good manners of the River Room.

Outside in the foyer the two of them shook hands. Mariel didn't feel a frisson this time. Ben didn't attempt to kiss her, and she took a step back so that he wouldn't have second thoughts. They were being very sensible, very adult.

'Try Sondheim some time,' he said.

It was only in the cab back across the river (he had smiled at the extravagance) that she realised there might have been a sly dig in the 'Sondheim' suggestion. The lyrics were so clever, the music so assured, but there was a coldness, a detachment, an astringency he must have thought she was suited to.

She wanted to think he was wrong about that, but couldn't be quite certain.

Ursule Kroll

Kroll was now living in dread of the daily post.

On a sheet of crested notepaper from the Count, in an envelope bearing an official mark of the Christian Democratic Union of Germany, she read that the dowager Countess was very ill, and that he would be in touch concerning those matters they had discussed – 'so pleasantly' – over lunch. Not a word about what had followed upstairs.

She left his letter on top of the in-tray.

Next week he wrote again, proposing another lunch '*à deux*'.

She realised what she had to say in reply, so that she left no room for doubt.

It is my conclusion, she wrote, *that there is nothing further for us to discuss. I have changed my mind since we spoke. I appreciate the great kindness of your offer to assist me in resuscitating my career. However, I regret that after careful consideration I am unable to avail myself. I must insist that in this regard I am quite determined and inflexible.*

It broke her heart to write that letter, and she had to make several copies, because her tears repeatedly blotted the ink. She was signing everything away, she understood that. Perhaps she would be able to carry on making records; recording was only half a career, though, if your public couldn't see as well as hear you.

Assuring you of my warmest regards, Ursule K.

She sealed the envelope and posted it herself. It was her closing statement, in print, and it couldn't be erased. Yet, as she knew quite well, it really explained nothing to him.

She received another two photographs in the post – one detailing a night express train's destination board MÜNCHEN-NÜRNBERG-LEIPZIG, the other showing a coffin being unloaded from a luggage car on to a cordoned-off section of a station platform – and she was as indignant as she was alarmed.

This time she waited two, three weeks.

When she sent the money, she typed on a slip of paper FINAL INSTALMENT.

A year later, Nagel was knocked from his motorbike in a street scramble to take photographs, and later died from his injuries. But Kroll simply couldn't believe that there might be an end to it.

She had imagined him developing the prints himself in a lab, watching them evolve diabolically from their basin of solution; she had pictured him pegging them up to dry and quietly smiling at his own villainy.

He had got the end he deserved.

But she wasn't easy, even so. Despite her return to Vienna, she would never be easy again.

She was introduced to the businessman Hermann Schikele, across a table at a *bal masqué* at the Jagdschloss Grunewald, and they spoke for a while. He was wearing a harlequin mask, while hers dazzled with paste jewels and feathers.

'Businessman' and 'importer-exporter' were euphemisms in common usage in 1954: a kind of warning not to enquire any further, and to find other partners to dance with.

Kroll thought no more about the man. Then, on a visit to Vienna from his home outside Munich, he called her and invited her to lunch. Put on the spot like that, she couldn't think of a good enough reason to decline the invitation.

He brought along a couple he knew, perhaps to put her at her ease. But Kroll sensed that the pair were on hand with the brief of 'assessing' her.

They all four reminisced. She now found herself much more in sympathy with her host; many of their values coincided. They wisely kept off the subjects of 'business' and her own premature retirement. While the world outside the doors of the Imperial carried on its vulgar way, they relished perfect times.

Hermann Schikele proposed to her one evening, in the garden of his mansion at Starnberg am See. Kroll thought she might have misheard, and he laughed when she asked him to repeat the question.

He said to her, wasn't that one of the tricks of the girls in the songs, so that they could live the moment twice over?

No, he explained, he wanted her to marry him.

She hesitated, which he thought was another charming ploy of the songs. She was telling herself what she knew to be true, that she didn't love him. But how many marriages began with love and later lost it? She had no notion of finding love with him, but he was rich. He might not have loved her himself, so where was the deception?

'Very well.' She seemed to be listening to someone else, not herself, saying the words. 'If you think you want to take me on, go ahead!'

You could have heard his laughter in Munich.

So she would be a kind of marionette. After all, she had to think of her future.

His past was kept conveniently shrouded. He had been adept at business in the 1920s, buying up failed factories and somehow steering clear of trouble himself. He chose to donate to the new nationalists, and again it was an adroit choice. He was included in

their plans for war, and was supplying munitions well in advance.
The Allies had wanted to prosecute him for employing slave labour,
but he had paid the best lawyers, to tangle the deeds of ownership
to the factories; thanks to their obfuscations and Swiss citizenship,
he got away with his life and the greater part of his fortune.

They didn't discuss those things.

Hermann went regularly to 'meetings' in Zurich. His new wife
discovered something else he hadn't mentioned to her, the full
seriousness of his kidney condition. At Starnberg she played the
role of the cordial, attentive hostess, as if – even though she'd had
no rehearsals in this part – it was one of her great stage triumphs,
exhausting her physically and mentally just as the parts of Mélisande
and Arabella had done.

Her husband died suddenly, not of his kidney disease but from his
injuries after his car crashed on the Rapperswil road. The 300SEL was
being driven by a hustler he'd picked up on the Bahnhofstrasse.

The boy broke his leg, but lived.

Life belongs to the young, the widowed Frau Kroll-Schikele said
to the Swiss lawyer.

'Indeed it does,' the man was obliged to tell her a few weeks later,
quoting her own words back to her just a day or two before the will
was due to be read. Apparently there was another widow, still only
in her mid-thirties. She was living, thriving indeed, on an *estancia* in
Montevideo, which Hermann Schikele had bought as a bolt-hole.

After the shock, and the anger, Kroll met Maître Durieux again
to pursue legal matters.

'Some waitress or shopgirl, I presume, who trapped him in her
web?'

'No, the daughter of a German wine importer out there.
Legitimately married to him. And a Catholic, unfortunately for
you.'

'Oh.'

'She's a mother. They had a daughter.'

'Hermann's?'

'She looks like him.'

'Poor girl. He wasn't a looker.'

'Good enough to pull the boys, though.'

'That was his money,' Kroll corrected the lawyer. 'Anatomically he was nothing to write home about.'

'He's dead already.'

'I'm quite aware of that.'

'Let's not kill him twice.'

'Touché, Maître.' Kroll smiled archly.

There was a contest over the will. It wasn't very dignified. Maître Durieux did his best, however, which was only what Kroll expected, given what he was being paid – by both parties.

The Schikele estate was divided unequally: two-thirds to the first wife and her daughter in their eucalyptus garden by the Rio de la Plata, one-third to the widow in King Ludwig's stamping ground in Bavaria. Fifteen per cent of both sums passed in fees to the lawyer, who assured them that the business would have dragged on for years and gone to court in two, feasibly three, countries but for his ministrations. It was a speedy conclusion, settled out of court, and Kroll was persuaded that even one-third of the total estate (less fifteen per cent) was a fortune by anyone's calculations.

And at least there was nothing for the rent boy, not a single mark or Swiss franc.

'Be philosophical,' Maître Durieux advised her cryptically.

Yes, she had sampled marriage, and doubted very much that she would want to do so again. But she had been rewarded for her three and a half years as a hostess, on call for whomever her husband chose to invite, and it was time to claim a life back for herself.

If only, a voice nagged away inside her head, *if only it were so simple.*

Mariel Baxter

Mariel and Ben had no further contact beyond a couple of letters and a postcard.

There were some WORLD EXCLUSIVE tags for Ben Tompkins over the next three or four years. But he must have got bored by it finally, by the unending need to view everything in a positive light.

Some of the artistes, he wrote in his first letter, were assholes of the first order. He was running out of tactful euphemisms. Any idea where he could get a new thesaurus?

The purpose of the earlier postcard was to confirm that the manuscript was withdrawn from offer. Mariel didn't know if that meant for ever. She replied, to establish that point with him.

I don't have any plans to be an author, he wrote back. *I'll stick to jazz. You should try it some day if you get tired of that sodding little nut tree.*

She took that for an acquiescent affirmative.

The sopranos and contraltos were bad enough, without the counter tenors weighing in, including that bitch Hamlin, with his photo-spread New Orleans lifestyle and no sign in any of the pictures of the rough trade he dredged up, there and in every city he toured to. He had teamed up with Traverso, the Australian director, and together they talked about shaking up the system and giving those diva-egos a run for their money. Pots and kettles, wasn't it?

She had lost the Eurydice role to him, and she had a notion that she only got *Vanessa* in Houston because the principal patrons objected to the desecrations being planned on Barber. Hamlin in *Semele* in San Francisco (where else?) got the go-ahead, but both she and Hamlin lost out with the Chicago *Iphigénie* because their rival supporters, rather than concede, allowed the role to go to someone else entirely, a Taiwanese coloratura who satisfied no one in the end. (Jesus Christ, Mariel could have told them *that*!).

How could anyone imagine the Arts were elevated? Sublime music, yes, but primitive base passions.

In 1998 she was – still – in a position to call Dieter Spengler and suggest lunch. In 1998 Dieter was – still – sufficiently in awe of her, one of the stars of their roster for more than a decade, to say yes, he'd love to, and why hadn't he thought of it beforehand.

'So we'll do lunch!'

'If you allow me to take *you*, Mariel.'

Dieter guessed she must have an ulterior motive.

'I thought you were off to Le Châtelet,' he greeted her.

'Tomorrow.'

'Korngold?'

'*Das Wunder der Heliane*.'

'Undervalued. Last great German opera?'

'The music's glorious.'

'It's always lovely to see you.'

'I did want to see you before I left.'

She had heard that they were planning a series of reissues for 2000. It was to be called *Meistersinger*, concentrating on neglected stars of the past. Ursule Kroll was to be one of them. When Mariel first heard, the blood ran cold in her veins.

With Dieter it was best to cut to the chase. (Deep breath.)

'I feel it's not what the company should be doing. There's so much *new* talent to bring on.'

'Snapping at your heels, you mean?' Ha ha.

Mariel smiled at him.

'No, really,' she said. 'What would be good and interesting for the millennium would be to sign up some fresh faces.'

'We've got hold of a lot of tapes. German mostly, and also French.'

'It's archive.'

'That's the point.'

'But it sends out wrong signals. It gives you a retro image.'

'You must listen to the old names yourself?'

'*Some* old names, yes. They're famous because they're so good, they're timeless. There are reasons why other people *aren't* remembered.'

'It may just be their rotten bad luck.'

'Hmph.' She wouldn't allow herself to look convinced.

'Are you being quite honest with me, Mariel?'

'Why – why d'you say that?'

'*You* would like to do some of the old repertoire, is that it?'

'What?'

She watched Spengler as he sat picturing the finished product, getting it shipped out to the stores.

'That's not a bad idea, you know.'

'It's *your* idea, Dieter. Whatever it is!'

'We get you to sing the songs of 1900. Another could be a tenor. Piano. Chamber. And so on.' He lit a cigarette. 'Yes, I can see how—'

Suddenly they were away from Kroll and other neglected singers, and the haul of unremastered tapes.

'We'd need another title, probably. I saw "*Meistersinger*" in Germanic typeface.'

'Zeitgeist,' Mariel said, off the top of her head.

'"Zeitgeist"?' Spengler repeated the word half-a-dozen times. 'Yes. Yes, I like that.'

Mariel smiled at him seraphically. She hadn't been intending to promote herself: only, yes, to deny Kroll *her* due.

'I wasn't meaning—'

Spengler shook his head, mock-seriously.

'Sure you weren't,' he said.

'But since you're so very kind as to suggest it—'

Cigarette hanging from his bottom lip, Spengler laughed.

Mariel felt generous enough to laugh along with him.

Ursule Kroll

From Starnberg am See Kroll returned to Vienna.

She hadn't realised until she tried to escape that Vienna was the place which held her. She hadn't yet earned the epithet *Wienerische*, and perhaps she would never be considered as such, but she felt that it was where she was meant to be.

Her life as Frau Schikele had been an interruption – and an aberration, it seemed to her, as she settled back into her Vienna ways.

Here she was recognised for her musical achievements. Her voice was her *raison d'être*. When approached and asked, implored, to teach the most gifted pupils that Vienna had to offer, to give them the benefit of her unique experience – how could she not consent?

News reached her in Vienna, in 1962, that Sabine Hebbel had died.

Obituaries appeared in the newspapers. They were reverential. They also named some of her pupils. In one, the best-known was Ursule Kroll. In another, foremost among them were two names, Alina Giebisch and Ursule Kroll.

Her heart seemed to stop beating when she saw the association of their two names. She found herself struggling for breath. Her eyes were very tight in her head.

Five minutes later she had recovered. The newspapers were already in the wastepaper basket for Brigitte to take out with the household rubbish.

Life didn't stop here in Vienna, even though, according to one fulsome third-rate obituarist, 'a light has gone out in the façade of the noble house of German music-making'.

She put on her coat, checked she had keys and went out. Fräulein Hebbel, Kroll realised, had been the one to warn them against mollycoddling; she mocked those singers who swathed themselves in scarves, who protected their ears with mufflers.

'There's nothing wrong with our Hamburg air. It's pure and refreshing. Take good deep draughts.'

Kroll used to go walking on the afternoon of a recital. If it was raining heavily, she'd stand under cover to get fresh air into her lungs. Dampness never seemed to do her any harm. She had grown up in a chilly house with badly fitting floorboards and must have become immune to the elements. Her mother's and father's families had had their medical problems but arthritis wasn't among them.

On the afternoon of reading the obituary in *Die Zeitung*, Kroll walked as quickly as she could. But after a couple of blocks she slowed. She couldn't escape.

The experience of Sabine Hebbel would continue to cling to her; the past would always exert this mordant hold.

She carried on walking, at a more sedate pace. A few strangers recognised her, looked twice, smiled, and one or two of them – as inevitably happened – would open their mouths as if they were about to speak to someone they thought they knew.

For years she had carried more of Sabine Hebbel about with her than she ever cared to acknowledge, even to herself. Every time she had stood on a platform to sing—

What she sang, and *how* she sang—

Without Fräulein Hebbel she would have been a different artiste altogether, perhaps not one at all.

At the outset of her career, Fräulein Hebbel would come to concerts or opera productions unannounced. A few pages of notes – criticisms, frequently blunt, and suggestions, *Next time you must ...* – would arrive in the post. They annoyed Kroll, but at the same time she read them from start to finish, several times. Her performances altered, and improved, because of them. But never, not once, did she concede that she had read the notes or acted on them. Fräulein Hebbel would have known, however, having the proof of her own years or reading press notices, that her advice had been heeded.

In a sense, Sabine Hebbel's being dead didn't matter. Kroll knew it had been impossible to walk out of her shadow. That was part of the deal, the bargain struck. Latterly, she couldn't spend time in the same room as her, but what sort of life would she be living now if she hadn't travelled to Hamburg years ago and knocked at her door?

The influence of Sabine Hebbel was ineradicable. For anyone skilled enough to look in the right places, it was fixed there as indelibly as a watermark on paper.

One evening in 1959, she handed her sable coat to a cloakroom attendant at the Hoftheater in Stuttgart.

'Good evening, Fräulein Kroll.'

Recognition was rewarded, as ever, with a brief smile.

The woman in her tweed uniform returned with a numbered disc. Kroll took it from her and dropped some small change into the dish.

'Have you been back to Tegernsee, madam?'

Kroll turned back round at the question and stared at the speaker.

'I used to work at the Excelsior Hotel. I tried to please our guests.'

Kroll blinked, looked away. She glanced left, then right.

'I remember,' she said, *sotto voce* so that only the woman could hear. Her eyes were drawn back to the face, to the mouth. The tip of the tongue appeared between the rows of teeth.

'I remember very well.'

'I met with your satisfaction?'

'Indeed.'

The following year, in 1944, Kroll had returned to the hotel, after recording a series of lieder programmes for radio in Munich with the ominous title 'Testament'. She had booked the same suite for herself. The staff, she discovered, were regularly moved from floor to floor of the sprawling hotel, but because Madam insisted, Brigitte Brank was given the job of attending to her accommodation.

The second visit lacked the surprise element of the first. The business in bed seemed less impulsive, more mechanical, more blasé. The girl had trimmed that prodigal bush, exposing her labia; she wanted Kroll to watch as she made a show of pleasuring herself with a rubber dildo, and using words that an uncouth man might.

Kroll also suspected that the under-manager who called by the suite one day had an inkling of what they were about. She wasn't especially sorry to leave. Brigitte wanted to keep in touch, and was upset when she didn't give her a forwarding address.

'I finish work at midnight, madam. It's very late, I'm afraid.'

Kroll didn't want anyone in the foyer of the theatre to hear.

'I shall be dining at the Kurfurstenstube,' Kroll said, adding, 'with friends.'

She was being entertained by one of her most devoted admirers in this part of the country. His wife, who had first brought the singer to his attention, was now in a sanatorium in Kronberg, and Kroll realised he meant her to be more than a social scalp tonight.

She made a getaway from the restaurant at nearly one o'clock, deftly escaping from the lecher's clutches. She hadn't forgotten Brigitte, but presumed she would have given up and gone off home.

The woman was waiting outside on the street. When a taxi arrived, Kroll had her come with her.

Relieved to be free of Herr Schiesser, Kroll might have chosen to celebrate. But she saw little that was desirable about Brigitte now.

Kroll told the driver to stop so they could get out and walk and talk.

'So, you're a reformed character with your gentleman?' the woman teased her.

It was gross impudence, of course, but Kroll accepted her humiliation.

'I don't retrace my footsteps. Ever.'

Brigitte nodded.

'I cut a picture out of the newspaper. Your wedding.'

'Why on earth—?'

'I was always looking for things about you to read.'

'No more weddings.'

'I read how you were with those bastards, madam. The Allied lot. You're a very proud lady.'

'I don't retrace my footsteps. But what is in the past – I won't apologise for. Never.'

That might have been the end of that. But another suspicion was gnawing at Kroll's mind, when the woman brought up the subject of continuing hardship: her crippled and blind mother, a wilful daughter she was paying to have nuns keep in order, a harsh Jewish landlord. Kroll wondered if she caught the tincture of imminent extortion, blackmail, darkening this exchange.

Perhaps not, to judge Brigitte quite fairly, but Kroll had heard too many tales of celebrities – Sapphists, especially – with reputations now irreparably sullied.

Would she otherwise have suggested what she did?

She had recently been interviewing for domestic help in Vienna. She already had a maid, who came three mornings a week, but the apartment required more thorough attention.

And labour was still, on Swiss money, comparatively cheap.

A month later Brigitte was in place, as housekeeper.

It was hard to believe this was the same Brigitte. Her figure had grown heavy and lumpy, her face was coarse and now very definitely plain. Her hair was lank and colourless, where once it had been her best feature, shiny and a rich auburn colour.

Hard for Kroll to believe she had played with that hair, caressing it, before burying her face into the curves and folds of the girl's body, which, she was surprised to discover, smelled sweetly everywhere of soap. (The thick muff too, auburn-coloured as her head.) If the girl was shocked back then in 1943, it hadn't manifested itself as a rush of perspiration. No, Kroll thought, you can deny it all you like, but I'm not the first woman guest you've done this with. Kroll hadn't had to instruct the girl in what gave her pleasure, because she knew. Mouth, tits, thighs, belly, arse, cunt. Kroll's breath came faster and faster. The girl's tongue darted in and out of her slit, then a finger slid in, to the knuckle, two slick fingers; they probed her, corkscrewing inside, round and round, slurping wetly as they pushed apart those silken walls and sent tremors of pleasure pulsing to every part of her.

Their bodies melted together. Pleasure taken and pleasure given was indistinguishable.

Brigitte turned down the bed for her in the evening, and laid out her nightdress. She drew the curtains, lit the lamps, checked that the radiators were on or off.

'Will that be all, madam?'

The question was always freighted with emphasis, Kroll felt.

One evening Kroll faltered.

In seconds Brigitte had crossed the room, and was undoing the cuff buttons on her tight sleeves.

'What are you—?'

Brigitte sprang back.

'I can manage,' Kroll said, 'you don't need to—'

The sudden elation on Brigitte's face evaporated. The features were left, blunt and peasant-like. It was strange to think that she'd passed muster as a theatre hat-check girl just weeks ago. But perhaps, Kroll had wondered to herself, there had been other opportunities in the opera house: with the cast or the crew, or in the lavatories during a performance.

Brigitte's eyes passed over her, from her breasts to her waist to the level of her crotch to the tops of her legs, concealed beneath her skirt.

'But', Kroll said, 'I *would* like you to brush my hair.'

'What?'

'Will you do that for me?'

'Brush your hair? On your head?'

Kroll ignored the vulgarity, her presumptuousness.

'I'll take it down for you,' she said, starting to remove the combs in her chignon. 'I don't make a good job of brushing it.'

'Why should I be any better?'

'Because I think you will be.'

Brigitte stood motionless for ten seconds or so.

'Which brush would you like me to use? Madam?'

'I'm not madam in the house, Brigitte.'

'What are you, then, Fräulein Kroll? It's only in my nature to say "madam".'

Kroll hesitated. Her Christian name was out of the question. Even at their most passionate moments between the sheets of a hotel bed, names had been unnecessary.

'Nothing, if you prefer. You know who I am.'

'I know what I know, mad—'

That was the last time she would ever forget herself and try to use the word.

'Now let me see what you know about brushing hair. Will you?'

'How many times?'

'Is there a number?'

'In a fairytale, isn't it a hundred?'

'That seems a lot,' Kroll said.

'Have you something else to do?'

That sounded almost like a reprimand. Kroll was willing to be contrite.

'No. *This* is what I want to be doing. Having you brush my hair.'

'One.'

Kroll sat taller in the chair.

'Tw-o-o,' Brigitte spoke beneath her breath, pulling the silver-backed brush down.

Kroll tried to keep her spine ramrod straight, without touching the chair back, just like the old dowager Countess at Schloss Esterhofen.

'Th-rr-ee.'

The Viennese had a fascination with death, a mania even.

They liked to prepare for their life ahead: wording of the newspaper death notice, which cemetery, location of the lair, expense and grandeur of the headstone, likely provenance of floral wreaths.

Kroll would listen to Brigitte's description of some funeral she'd just seen going through the streets. As soon as a death loomed, friends and colleagues would fix on the big day. There was no subterfuge about death in Vienna. It was the details of the (still) living and breathing existence which were clandestine.

Such were the priorities here.

A piece of music heard in Vienna – say, a trio playing in a café – didn't sound like the same piece of music played anywhere else. So many had performed it here, the music was shadowed and blurred by its associations. How could the music – even a waltz – not seem somehow melancholic, as if it was pining for its own past?

By the time Kroll realised what Vienna was like, she felt it was too late to move. Anyway, where would she go? In a sense, Vienna was entirely appropriate, given that her glory days were over.

Scattered all about Vienna, in its leafy suburbs, were musicians – singers most of all – once well known and now likely to be living in comfortable, discreet seclusion. This city had always represented the apogee of Germanic culture; it was for that very reason it existed, with its museums and galleries and its opera houses and concert halls. The spirit of Germanness belonged here, it was in the very air that you breathed.

Every year's passing seemed to make it more difficult for Kroll to move. She did once broach the practicability with Brigitte.

'Who would you find to look after you in the mountains, tell me?'

Clearly Brigitte wouldn't be coming, she was making that quite clear, without being required to speak more testily on the matter.

In Vienna Kroll felt that she could be as public or private as she wished to be. Vienna knew to respect reputations, and also to be equivocal; it seldom condemned.

Finally, having put half-baked notions about mountains and lesser cities out of her mind, Kroll understood that this was the only place she could possibly be living, without ever making the mistake of calling it 'home'.

Her home was in the music of the composers, in the words of the poets, in the eminence and honour of the fatherland.

Mariel Baxter

Insomnia struck her in 2001. It stayed with her for three years. Finally acupuncture helped to release whatever it was that was keeping her from sleeping.

During those long, long nights Mariel would retrace her steps round Vienna. She made endless circuits of that city, to which she had never returned, but of which she had greater recall than any other place between Benton, South Carolina and New York, her home on and off for the past decade.

After her broken nights started, someone told her about Alva Anderssen.

'I don't need a therapist.'

'That's what we've all said, Mariel.'

'Honestly.'

'And we've all said "honestly" too.'

Three weeks later she rang the number. The woman at the other end sounded sympathetic, but didn't pitch for her business.

'Would you like to drop by some time, Miss Baxter? Or could I come and meet you?'

They had a rendezvous at the Russian Tea Room, among the stagey red plush and gilt. Appropriately enough, Alva Anderssen had trained in Stockholm as an actress. 'In an earlier existence.' They got along fine. Dr Anderssen, as she had styled herself when reserving the table, produced a pocket diary.

'What d'you say I fix something up? Just say when would be good for you.'

It took six adjustments to find a time which suited them both.

At long last, with her first psychiatrist's appointment booked, Mariel Baxter felt like a genuine New Yorker.

Mariel spoke towards the window, and its view of treetops and the East Side across the park. She would get to measure time by the seasons, by the colour of the leaves on those trees by the reservoir.

Dr Anderssen's habit was to sit side-on to her. Sometimes she wouldn't look at her patient at all, letting her eyes travel from her notes over towards the bookcase.

'You *like* sex, Mariel?'

Was that a valid question? She'd thought she was paying for a professional service.

She had told Dr Anderssen – no, the Christian name wasn't an option for her – about her predilection for married men, or men already in relationships. They'd worked their way through the lesbian programme – had she seen such and such a movie, was she an Ellen DeGeneres fan? – and they'd discounted that, which wasted most of one session.

Next time, just as Mariel was planning how to say she wouldn't be coming back, Dr Anderssen tricked it out of her: she'd had an abortion and they'd fucked up.

'So to speak.'

'Let your anger out, Mariel. That's good. It's what I'm here for.'

The first touches of russet were on the trees across the street, among the yellow and gold leaves. Mariel longed desperately for spring. She wanted to be on the other side of this winter, with its frosty mornings and short days, lamplit afternoons and sleet caught in car headlights. Just that very morning she'd read a travel article,

'Christmas in Vienna', about the street markets; it had been another hole in reality to fall through, and so here she was waiting to be given a helping hand, to hoist her up out of it again.

A couple of years into therapy she spotted Dr Anderssen's partner in the men's accessories department of Bergdorf Goodman. He was trying to decide between a red or yellow scarf.

'Which d'you think?' he asked her.

'Is that the choice?'

'I guess.'

'Neither, Mr McLain.'

She suggested French lavender.

'You reckon?'

'Oh yes.'

'I don't know if Alva will like it.'

'You'll be wearing it.'

'And she'll be looking at it.'

'If you can afford her professional fees – why don't you sit down and talk it over between you?'

He laughed. Then, after a little more thought, he made a face.

'You don't like that colour?' she asked him.

'Yes, I do.'

'So?'

'This is my money. Scarf money.'

'In that case, you get the scarf *you* want.'

Mariel told him she was going to have a light lunch upstairs, would he join her? They sat on stools at the counter, and she heard whispers of 'Is that her? Mariel Baxter?'

Marc was younger than his other half. Seven, eight, even ten years maybe. It occurred to Mariel that there would always be a danger in those relationships.

She was between them in age. If she felt slightly fazed herself by his air of youthfulness – he was fresh-faced, with a head of thick hair – it had to be worse for his partner, who looked her fifty-four years. The woman must always be wondering about other people's reactions, women's and men's, not knowing where the next threat to their fidelity would come from.

Marc told her that the good Doctor A. had done all the running. She used to literally chase after him; she'd patrol the grounds of the research centre, watching the windows just for a sight of him.

'Should you be telling me this?'

It struck Mariel that he was the passive member of that couple, and might have been equally at home in a gay relationship.

She guessed he wouldn't have slept with her if she hadn't been who she was: Mariel Baxter. That would have been true for half the men she'd known.

'So what is *my* attraction?' he asked her.

'That lavender scarf.'

'Why not just buy one for yourself?'

'It suits your colouring better than mine.'

He must have realised quite well what his attraction was. He was her psychiatrist's bed mate. This was Mariel's revenge, of a considered eighteenth-century kind. She was setting the record straight between her and Alva Anderssen, getting even. It wasn't complicated. No psychiatrist was needed to explain the issue.

She came to her next therapy session wearing an identical scarf to Marc's.

Perhaps that was her misjudgement.

From there on, they went downhill. The more she cooperated, the more assiduously her inquisitor eviscerated her answers.

It was like a war every second Tuesday afternoon, if she was in town. But Mariel wouldn't give in. Even after she and Marc had found reasons for not being able to see each other any more, she kept on her appointments with his partner. This felt like a fight to the finish. They were in this right down to the line.

Ursule Kroll

She continued to be stopped in the street by elderly strangers.

'You won't know me, Fräulein Kroll, but—'

And they would tell her how much pleasure her recordings had given them, or ask her if she remembered such and such a recital or production, which they'd had the privilege of attending. They had heard all the Reichssenddungen, the national broadcasts, and the Mozart series with Krauss and Knappertsbusch conducting.

For a few moments they would talk. But Kroll would never let those exchanges turn into conversations and risk losing control of the situation. If possible, it was best not to stop walking. Sometimes, though, she was accosted at a lunch table or in a café. If she had company, a cue sufficed to bring in a third voice; if she was alone, she would shake out her newspaper, as if she must return to the solemn affairs of the world, which – will you please excuse me, sir or madam – were already weighing quite heavily on her arms and wrists.

She also had her appreciation societies. There were half a dozen across Germany and Austria. In addition, there were other voluble fans, private and unaffiliated: a clique here in Vienna, and others in Cologne and Hamburg. Not all were wealthy, but they wined and dined her and sent her outsized bouquets on her birthday and the finest comestibles from Paris (Fauchon, Dalloyau) and gifts of favourite perfume ('Vol de Nuit', 'Arpège') at Christmas time.

She realised that she wasn't forgotten, and deservedly less so than the other big stars of the past who had settled in the green Viennese suburbs – and who, like herself, neither apologised for their behaviour nor accepted the new regime.

Vienna comprised different cities through time. One was particularly special to Kroll: the Vienna she discovered when she moved here shortly after the war, burned-out and rubble-strewn. She remembered it in black and white, and the contrasts were extreme. Its inhabitants were down-at-heel aristocrats and low-born opportunists who would stop at nothing. The ghosts of its past were also there, given refuge, just as she was. The music had survived, Ländler as well as lieder, and she felt she'd had no small part to play in bringing that about.

The spirit of Germanness lived on, bloodied and battered but unbroken.

It happened a couple of years after Brigitte came back into her life.

She wasn't concentrating on what she was doing, and had to turn the little key in the lock of the drawer several times. Once she got inside, she realised that the contents weren't as she'd left them. The pile of silk squares wasn't in the order she kept it in. The Ferragamo one now on top – a gift – had a pattern of autumn leaves she had never cared for; it reminded her of the accompanist who had bought it for her, hoping to be in favour with her, and had been kept at the bottom of the pile.

The scarves had been replaced upside down.

Beneath the silk squares she kept Nagel's photographs, in an envelope. She might have destroyed them, but some perverse curiosity had prevailed.

The glue on the envelope's seal had dried, so she couldn't tell if Brigitte had needed to prise it open or not.

Who else could it have been?

It was possible that Kroll had left the drawer unlocked, and so the blame was hers for putting temptation in Brigitte's way.

She studied the woman's expression afterwards, but couldn't detect any difference. That was the skill of the cunning expert, of course. Years ago, as a hotel chambermaid in Tegernsee, Brigitte had perfected her art.

So now she had seen what she ought not to have seen.

Photographs of a villa. A deserted garden, a lake beyond. The name 'Zdenka' on a gatepost. Would she merely suppose that it was another villa, another garden and another lake, the Starnberger See?

Brigitte wasn't stupid. Kroll wouldn't have taken her on if she had been. The Fates too had played their part in bringing them together, recognising that they deserved each other.

Brigitte did appear more withdrawn this afternoon. Her silence was that of private thought, not obtuseness.

It was too late to remedy the situation, Kroll realised.

It could have been that she had disturbed Brigitte, and Brigitte was simply irritated with herself for failing to cover her tracks any better than she had.

A cunning woman, more than anyone, has – if not honour – her vanity.

The Fates had paired them off, certainly, meaning to have their cruel Olympian fun with them both.

Mariel Baxter

One morning last September, at home, Mariel opened her mouth to sing. What came out was a gross caricature of a soprano voice, ripped and torn.

She tried again, and the same thing happened.

She stopped, too terrified to try again that day.

The following morning, tensed up, she breathed deeply. She opened her mouth. Nothing at all emerged: or something so faint and poor that she couldn't recognise it as her own.

It took two weeks to get back her nerve, and to find a respectable copy of the voice on her recordings.

From this point on, Mariel knew, she would always be afraid that the same affliction might occur again.

She had a reprieve. For four months her voice held up. She almost started to forget about the earlier scare.

On a flight to Santa Fe she was seated in front of a man with a sneezing attack. She tried to move her seat, but an officious woman attendant told her to stay where she was.

'The captain's switched on the seat belts sign.'

'Yes, but—'

'We're scheduled to hit some turbulence shortly.'

No exceptions.

She attributed the roughness in her throat soon afterwards to the sneezer. But she'd had colds before, even doses of influenza, and could still sing. Her voice this time was small and hollow and at least a semitone out of tune: sharp or flat, but off its perch on the stave. She couldn't control the volume: too quiet for the most part, but just now and then it flared up.

Litvinoff's released a statement:

> We regret to announce that our client Mariel Baxter is currently indisposed with a viral infection. She has been advised to rest, in the interests of a speedy recovery. We would ask you to respect our client's privacy during her period of indisposition.

L.L. had decided it should seem as if they were being upfront, which was precisely what they *weren't* being. 'The art of economical amplitude,' he called it.

'Overuse,' was the consultant's verdict.

He shot from the hip, but made it seem like he was doing her a kindness.

'You had this wonderful gift, and early on you did all you could with it. Some roles were difficult for it, but you persisted, to show that you could do everything. Yes? You're not the first, ma'am, and I know for sure you won't be the last.'

Dr A. must have found out what was happening with Marc. Perhaps it didn't surprise her. But she nursed her jealousy. She did jealousy better than anyone she treated. She was jealous to a Proustian degree. She was the spirit of disembodied Marcel afloat in Manhattan. She still ran after her lover, she trailed him in cabs. Once in the office Mariel had seen a pair of small 8x folding binoculars, and she had asked, laughing, if they were for watching the birds, thinking Hitchcock, thinking *Rear Window*.

But the psychiatrist's response afterwards was very simple and direct. She picked up the phone and got through to someone who she knew would never keep a secret. She talked, about nothing very much, waiting for her moment.

'Did I ever tell you that Mariel Baxter's been coming here? This is all in strictest confidence, of course. You'll never guess the big problem she's got—'

2008

A quarter past eight.

Brigitte was waiting, waiting to brush her hair.

Kroll seated herself in front of the glass.

All her life, it seemed, she had been sitting in front of mirrors preening herself. Yet the person she found she was looking at, this old woman, was unrecognisable to her, to the person she still was inside.

She always unpinned the hair herself, and let it roll down her back. Then Brigitte gave it a hundred strokes, smoothing it and burnishing it with the bristles of the brush.

'Such – beautiful – long – hair.'

It had become an earlier and earlier end to every day. Now they would start at a quarter past eight precisely. Gentle lamplight allowed Brigitte to see what she was doing, although decades of practice really made that unnecessary: she could have unfurled the hair and combed it out even if she'd been struck blind.

'Rapunzel, Rapunzel, let down your hair—'

Brigitte always counted to herself. Even when she was praising Kroll's hair, she was counting. One hundred strokes. Some evenings she might think she'd missed two or three, if she'd been distracted by something, and would add another few by way of compensation.

Kroll would sit in front of the glass, watching herself, watching

Brigitte. Brigitte would steal glances at her, standing over her like a protectress; as if, this way, no harm should ever dare come to her.

*

'You know your way round this place.'

'Vienna? I don't know.'

Mariel looked out of the cab, through the rain on the glass. The driver spoke good English. Changed days.

'You don't have a map.'

'It's in my head,' she said.

'You've been here before?'

'Somewhere called Vienna, anyway.'

'Pardon me?'

'I – I lived here for a while. It was a long time ago.'

'Because of your job?'

'No, I was a student.'

'What's different about it?'

'The buildings are much the same. But the people have gone.'

'The people you knew?'

'The people I *thought* I knew.'

*

She had him drop her at the Café Glockenspiel.

The Mozart mural was still in place. In most other respects, she found it altered. They had lightened the panelling, the mirrors had a bluish tint, the tables had heat-resistant tops and the chairs were plastic-finish bentwood meant to look 'belle époque'.

Mariel held the coffee cup in her hands, warming them. She looked into the blue-toned mirrors, half-expecting Die Gruppe to appear. Then she remembered something else, the incident of being watched from outside by the faceless woman in the belted mackintosh, and she turned and looked across to the window, on to the street.

All she saw there was her own solitary reflection.

*

On the mantelpiece in Kroll's drawing room, gilded Atlas held the world on his shoulders. The globe contained a clock face.

Time – Kroll had the evidence in front of her, day in and day out – was a burden, quite literally. Her body was becoming increasingly unequal to the task. It surprised some people that she was still breathing. Look in the Viennese suburbs, though: a sense of injustice was keeping as many, like her, defiant and alive as it had defeated and taken to an early grave.

The Semmelrogge family lived long, at least.

Kroll had a sister, older than she. Two brothers were alive, and one was still working in his electrical goods shop.

She didn't see them. She hadn't met any of them for forty years, after Peter's wife had come looking for her, hoping she would help out financially. (If she had helped them, there wouldn't have been an end to it.)

The public had been told she was an only child, from an old Prussian family. All families are old, as Frau Fleissner once said: and in a sense she *was* alone, since she'd constructed an identity entirely to suit herself.

In her mind she was no age in particular. She had seen her country brought to its knees and pick itself up again; she was aware of today's atmosphere of discontent and xenophobia. Nothing under the sun – hidden by grey northern clouds – was new. It all passes, but only to come around again. She had the years and perspective to judge these historical developments, but when she found herself thinking of Hamburg – clearer to her now than what happened yesterday – she felt she was inside the twenty-year-old's body and mind, experiencing the city all over again. She didn't need virtual reality and cyberspace, those concepts which others spoke about so glibly. They were only what she was perfectly capable of doing for herself, travelling across time and from one end of this great land to the other in the blink of an eye.

When she wasn't flitting about the staging posts of her life, she was having to deal with her physical infirmities. Arthritis hadn't spared her after all, and she was prescribed statins and betablockers for circulatory problems. Her joint pains and heart palpitations repeatedly humiliated her, forcing her to stoop and stop in her tracks, and making it all the more necessary for her to imagine she was elsewhere.

Mind over matter. Hundreds, thousands of times in the course of a day: every day, and every shapeless and merciless night following in its trail.

*

Mariel smiled at herself.

Fifty years old, and a life littered with failed relationships, if they were even that.

No, don't smile.

She stood in front of the mirror, taking a long hard look. At her hair, in particular.

The colouring needed a top-up. *She* knew she was steely grey beneath the pretence of bronze-highlighted butterscotch, but no one else was meant to guess.

She was having to replenish more regularly, as if the evidence of the years would not be denied. Run as fast as she might, but time would always catch up with her.

*

Kroll would put off the moment when she pressed the switch on the bedside lamp, delaying it for as long as possible. (If she left it on, she got no proper sleep at all, continually being pulled up to the surface.)

She lay there in the darkness of her bedroom.

She tried to think of something completely unimportant, anything which her mind could scoop up. What had happened in the course of the past twenty-four hours? She could only think that her American visitor hadn't come, and that today had seemed unending to her.

But she couldn't postpone the inevitable. No image she could conjure up was vivid enough.

She was in the power of the involuntary.

She closed her eyes.

It was there, waiting for her.

She saw a villa.

Fräulein Steinicke's property on Lake Konstanz.

Villa Zdenka.

She had never been there, never even set eyes on the place. Yet she was familiar with every room, as if she had lived in it herself.

The villa. The garden. It's November. An expanse of cold water behind. Night. Moonshine. The last light goes off in the house.

Donnerstag

Thursday

2008

Breakfast in the hotel coffee shop.

Nikolaus Harnoncourt looked at her sternly from the cover of the music magazine. She still hadn't thrown it out.

It opened at that *other* photograph. Cara Michaels, breasts heaving and barely contained inside her dress, stubby nipples outlined beneath the sheeny fabric. And in the column alongside, a selection of her insights on her art. Jesus Christ! Graf-Rhena-Strasse was easy compared with the agony of reading crap like that.

Mariel turned the pages with her thumb.

She found she'd strayed into the jazz section and was about to close the magazine resentfully when she got another shock.

A photograph of Ben Tompkins. He was playing with some colleagues. He was bearded; his crown was bald and he had his hair (still) long at the back, over his collar, to compensate; he'd put on weight. And was wearing glasses, big let-it-all-hang-out green frames.

She knew he'd turned into an American. He'd lived with a jazz chanteuse for a while. Then he got entangled with the wife of a congressman, encountered at a benefit. After that, she'd heard, there was a string of women; wannabes, and over-the-hill types willing to do anything – then there was the business with the jazz legend's young widow, which shattered the image that jazz was racially integrated when the black-is-beautiful lobby bayed for her blood and some of the MOR stations which played him as crossover took him off their playlists. A couple of years ago he'd married a girl young enough to be his daughter; was she still in the picture?

Mariel sucked in her mouth. She wasn't winning this morning – not like Cara Michaels, or even Ben Tompkins. She pushed her chair back and got up. She handed the magazine to a waitress and asked her if she could please throw it away.

*

Every morning Brigitte brought in a newspaper with breakfast. Kroll would pick it up and open it only after she'd swallowed the first two pills in the line of pills, drinking a little water to ease them on their way.

The newspaper, and opening it, had become a formality only. She had stopped being much interested in the world's affairs quite a few years ago. The newspaper reminded her that the world existed, but did little more than that. If she wanted to learn more, she had the radio voices to tell her. She'd had Brigitte get rid of the television set; she'd got tired of copy-cat 'Black Forest Clinic' serials, and irritated by the liberal bias of the news programmes.

The newspaper was really a talisman. As long as it continued to be brought in with breakfast and her seven pills and the glass of water, so long as she picked it up and turned the tops of just a few pages, then the external world didn't touch her but left her alone.

But even that now seemed like too much effort.

This morning Kroll left her *Kronen Zeitung* on the table. She had matters to think about, and to *not* think about.

Her coffee cooled, and for once she failed to notice.

*

As the taxi approached Favoriten, a girl sailed past them on a red bicycle. Mariel jerked her head round and looked out of the rear window. Blonde hair trailed behind the girl. It *couldn't* have been her, not Zoë, but for a couple of seconds Mariel was caught on a time loop.

*

Kroll was conscious of Brigitte moving things about, and of the back door in the kitchen opening and closing.

The sounds were a vague distraction. But it was better than having Brigitte hanging over her, finding something to complain about.

In the drawing room she sat quite still, trying to sharpen her thoughts for what lay ahead.

*

Only once, Mariel was recalling in the cab.

At a recital in Minneapolis.

There was a sizeable population of German descent in Minnesota. They might not have been classical music nuts, but they came out: to show solidarity, maybe, and to hear the language being sung.

A man was waiting for her outside the concert hall, where the Baxter fans and the autograph hunters collected. He had a double-barrelled aristocratic-sounding German name which she didn't catch. He was tall and distinguished-looking, with silver hair and a winter tan.

He patiently stood in line until she turned to him.

'I was reminded of someone tonight,' he said.

His English was very good, but spoken as a German would speak it. (His coat was the German sort, Mariel registered: green loden, cut full with a back pleat.)

'You were?'

'I could believe I was listening to Ursule Kroll.'

Mariel wasn't prepared. She struggled to keep a pleasant expression on her face.

'But it's a long time ago,' the man said. 'In the United States only my friends have heard of her.'

'She – she was very famous in her homeland.'

'You know about her?'

He seemed surprised. Mariel was relieved; she guessed that he didn't know the details of her early career.

'You're an admirer?' she asked him.

'I knew her before she became famous. I've always taken a great interest, as you can imagine.'

He was very charming, in that effortless way only the well-born are.

'Do you – do you still–?'

'I hear about her. She will outlast me. Her parents lived to be old. That was our good air in Wendland.'

Her car had arrived.

'I enjoyed my evening,' the man told her. 'It took me back. Thanks to you.'

'I'm glad.'

'You are quite at home with those songs. They might have been written for you.'

'Thank you,' she said.

And that was how the encounter ended.

Should she tell Kroll about it? But Kroll would want to know what she'd said to him. She would probe to discover her exact words.

'You mean you didn't tell him? You *denied* me?'

No, she wasn't going to allow Kroll the pleasure of putting her into the St Peter role again.

Brigitte looked into the room.

She stood there, as if expecting a response.

'You've been very busy,' Kroll said.

'I'm always busy.'

'Were you moving things?'

'What would I be moving?'

'I don't know. I've just been sitting here.'

'Doing what?'

'Collecting myself.'

'For *her*?'

'For her, yes.'

Brigitte's opinion was all the clearer for not being spoken.

'I've been able to hear you. Being very busy.'

'Nothing special. Why would it be any different, eh?'

Kroll knew when Brigitte was being evasive. Brigitte, canny soul that she was, must know that *she* knew that very well.

It was just another of the games they played.

From the top of the road Mariel sniffed out bonfire smoke.

Two hundred years ago, in the time of Schubert, the air of Vienna would have smelled the same.

The bonfire was in the grounds of Kroll's apartment block. A gardener was feeding, first, an armload of garden refuse into the brazier, then a brown paper package from a cardboard box filled with similar packages. Mariel stood watching from the pathway as he stoked the burning wood beneath the brazier and fresh flames flew up.

Something made her glance towards the building. A figure – Brigitte's – let the net curtain fall at one of the windows in the apartment.

Mariel delayed a few moments. She hadn't thought what she was going to say. Instinct had brought her. According to Kroll's lessons, instinct had to be curbed: singing was the considered recollection of past emotion, head taking a lead from heart but ruling it. She realised now how difficult it must have been, explaining such a concept to someone so young and callow as herself.

That excused nothing, though. But at least, twenty-eight years on, she could manage to recognise a perspective other than her own.

She suggested to Kroll that they go out.

'Go out where?'

'I don't know.'

Anywhere really.

The apartment felt just too oppressive to her today. Was it ever aired? The netting at the windows was a heavy filter of daylight.

Kroll considered for a few moments.

'Very well.'

'Only if you want to.'

'Of course.'

Of course only if I want to.

Mariel waited for Kroll to get ready. Brigitte was summoned. Twenty minutes later Kroll reappeared with her face made up to confront the vigilant eyes of Hietzing.

Outside Mariel commented on the bonfire smoke, and drew an admission from Kroll that her sense of smell wasn't what it used to be. Kroll didn't seem to have smelled the smoke at all. Mariel pointed, and for a few seconds they both watched the brownness smudging the air.

The concession from Kroll about the failure of one sense (at least) had been quite unexpected.

This afternoon she looked least like her former self: she was smaller, thinner, and somehow – for all the artifice applied to her face – *unprepared*.

'Can I—?'

Mariel offered her arm.

'What is it?' Kroll asked her.

'D'you want to—?'

If Kroll was going to snap at her, as she would once have done, she had obviously changed her mind. She shook her head.

'No, thank you. I shall cope by myself.'

Mariel smiled at her.

'Which way?' Kroll asked.

They stopped out on the sidewalk. Kroll turned her head. To their right, the silver-haired man with his green coat and hat was walking off beneath the trees. Kroll stood, a little unsteadily, watching him before she pointed in the other direction with her stick.

'This way,' she said. 'We shall go left.'

They walked no further than to some railed gardens.

A nanny was pushing her charge in an old-fashioned pram, and a couple of boys sailed yachts in a pond, and the scene resembled some kind of faux-naïf painting.

An original Michel Delacroix had hung on the walls of Dr Anderssen's study: a subconscious celebration of what those sessions cost.

At least Kroll appeared pacified for the moment.

The sun was shining. The air had warmed up.

Mariel wished she could be pacified too.

Vienna was a city of distances and perspectives, Mariel was thinking. It was designed for carriages bowling along.

Smaller, less ostentatious cities were better to travel on foot.

'In America nobody walks,' Kroll said.

'Not true,' Mariel corrected her.

They proceeded slowly, taking small steps.

'You drive everywhere.'

'That's a generalisation,' Mariel smiled back. No, she wouldn't be provoked, not today.

'Some days are too long,' Kroll said, 'no?'

'I understand.'

Kroll was looking at her.

'Even a fine apartment', Mariel said, 'can seem like an enclosure.'

Their different experiences had brought them to the same conclusion. They agreed about *that*, at any rate.

Ursule Kroll

1972. A table reservation, in the name of Niklas-Schwarzenberger. And where else in Vienna would he have chosen but the dining room at the Palais Schwarzenberg?

Full circle – almost.

'We spend our lives, it seems to me, not saying what we think.'

'It seems to me', Kroll replied, 'we spend a lot of time talking, even so.'

'I learned', he said, '*not* to write things down. In case they incriminated me. I thought I'd try to write you a letter, but – the paper was very white. It was like looking at the north face of the Eiger, or Pitz Palu.' He laughed. 'Do you understand?'

She nodded.

'You've never spoken publicly, in the press,' he said. 'You haven't come out and told us what your feelings are.'

She didn't need to ask what he was referring to. About having had her career taken away from her.

'Even if I'd been quoted accurately – which I doubt – those are private matters.'

He was looking at her very intently. For a moment she wondered if he knew more about her than he was supposed to. She held her breath. But when he reached out on the tablecloth to touch her fingers, she realised that her hidden life was still a secret from him.

'I wasn't much of an opera fan,' he said. 'In the days when you went off to see *The Gypsy Princess*, I thought I was much wiser. I didn't know the difference between being wise and being cynical. I didn't believe in happy endings. I've seen very few of those in my life.'

Kroll was puzzled. It was as if, for him, her seeing the Kálmán had marked some landmark in his experience at Esterhofen; whereas her Damascene moment had been walking into the stables on another afternoon and disturbing him and his lover when they were hard at it.

Where was all this leading to?

She watched as he withdrew his hands.

'Klara died last autumn.'

'I had no idea. I'm very sorry.'

'I wasn't faithful to her. In the physical sense.'

Did he really have to tell her that?

'I wouldn't have been able to keep on Esterhofen without her father's money. Or been able to entertain in Berlin, and grease palms, and all the rest of it. Being married to her was the complication, you see.'

Kroll couldn't help smiling.

'Yes,' he said, 'the cynic never quite dies, does he?'

'If you say so.'

'I tried, I *tried*. To be a decent husband. Not as good as she deserved, but—'

His fingers touched hers again. At one time that simple contact would have sent a bolt of current through her.

'She took a series of strokes. Her family didn't want people to know she was being cared for. Whenever I went back she asked me to read her stories. The stories she'd been told as a child. Fairy tales. It was – it was pitiful.'

Momentarily his eyes shone moistly behind his lenses.

Kroll sat very still. She was aware of the risk she was running. She didn't move her fingers.

'Politics,' he sighed, 'I can do without. Business is enough for me, and running Esterhofen. So I don't have to think of my public profile any more. What a relief!'

Was that the real reason why he was talking to her? She couldn't harm his career now. But as a consort for a politician in the new Germany, in its age of boom, she would have been completely inappropriate.

The unspoken inference irritated Kroll, and she drew back her fingers. He was left staring at the cloth where her fingers had been.

She watched his face. He seemed entirely at a loss.

Did he imagine that he might genuinely be in love with her?

She was shocked. She couldn't think straight. When he asked her if they could see each other again, and rhymed off a list of restaurants and high-minded entertainments awaiting them in Berlin, she heard herself inventing excuses why not.

The next time he was in Vienna he rang her, and she could only suggest a park close to his hotel.

'I'll wait for you there,' he said, 'shall I?'

It wasn't what he had intended, clearly, but he told her chivalrously that it was a lady's choice.

They could go walking, was her immediate thought, anything rather than being trapped at a restaurant table or in a theatre seat. It was the closest she could contrive to a turn in the country. Trees, greenery, flowers, water, sky, quiet – and Schubert's ghost, watchful, pensive, hovering about them.

The little park, she discovered as soon as she turned the corner of the street, had become a temporary fairground.

In the middle stood a carousel. Dodgem cars went careening while lurid lights flashed, bells rang and organ music blared.

She saw him standing in the glow, watching the antics of the dodgem drivers. The drivers spinning the steering wheels actually had no control; the pretence was that they did. He watched with a blank expression. Screams, laughter, bells, and that ceaseless music, like an organ grinder's but so much louder.

It was a hellish place.

She continued to stand twenty or thirty yards from him. The mechanical music was holding her rooted to the spot, she felt. She was remembering the musical box in her childhood home, how she used to lift the lid and the little spiked drum would start to turn, with a pretty tune being plucked out of it.

The carousel spun to the din of organ pipes. The music was shapeless, it was impossible to detect a tune.

She always needed a melody. Music, otherwise, made no sense to her, it was like Litzmann's cacophony of sounds.

Brash colours fell on to the crowd of spectators. Bells clanged, a whistle shrieked, while the organ ground out its scatterfire of notes and the dodgem cars spun and people screamed and yelled and laughed as the cars crashed into one another. The cars were attached to upright poles, and where the poles were connected to the ceiling of the carousel orange sparks crackled.

She stood watching him, a dapper figure in his green loden coat and hat, with hair now silvering. He hadn't seen her, she guessed. He was waiting for her; he would always be waiting.

She noticed how he turned to look at a girl who was weaving between the bystanders. The girl was slinky like a cat, wearing cheap gaudy clothes, with red bruise marks on her heels from uncomfortable high-heeled shoes. She could only be up to one thing.

He continued to watch her. He made no bones about it. The girl glanced at him and walked on, glanced again, let her eyes rest. She smiled. But he didn't know what was patently clear to Kroll, that the girl wasn't smiling for his benefit. It was a mocking smile.

She was a trick all right, but for the women who were in theknow this park was a pick-up spot. Kroll felt herself dampening as she observed the two of them, in their utterly pointless encounter.

She would inform him later that, yes, indeed she *had* stood him up, but it was all for the best. She wasn't likely to ever make him happy. She was too settled in her ways, and if she had wasted his evening then she was very sorry. Maybe in time he would find it in him to forgive her?

She knew that he would, because he wasn't a man given to petty grudges. The two of them went too far back for that.

Kroll melted into the crowd. She found the girl close to the Damen. It was several years since Kroll had played this game. The woman who oversaw the conveniences was the same pander who used to be here, still keeping one eye trained from the arched doorway (the other eye was glass). She didn't object to street trade if it was accompanied by a lady like herself. A big tip in her saucer on the way in meant you were left in peace, with regular flushing from the adjoining stalls to conceal the sounds of lovemaking. (Some old Viennese habits didn't change, thankfully.)

The girl knew just what was expected of her. She went down on to her haunches, raising Kroll's skirt and running her hands up the insides of her thighs. Kroll shivered with anticipation. The girl's tongue appeared between her lips, flicking left and right.

Leaning back against the panel with her eyes closed, Kroll was picturing Christine Duringer. It was that woman's tongue which was darting in and out of her wet pussy, and her head which Kroll was now cradling, her hair which she was bunching with her fingers, holding the two of them close, *close*, while the breath building inside Kroll seemed ready to crack her ribs.

Mariel Baxter

Two or three people in the press had gotten to hear about Mariel Baxter's voice. They knew she'd been to see a medical consultant, the best money could pay for.

She believed she had kept the problem a secret from her musical colleagues, even from Lou Litvinoff. An outdoor production of *Of Mice and Men* at Tallahassee might well prove to have been her swansong. Her subsequent cancellations had been put down to tiredness and a stubborn viral infection. Nobody had disputed her. She had pulled out of the Met's *Arabella* before rehearsals began, before anyone she was due to sing alongside heard her and got any ideas of self-aggrandisement.

It suddenly came to her, turning the Swissotel Drake corner of East 56th Street on to Park Avenue, looking into the Fauchon window and seeing those bitter-tasting coffee beans dipped in chocolate, which got some people through their long days. Bitterer than coffee beans, than the darkest almonds –

Alva Anderssen.

Ursule Kroll

But sometimes it would seem to Kroll that Vienna had let her remain in a state of suspended animation.

In summer, when the fountains played, she would hear Mozart in her head and think of Maestro Böhm's comment that to listen to Mozart was to drink at the fountain of perpetual youth.

The music was in her veins. Thank God for that. Like embalming fluid, it had preserved her.

Thus far.

She had lived three times as long as some of the composers. For more than half her adult life she had been deprived of the means to a career. Such staggering success as hers must have a cost, people said to console her; but they would never know the whole truth of it.

No, they would never be *allowed* to know.

Mariel Baxter

There had been only one place left for her to go.

For twenty-eight years she had resisted. Invitations had come to sing with the Staatsoper, and with the Philharmoniker, and with the Symphoniker. The New Year's Day Concert at the Musikverein had been mooted in the late 1980s, with Leonard Bernstein on the podium. Lou Litvinoff told her she was insane to turn everything down in Vienna, and she could only answer him, yes, quite possibly I am. (She would then agree to whatever he lined up for her elsewhere, to appease him, but only confirming for him her own perversity.)

2008

She'd said it.

She had said what she came to Vienna, to these primped public gardens, to say.

'I don't know what to do,' Mariel confessed simply. 'My voice is all that I have.'

Kroll didn't speak.

Mariel listened to the silence. She had spoken as plainly as she could. There was nothing more to be said. She had told Kroll the worst that one singer could admit to another. She was left wholly vulnerable and exposed. She had put herself into Kroll's confidence completely.

Not having her voice meant she was emotionally bereft.

'Dancers don't dance for ever,' Kroll said. 'It's the fate of interpreters. Pianists, sometimes they're lucky, their fingers stay agile. Even if the voice stays strong, it isn't so accurate.'

'It's like a race against time?'

'A singer should be judged also by how she reacts to her voice changing.'

'She should stop, you mean?'

'That isn't for me to say.'

'You had so much advice to give me at the beginning.'

'You think this is the end?'

'Isn't it? If I can't rely on this instrument—'

Kroll shrugged.

'What about – what about your own voice?' Mariel asked her.

'I was careful what I sang. It would have lasted longer. But I wasn't permitted. It's a different situation from yours.'

'I was told I sang too much.'

'Impossible.'

'Not the right things.'

'Did you feel you weren't singing the right things?'

'Not at the time, no.'

'Then they were probably the right things.'

'I only sang music I thought I understood.'

'Don't feel angry with the music.'

'I'm not angry.'

'No?'

'With the press, yes.'

'Only the press?'

'Okay. Doctors. Directors. Other singers. Rumour-mongers. Publicists telling me I should—'

Kroll seemed disinterested now. It was as if she didn't want any more information. Mariel wondered why she imagined Kroll would be willing to instruct her about what to do.

She tried to draw Kroll back into the conversation.

'You never mentioned Alina Giebisch.'

Kroll's body froze for an instant.

'When?'

'When I was coming for my lessons.'

'Why should I have done?'

'You knew her.'

'Yes. I knew her.'

'Knew her well?'

'At one time, yes.'

'You sang together?'

'I sang with so many people.'

'You made a record with her.'

'I made dozens and dozens of records.'

'A record of operatic duets.'

'If you say so.'

'Only one record?'

'I forget.'

'I could only find one.'

'Then it must have been one.'

'An LP, I mean. That would have been compiled from old 78s.'

'You make me sound ancient.'

'I'm sorry, I wasn't intending—'

'But that's what I am, isn't it?'

Kroll's smile, Mariel felt, was an attempt to escape from this line of questioning.

'She didn't continue,' Mariel said.

'Didn't continue what?'

'Singing. Making records.'

'She died. She died in an accident.'

'An automobile crash?'

Kroll nodded.

'You and she were friends?'

'We were students together.'

'And later?'

'Later?'

'Did you stay friends?'

'I tried to be a friend.'

Mariel sensed there was an undertow, flowing hard against the top current.

'You sounded very alike.'

Kroll sat on the bench quite still now.

'I once heard the record of duets,' Mariel told her.

'It must be a rarity now. Quite valuable.'

'On vinyl.'

Suddenly Kroll was as still as a jungle cat.

'There's a lot which hasn't been released,' Kroll said. 'Who knows why? Can you enlighten me?'

Mariel forced her mouth to a dry smile.

'I don't understand the recording industry.'

Kroll raised her eyebrows.

'No?'

'No.'

'That does puzzle me,' Kroll said.

'Why does it puzzle you?'

'For a successful career you need to have the right people on your side, don't you?'

'But', Mariel threw back at her, 'I expect that was just as true for you.'

Kroll paused, with her famous instinct for the telling beat, before she spoke.

'Perhaps we two have more in common than you like to think.'

Mariel was suddenly the one being wrong-footed.

'I would need to know more than I do,' Mariel said, 'to judge.'

'Know more about me?'

'Yes.'

'Or about yourself?'

'I've had to live with this person for fifty years.'

'With Mariel Baxter?'

The briefest smile passed over Kroll's face.

Who *was* this Mariel Baxter? Not a doppelganger, but a monster nonetheless. Larger than life, but somehow less real.

Kroll reserved her fusillade for the return journey to Graf-Rhena-Strasse.

'You know Dieter Spengler?' she asked.

Mariel stared ahead of her.

'You belong to his roll of artistes. That is still the case, I suppose?'

'Yes, that's right,' Mariel replied, with a falsely bright voice. 'How – how do you know all this?'

'We have an acquaintance in common. Professor Welspricht here. There's a line of communication, you see.'

'Ah.'

'And so I get to hear about his job. Your Herr Spengler's achievements. Also, the schemes he doesn't manage to get off the ground.'

Mariel didn't speak.

'But you know about those, don't you?'

'Do I?' Mariel said, disclaiming interest.

'Oh yes, I think you must.'

'If you say so.'

'It's what *you* say, I believe, which counts with Herr Spengler. Or which *did* count when he asked you. He wanted your advice.'

'What about?' Mariel bluffed her.

'A project.'

'A project?'

'His big millennium idea.'

'What was that?'

'The one you didn't care for. The *Meistersingers*.'

Mariel stared ahead of her again.

'Werner Welspricht was telling me. He wondered why I hadn't been consulted.'

'It hadn't reached that stage.'

'You remember now?'

'I remember, yes, vaguely.'

'You didn't approve?'

'I thought – for the millennium – they should take on some new singers.'

'That didn't make you uncomfortable?'

'Why "uncomfortable"?'

'Those other singers—'

'No, not at all.'

'Following along so close behind you?'

'Why should I mind?'

Kroll smiled from a position of greater wisdom.

'I could have been displayed in the record shops,' Kroll said, 'just like yourself.'

'I didn't make that decision.'

'They wanted to know what you thought.'

'Sounding me out, yes.'

'And if you'd said to them, "What an excellent idea!"'

'I tried to establish the priorities.'

Kroll pulled a face at that.

'*Your* priorities.'

'For the company.'

'That was very selfless of you.'

Mariel pressed her lips tightly together.

'You're going to tell me', Kroll said, 'how selfish my generation was by comparison.'

'No, I'm not.'

'It's true. We did have to think of ourselves. All through the war we had to believe we wouldn't be silenced.'

'*You* weren't silenced, not then.'

'Certainly I wasn't. Not when the great songs I was singing needed saving.'

'You want me to tell you how grateful I am to you?'

'No. But some small acknowledgement – public acknowledgement – that would have been useful. A recommendation, at any rate. Coming from Mariel Baxter herself.'

'I did – I did what I judged best at the time.'

'That could be said of us all, I think.'

Mariel realised that Kroll was talking about her own life. But by saying what she had done, Mariel had helped to trap herself. Kroll was telling her, very firmly, that neither of them could claim the moral high ground.

Back at Graf-Rhena-Strasse Mariel smelled the woodsmoke still, even though it wasn't visible.

A late spring day took on the semblance of fall.

'What are your plans?' Kroll asked her.

'I'm leaving on Saturday.'

Kroll offered no reaction, not even relief.

Mariel thought she heard footsteps and looked behind her, but there was nobody.

Kroll did the same, but her eyes watched the empty sidewalk for longer.

'Tomorrow is Friday, yes?' Kroll said.

'Shall I ring you?' Mariel asked, after a moment's pause.

'When?'

'Tomorrow. Late morning.'

'If you have nothing better to do.'

'I don't have anything better to do.'

'Very well.'

If Kroll hadn't wished it, Mariel realised, she would have said so. She wouldn't have let her trademark Prussian courtesy get in the way of a 'no'.

Mariel went into the building with her and pressed the button by the elevator door.

Hydraulics sighed distantly, and cables started to pull.

Nothing more was said except goodbyes: polite and non-committal.

After everything, Mariel was thinking as she walked away.

'Goodbye, then.'

'*Auf wiedersehen.*'

She was suddenly exhausted. She had kept going for four days.

The end of the week, and that two o'clock return flight, seemed a remote finishing line. And not even that, because in a sense – if nothing was resolved – she was returning to a future much more difficult than her past.

*

'Brigitte!'

Kroll screamed out the name again.

'Where's everything gone?'

Brigitte materialised, standing in the doorway of the dining room.

'Where's what gone?'

'The letters. The photographs. Where are they?'

'Where they should've gone years ago.'

'What are you saying?'

'The truth, God help me.'

'Where are they?'

'Not here, anyhow.'

'What's happened to them?'

'They're gone.'

'Answer me!' Kroll was shrieking again, oblivious to their neighbours in the block. 'I know they're gone. Where?'

'Up in smoke.'

'What?'

'Burned.'

'*What?*'

'I got the Croat boy to burn them.'

'You? You?'

'You should never have kept them.'

Kroll was fighting for breath.

'That – that was my – *my* business.'

'You want the world to read all that stuff?'

Kroll stared at her.

'What?'

'Just giving them reasons to drag your name through the mud again.'

Kroll didn't speak, didn't know what to say.

'These are your secrets now. They won't know now.'

'I'll never see them again.'

'That's why. Can't you see that, for God's sake?'

Kroll stood supporting herself at the table.

'Answer me, then.'

Brigitte waited. She waited a long time. Finally Kroll found herself nodding.

'Well—?'

'Yes,' Kroll said.

'I can't hear you.'

'Yes,' she repeated.

'Again.'

'Yes.' Kroll sighed, as deeply as she dared. 'Yes, Brigitte, I do see.'

*

The taxi stopped, as requested, at Katrin-gässchen.

Yes, this was definitely the street. But the little record store, where Tomas used to play her his collectors' discs, had gone.

The street was pedestrianised. Mariel stood in the middle of the new cobbled precinct, looking round her. She listened to the dull fall of feet, ambling casually, where there used to be the purposeful hubbub of cars and vans and motorbikes.

*

Kroll returned to her bedroom. She tried the drawer in the chest. It was locked, but that didn't mean Brigitte hadn't somehow been able to get at it. Her heart was beating very fast as she turned the key in the lock and pulled the drawer open. She felt with her fingers.

It was there!

She eased it from beneath the soft weight of cashmeres and woollens, where she'd taken to placing it. A heavy silver frame, with the precious photograph inside.

She used to keep some yellowing pages with it: words written by Paul Ehlers, one of her earliest devotees, to commemorate the fiftieth birthday of the one he called 'the Saviour of German Music'. But she had come to know them by heart.

We longed for the man in whose pure hands the power resided to cast out the desecrators from the temple with a whip! And this man came. He came with a mighty sword as a sovereign of the German people and of German art.

Unlike the singers who would supersede her, she had committed to memory the lyrics of every song. No hand-held score for Kroll. Fräulein Hebbel had merely expected her to be word-perfect in all her operatic roles, without a single slip.

Like a thunderstorm in springtime his words and deeds covered the holy German land and sent flaming lightning to punish the robbers and secret masters of the Germans: the Jews.

*

She asked in a tobacconist's.

Had Tomas moved premises?

All she learned was that the record shop had been there one day and gone the next. Five or six years ago. No explanation offered. Sign up on the door: they'd ceased trading. The stock had been moved out overnight, and it hadn't been possible to contact the tenant.

Mariel was satisfied with that report. It made the past *truer* somehow, because it no longer existed. She was purely reliant on memory now. Facts couldn't be proved or disproved. One small portion of the past, *that* one at least, was conserved intact.

*

'Have you laid them out, Brigitte?'

'Why should I not have laid them out? I always lay them out.'

'Yes,' Kroll sighed, 'you do.'

Brigitte looked round and fixed her with a stare. Kroll understood that she still hadn't been forgiven.

'Have you any reason to complain?'

'No, of course not.'

Brigitte shrugged. Why should I care?

Kroll walked past her and into the kitchen. She stopped at the table. The tablets were laid out for the morning, as usual. The big white one, the pink one, the blue one, the white heart, the yellow oval, the annoying round red one that rolled about. And an aspirin in the brown glass bottle.

She was having difficulty focusing her eyes today.

She laid her index finger on each of the pills in turn. All to keep her, more or less, alive.

For what?

Brigitte collected her things and paused at the front door in her belted mackintosh.

'Good night,' she said.

'Good night,' Kroll replied.

Normally they both turned away at that point. But this evening something made Kroll linger, and Brigitte did the same.

'Is she coming back?'

'I don't know,' Kroll answered simply.

'I wish she would go.'

'I know you do.'

'She should never have come.'

'She thought she needed to come.'

'"Needed to"?' Why?'

Kroll shook her head.

'She didn't tell you why?'

'She gave me some reasons, yes,' Kroll said. 'But—'

'But?'

'She leaves on Saturday.'

Brigitte heard, and crossed herself.

*

Conrad Niklas-Schwarzenberger.

A red line had been run through the name.

He died in 1987. Twenty-one years ago.

At the end of every year there used to be a Christmas card: from Esterhofen, or from some resort – Acapulco, Cancun, Guanacaste – he'd taken himself off to, or later from Minnesota. His little joke was that he called her 'Maria', and signed himself *Ever yours*. The form didn't alter, not once in all those years.

*

She found a big record store still open and went in.

'Right, Mariel,' she instructed herself, 'this is what you do.'

She collected all the Cara Michaels CDs and DVDs in the racks. She took herself off to the different departments, enjoying this game of redistributing Cara Michaels about the premises more and more.

Country and Western. Funk. Easy Listening.

'No one easier,' she told herself. 'Miss Easy-Lay.'

Self-help. Urban. Gay Interest.

She headed off for another DVD section with the final two copies.

To Comedy. Where else? That digitally enhanced little tramp was just a joke.

She felt better for it. The other customers heard her laughing, and looked up at Bill Murray on the screens. Maybe something about *Lost in Translation* really did get lost?

*

Kroll didn't want to go to bed. She checked that the front door was locked, then she returned to the drawing room.

In her dressing gown and embroidered slippers, she remained sitting on a high-backed chair.

Villa Zdenka's garden runs down to the lakeside. In mid-November conifers and evergreen shrubs prevent those out on the lake from seeing in, but allow the villa's occupants to view the panorama.

She sees it in her mind's eye, as if she had actually been there for herself instead of relying on photographs, Fräulein Steinicke's and those ensuing ones from the Intelligence files. In darkness the scene is more real than the lit room in which she sits now.

Lights spell danger. The cars that glide along the avenues of Lindau have slitted caps fitted to their headlamps. As they approach the lake, the drivers switch off their mainbeam altogether.

The front gates have been locked and chained, but there are ways and means of dealing with such obstructions. Similarly, it doesn't matter that the villa's doors and windows are snibbed and bolted. If they intend to, then enter they will. No amount of naïve ingenuity will stop them.

The time between then, when those events happened, and this present moment seems to have been a dream. Nothing is left now except a few mementoes overlooked by Brigitte.

Kroll gets up, turns on all the lamps in the room, goes into other rooms turning the lights on, until the apartment is ablaze, like some grand ocean liner sailing through the night.

She returns to the drawing room. She can't face bed and the heavy drapes and having to wear an eye-mask.

She seats herself again. She loses track of how long she sits there.

The villa is waiting for her. It's bathed in moonlight, yellowish-blue.

She hears voices, shouts, a woman's scream, the scramble of heavy boots, a door being kicked down, a gunshot, a group of men cursing at one another, the reinforced toe of a boot aiming at wall tiles and smashing them out of sheer frustration.

It all happens inside her head. Sounds which create pictures. She can't not hear, not see. Everything is played out in front of her, and she's helpless to change anything.

Freitag

Friday

2008

Kroll started awake. Sunlight was shining directly into her eyes. The lamps were still on.

Her limbs felt stiff. Her head ached badly. Now her eyes were hurting with the light.

She pulled herself slowly to her feet. She screwed up her eyes, to read the time on Atlas's shoulder. The hour hand was at V.

Drawn by the light, Kroll walked over to the window still in her dressing gown. She pulled the hem of net curtain apart with the fingers of one hand. Already dust danced beneath the trees. She was about to turn away, but stopped. A figure was standing down on the pavement. It was the man in green. She couldn't make out his face, but he was looking this way, towards the apartment building.

Her instinct was to turn away. But she stood continuing to watch him. She was fascinated, and panic-stricken too. She noticed that her hand was shaking, and she let the curtain drop from between her fingers.

He had been waiting, waiting patiently, for this ominous day to dawn at last.

*

Mariel didn't call the apartment at the time she'd said that she would.

She distracted herself with an e-mail.

> *To: Lou Litvinoff*
> cc:
> Subject: Sands of Time.........
>
> Shalom Lou, Still here. Read this weeks ago, meant to
> send it you. Degas wrote, Everybody has talent at 25 –
> the difficulty is to have it at 50. Is it true or is it true? Be
> well, may your light shine for ever. M xx

That message written and sent, Mariel's mind turned to what she
was doing. Or rather, what she was *not* doing.

She was half an hour over schedule on the phone call.

Ursule Kroll only knew that she was staying at a hotel in the centre
of town, and didn't have a contact address or phone number.

She wasn't sure why she was holding back. It was a reflex. There
was a streak of cruelty in what she was doing. That was the truth
of this relationship. It was a tale of malice and truculence, and
Schadenfreude – sometimes called 'unholy joy'.

Instead she rang late morning.

Brigitte answered.

'Shall I come today?'

'It's up to *you*.'

Mariel was determined to rise above the provocation.

'How is she?'

Brigitte hesitated.

'She's still asleep.'

Mariel glanced at her watch. Eleven fifteen.

'She slept badly last night.'

'Will she want to see me?'

'She never sleeps late, never.'

Brigitte seemed disorientated. This change of routine had thrown her.

'Let's play it by ear, shall we?'

'I don't understand.'

'I'll come by later, yes?'

She was due to return to New York tomorrow afternoon. She had just over twenty-six hours left.

When she got to the apartment, Brigitte opened the door.

She didn't appear surprised to see her, and simply stood back to let her in.

Kroll was waiting in the doorway of the salon, more shadow than substance. Mariel registered the strange effect, reminiscent of the first morning.

'I've come.'

That was all she could think of to say to her.

Mariel already knew she wouldn't be standing watching Kroll like this again. She had come precisely because not a single minute could be lost. By early afternoon tomorrow she would be gone. She was here about losing her voice, and about wanting a song.

Mariel Baxter

It was one of the lieder which Dieter Spengler had selected from the Kroll archive, which he judged especially worthy of mention.

'"Im Frühling".'

'"In Springtime".'

'Funny you mention *that* one,' Mariel had told him.

'Why's that?'

She hesitated.

'It was one that my professor in Boston was very keen on. But he didn't think he could teach me.'

'So you didn't learn it?'

'Right.'

'What do you think of Kroll's version?'

'There were others,' Mariel said.

'Whose do you like?'

'Gundula Janowitz.'

Spengler nodded.

'Schwarzkopf?' he asked.

'Yes.'

'Anyone else?'

'I've never heard Alina Giebisch sing it.'

'*There's* a name.'

'Yes?'

'What a tragedy that was,' Spengler said. 'What an end.'

'A car wreck, wasn't it?'

'Seems so. Otto Litzmann went out of circulation at the same time.'

'Litzmann? Who was he?'

'A composer. Jewish. "*Entartete Musik*".'

'A decadent?'

'He was protected for a while. But they were on to him.'

'*They*?'

'The censors.'

'And Alina Giebisch?'

'They were lovers. Or they may have married.'

'What happened to Litzmann? D'you know?'

'Does anyone know? It's a big world out there if you intend to make yourself invisible.'

Mariel blinked at the whiteness of the table cloth.

'You'll say, Mariel, we've had all this German stuff.'

'Sure.'

'I can't change your mind?'

'How many copies of *Meistersinger* are you going to sell?'

'Enough, maybe.'

'Just "enough", Dieter?'

'Hmph.'

Spengler looked a little chastened.

'That's the independents' niche,' Mariel said. 'They can price high, for aficionados. But it'll never be mass market.'

'Granted, but—'

Spengler's voice trailed off. He seemed to be acknowledging that she had common sense on her side after all.

Mariel touched his wrist consolingly and tried to keep a check on the big Times Square billboard-wide smile that was wanting to break out on her face, from ear to ear.

Long before, Professor Donsbach in Boston had told her, 'I've heard a Kroll recording of "Im Frühling". No one has sung it better, in my opinion.'

He claimed subsequently in an article that it was the finest of Schubert's spring songs. The trouble with many interpretations was that they took the emotions too far and over-complicated things. Kroll's version was surely the closest to what Schubert had intended, which, in Professor Donsbach's opinion, was to 'luxuriate quietly' in 'private melancholy'. The lyrics looked back tenderly, and the music – switching mid-way from G major to G minor – shrugged off time signatures.

No misfortune or suffering was so great, Kroll's voice promised, that it couldn't be made bearable by the sweet balm of memory.

2008

Mariel explained why to Kroll as best she could.

'Will you teach me that song?'

'I've forgotten—'

'You once told me the best singers have complete recall.'

'Is that what I said?'

'Yes.'

But Kroll shook her head.

'Please,' Mariel said.

'Schubert wrote six hundred songs.'

'But only one "Im Frühling".'

The song was more elusive and more desirable to Mariel than ever.

'Peter Donsbach said I would be judged by how I could sing a lied like that one.'

'The time to ask me was *then*.'

'I did. Why not "Im Frühling"?'

'There was so much else you had to learn. What difference does it make now?'

Mariel herself wasn't sure. It was an instinct with her, stronger than any other at this juncture.

'It's unfinished business,' she heard herself say. 'Something I didn't do when I was here. Which I can put right.'

There seemed to her something talismanic about the song. She had never sung it, although she had been asked to many times. The absence had left her repertoire incomplete. Her voice wouldn't allow her to sing it much longer, or to a standard which was anything like satisfactory to her.

Kroll averted her eyes.

'Please.'

Kroll looked this way, that way, as if she was searching for her escape route.

'Please, Ursule!'

Kroll froze at the use of her Christian name.

'*Please!*'

Mariel had brought the music with her. She placed her copy on the music board of the piano.

Kroll gazed at her with imploring eyes.

Mariel began to read the lyrics aloud.

'*Silent I sit on the hillside. The sky is so clear. The breeze frolics in the green vale where once, at the first gleam of spring, I was, oh, so happy.*'

Kroll picked out the melody on the piano and half-sang, half-spoke the words. She was managing to stay composed, thus far.

'*Where I used to walk so close by her side ...*'

Kroll faltered for a moment, then continued.

'*... and see the bright blue of the heavens mirrored in the depths of the dark mountain stream ...*'

She lost direction again, looking into that crystalline torrent, glacier melt, into the depths of the undeclared.

Her voice suddenly had a crack in it as she delivered, talked out, the next words.

'*... and she was part of that heaven.*'

It was only a run-through, Mariel told herself, so that Kroll could re-familiarise herself with the words. And to allow herself some vocal exercise.

She took over from Kroll.

'See, the spring colours already peep out from the buds and flowers. Not all the flowers are the same to me.'

Her voice was somehow bearing up.

'I like best to pluck them from the same stems as she did.'

She saw Kroll staring at the sheet music on the stand.

'For everything is just as it was then, the flowers, the fields; the sun shines no less brightly ...'

Mariel tried to picture the scene, tried to believe that she was there. Sympathetic transference.

'... the blue image of the sky ripples, just as friendly, along the stream.'

Kroll rested her fingers on the piano keys. The stream was rushing past her. She hadn't been here for more than half her lifetime.

Mariel watched Kroll, who was transfixed. She took up the burden of the song by herself.

'The happiness of love passes away, leaving only love itself and, alas, sorrow.'

The piano was silent, and Mariel had to remember the accompaniment, hearing it for herself inside her head.

At one level Kroll was listening to her, while at another she was somewhere else entirely.

'Oh if I could only be the bird ...'

Kroll knew what came next, as if the song flowed in her veins. The sadness was unbearable to her.

'Oh if I could only be the bird, there on the meadow steep!'

Lightness was the thing, Mariel realised, turning her eyes away from Kroll.

Kroll's face was all despair. What was this all about? Jealousy? Resentment?

Indignation carried Mariel the remaining distance.

'*Then I would rest here on this bough, singing a sweet song about her all summer long.*'

Kroll said nothing.

'*The happiness of love passes away …*'

Those words eddied and whirled for her.

'*… leaving only love itself and, alas, sorrow.*'

She blinked at the music open on the stand, caught herself doing it, and realised that the person who was in the room with her wasn't that special one, the beloved.

Mariel registered the confusion on Kroll's face. She saw a very old woman struggling to maintain her pride.

Kroll couldn't bear the American's pity.

She snapped the sheet music shut with the agility of a girl. She closed the lid over the piano keys.

I've riled her, Mariel thought. Kroll believes I've humiliated her.

Nothing changes. We're black and white. At one time, when I knew no better, I let her play havoc with my life. The old bitch. She won't get that chance again.

But now I can smile at her.

'Hey, we got there!'

Kroll couldn't understand what the woman was talking about. 'We'? There was no 'we', there never had been. Only once in her life, for a short-lived interregnum, did she say 'we'. That had been a truer time than any of the rest before it or since. But who would ever understand? The secret would go with her to the grave; there was no record of it written in her hand, no spoken confession. After the very last song, after 'Im Frühling', there could only be silence.

Mariel went to the bathroom before she set off back into town.

She hadn't used it before.

If there was heating, it was turned down very low.

A cruise liner, she decided, of a more stylish age. The porthole window of frosted glass. The yellow and black tiles on the walls, the marble finish to the floor. The wide yellow pedestal basin. The long deep bath. The chrome rails.

It was practical above all else, well-lit with mirrors to view herself from all angles. Nothing hid your blemishes under this degree of scrutiny. If you could leave this room feeling assured and resolute, it meant you were ready for anything.

Kroll was waiting for her in the hall: as chilly again and as matter-of-fact as the bathroom. Perhaps she thought it had been an intrusion, even though she'd felt obliged to say yes when Mariel asked her if she could use it.

The atmosphere hadn't improved since they'd tackled 'Im Frühling'. Or just possibly Kroll might have been feeling awkward about the finality of this leave-taking.

'I'll ring you before I go,' Mariel heard herself say, not having given the matter any thought beforehand.

Kroll didn't reply.

'Yes, perhaps you were right,' Mariel said. 'We *are* more alike than I thought we were.'

Silence.

Wasn't that what Kroll had said to her yesterday? But, to judge from her deadpan expression, she didn't remember, or had changed her mind.

'Thank you,' Mariel said.

'For what?'

'Your time.'

'Time.' Kroll repeated the word in a whisper.

They both knew that the days in Hietzing were lived quietly. But 'time' had another meaning for them both. It was the drop, the plunge, beneath them.

'Yes, I shall ring.'

Mariel saw how tired Kroll was. She was two hundred years old. Over three hundred, like Janáček's Emilia Marty.

There was no physical contact. No kiss. Not even a handshake. It wasn't Kroll's way, Mariel knew, although that wasn't a valid reason in itself.

She passed through the doorway, out on to the landing.

'I shan't take the elevator.'

When she looked back round, she couldn't see Kroll for a few moments. Had she gone? No, she was still there. But it was as if the afternoon had vaporised everything. Mariel kept her focus before she lost her again.

'The song,' she said, 'I'm taking away the song.'

'That's what you came here for.'

'Yes. But I didn't know if—'

'If what?'

'If you would be willing.'

Kroll didn't reply. Mariel made out a shrug: as if she was telling her she'd had no option.

A shadow appeared on the floor. Brigitte's, from behind the door.

The door started to close. The view of the hall narrowed to a long Klimt-like strip.

Less and less. Then the edge of the door met the jamb and the lock clicked. Mariel stood staring. This time it was the other way around, and *she* wasn't writing the script, as in 1980. The door had been closed, for the final time, and not by her.

Mariel recognised the sound of a rattling chain being hooked into place.

*

As ever, Brigitte brushed Kroll's hair. She was a little brisker than usual, as happened when she was displeased about something. Brigitte had a sixth sense for what was likely to disturb her; it was unfailing. As the brush was worked through her hair, Kroll could hear Brigitte's thoughts as if she was speaking them into her ear.

One hundred strokes, and then the brush was replaced on the dressing table.

The woman looking back at Kroll now from the glass was unrecognisable to her. It was the ancient Countess in *The Queen of Spades*.

*

Mariel went straight to the hotel bar. She needed a drink.

She searched for her phone in her bag and scrolled through the messages.

Several from Litvinoff.

She picked up a newspaper. She couldn't concentrate on what was in front of her, she didn't care what was going on in Iran or Afghanistan. She turned to the back page. What was the weather doing in the eastern States? Cloud over New York.

Over Africa little suns shone, but she had reason to believe there might be showers in Madagascar.

*

'Do you want me to stay?'

Kroll turned and looked at Brigitte. Brigitte was staring at her. 'What was that?'

'Would it be better if I stayed here with you tonight?'

It was the first time Brigitte had ever asked her that question. 'You too, Brigitte?'

'What do you mean?'

Kroll shook her head.

'You don't want me to stay?'

If Brigitte had insisted, Kroll would have said nothing to object, and then Brigitte would have stayed.

If.

'No. No, Brigitte.'

She wouldn't acknowledge the need, wouldn't let herself. All her life's cautions and refusals had been in preparation for this moment, she realised.

'Go now,' Kroll said.

Brigitte went off, just as she always did. There had once been intimacy, a very long time ago, but that hadn't led to closeness. Why should it? Their wants had been animal ones. Afterwards Kroll had had to learn to live by checks and restraints.

She didn't believe that Brigitte was even relieved to be off home. Brigitte was ever-protective, and would have gone to any lengths to defend her. But they had always been incurious about each other's day-to-day existence, the uninteresting just-getting-by routine.

Days were one thing. Her nights had turned into something different, Kroll realised. They were an endurance test, a trial of will, when she needed to forget so much more than she permitted herself to remember.

*

Mariel didn't want to leave the bar, so she ordered a second drink.

She took out her phone and looked again.

No new messages.

Several times she had caught different pairs of eyes moving over her.

Hotel bars like this one were a great cure for loneliness. Mariel picked up her glass of vermouth and soda and swallowed – once, twice, a third time. She returned the phone to her bag.

She got to her feet, just a little unsteadily.

A young man was watching her. He seemed to be trying to match her face to—

But she was out of that place before he had a chance to recognise her, and to compare the reality of Mariel Baxter with the image.

*

Brigitte had left out her tablets for her, on top of the kitchen table. Sometimes, if she couldn't sleep, she took them early.

Kroll scooped them up in one hand and crossed the room with them.

At the sink she emptied her hand. She turned on the cold tap and watched the water go spinning after the pills.

After that she walked from room to room. She left the lights off, seeing her way by blue moonlight and her sense of touch.

She couldn't get the Schubert song out of her head. She switched on a radio, she wanted to hear voices, chatter. The song persisted, though, and she turned up the volume.

She made for her bedroom.

She took off her dressing gown and laid it on the back of the chair, as was her custom. She did it automatically, just as she got into bed without thinking about what she was doing.

In bed she lay in darkness. She pulled up the linen sheet, placed her hands on top. Her fingers felt for the edge of the coverlet and held on to it.

In another room in the apartment the radio voices spoke on; it was just meaningless noise to her.

So much was passing through her mind. A blur of faces, places. She closed her eyes, tried to stop the cavalcade. People opened their mouths to speak but nothing came out. They turned away. Or a car drove off. A dodgem. A door closed on her. Gates were slammed shut. NO ADMITTANCE BY ORDER. Everyone was leaving, and she couldn't do a thing to stop them.

*

She couldn't believe what she was looking at.

A TV ad, dubbed in German, for Cara Michaels!

Mariel was so taken aback, she didn't have time to respond and change channels.

She confronted the crassness of crude commerce. This was what she was up against. No, worse, this was what had come along to replace her. There really was no competition, was there?

Who was Cara Michaels anyway?

Mariel even pitied her, trapped inside this cosmetically aided construction. Cara Michaels was all artifice. She was image to a degree to which neither Mariel nor even Kroll was subjected.

Even in the back of her stretch limos, or that black Phantom she was seen getting out of in the ad, she wasn't allowed to be alone with herself. Because if she was – presuming, that is, she wasn't extraordinarily stupid and could think clearly about what her agent and manager and the rest of them were doing to her – she would go stark raving out-of-her-head mad.

*

Kroll is in Berlin.

She's just been told that the car accident was set up. Alina had been dead for forty-eight hours by the time they got her some one hundred and twenty-five miles away to Nuremberg. They put her into a tourer and towed it to a forest between there and Schwandorf. They contrived to drive the tourer into a tree; the force of the impact sent it hurtling off the road and it caught fire on its descent.

A steel cabinet is unlocked. She's being shown the contents of a file. Documents, photographs.

13 November 1938.

They found one body on the bathroom floor. Litzmann had shot Alina Giebisch, at close quarters from behind and directly into the head, shattering the skull; then he had turned the revolver on himself and pressed the trigger. But the mechanism had jammed. When they grabbed hold of him he was screaming and writhing like some hellfiend.

It had been a prearranged exit in all likelihood: in the event of a tip-off, and there not being any realistic hope of getting away from the house and on to water.

Switzerland was no further than twenty miles away from the Villa Zdenka, tantalisingly close. They had already spirited a dozen friends away on night expeditions, across the lake. On this occasion, preparing for their own escape, the couple's luck ran out.

An overnight in New York, and then off to Maine.

She went to the island in the fall and the spring. Winter was too uncomfortable, Atlantic damp rather than cold. In summer the place became too busy and social.

On the island Mariel was left alone. The shopkeepers knew her, and she knew her neighbours, second- and third-generation offshore people who were quiet and uncomplicated. She had a garden, and a porch, and her books. She kept her TV at the back of a closet, so that she had to think twice about bringing it out. As with the radio, reception was bad. Her records and DVDs were all in the city, along with the means to play them. No computers.

It was a secret she kept from interviewers, and from her colleagues. In her mind she was moving through the rooms of the shingle house – the old parlour, the kitchen, the little study, the bedroom – and along the gravel paths, where she grew whatever would grow in this salt-wind garden. Escallonias, sea buckthorn, agapanthus, big scarlet and lilac Shirley poppies. In her mind, she settled herself in a creaky basket-weave chair and looked out at the view, over the sound, to the small ferry sailing across the horizon.

12 November. Seventy-two hours after Kristallnacht.

The telephone receiver was heavy enough, Kroll felt, to break her wrist.

She gave the number to the operator in a dry faint voice.

She held the list of names and phone numbers which she had been handed in the lobby of the Adlon Hotel after lunch, three months before.

She had to repeat the number into the mouthpiece, speaking more clearly.

On the list were the names of the SD internal security officers who would protect them all from the wrong sorts of people.

Plugs were being switched.

Kroll, in her other hand, crumpled the incriminating piece of paper into a ball.

'I'm connecting you to the Kommandant's office now, madam.'

'Pour your silver light, beloved moon ... where fancies and dream figures flee before me.'

An expanse of dark silver lake. The thick shade of conifers. The Villa Zdenka, with its blue-yellow walls. A last light goes off at a window. Shapes, shadows, they cross inside unlit rooms.

It was Otto Litzmann she had been telling them about.

She didn't mention Alina to them, or she hadn't planned to. Alina was incidental, a detail of sorts.

Jesus God. Why hadn't they seen that? It wasn't what she'd meant.

Not Alina.

Litzmann, yes. Poisoning the blood. The Reichsmusikprüfstelle were due to proscribe him. Otto Litzmann.

But not her. Not Alina.

'A precious thing I once possessed ...'

Litzmann is holding Alina close with the revolver between them and his finger poised on the trigger. They had made their suicide pact. There was no time for poison shared from the same phial. Bullets would do the job instantaneously. The worst of it would be the hiatus of a few seconds' before Litzmann could deliver himself from the world, before he joined Alina in whichever place he'd promised her they were going to.

It wasn't to be.

They finally overpowered him, carried him off. He was in prison for a year, in solitary confinement in the psychiatric wing. There were rumours that suggested he had fled the country and changed his name. In actual fact, he was stamped with a number and shipped out to a death camp at the first opportunity.

About Alina they panicked. A car accident was the best they could come up with given the pressure they were under. She was just recognisable from her remains (teeth, hair) for the coroner's report, so that everything in her case might be done by the rules and appear to be above board.

'*A precious thing I once possessed ...*'

Finally it happens.

Finally, at the darkest moment of the long dark night, the demons come to Hietzing and snatch Kroll, before she can even cry out from her bed, and they drag her down, down, down.

Samstag

Saturday

2008

A man who introduced himself as a doctor met her at the door of the apartment.

'Mariel Baxter?' He said the name without her telling him.

'That's right. I—'

She'd had an instinct to return to Graf-Rhena-Strasse. She had tired Kroll out yesterday and felt guilty. On the way here she'd brought some florist's roses.

'I saw you in Brussels.'

'Brussels?' she repeated.

'The Théâtre de la Monnaie.'

'You did?'

'The *Arabella* they recorded.'

'That's right.'

'Your Arabella is the best in the catalogue. The best since—'

Behind him she saw Brigitte. Her face was a hollowed mask. Something terrible had happened.

'Fräulein Kroll', the doctor said, 'is dead.'

Mariel's heart missed a couple of beats. This wasn't news, though. She had turned the corner of the road suspecting as much.

'How exactly—?'

She'd had a brain haemorrhage some time towards morning.

Mariel looked again at Brigitte. The woman's soul was in torment.

'Would you care to go through?' the doctor asked. 'To pay your respects?'

Mariel put down the flowers. She walked past Brigitte, who didn't attempt to bar her way.

'I have to warn you—'. The doctor started to speak, somewhere behind her. But she was already in the bedroom and could see Kroll's face from where she was standing.

She knew she wouldn't ever forget this moment, although for the rest of her life she would try to get beyond it. It would be the spur to do everything she still had ambitions to do.

Kroll was lying in bed. Her head was turned towards the door, as if she had seen a movement or heard a sound just as she was dying. Her eyes were open – they hadn't been able to close them – and still conveyed the horror of her last moments. It was as if she was staring into a charnel pit.

Mariel must have reacted, let out a cry, because she looked down and saw the doctor's hand on her arm. He was trying to lead her away, back to the hall.

'I'm sorry,' he said. 'I forgot that—'

'No. No, I had to see her.'

'This must be a very big shock.'

'Not – not really.'

'It isn't?'

The doctor closed the door of the bedroom behind them.

'The angel of death always flies close,' she said, 'to announce the end.'

'I'm sorry—?'

He was looking at her as if he realised that everyone in this apartment, apart from himself, was of unsound mind. Even her reputation couldn't protect her at this moment.

Mariel proceeded along the corridor, towards the front door.

She looked in at the kitchen. Brigitte was sitting at the table with her back to them, head turned to face the window. The netting at the window, with filtered daylight behind it, offered nothing but a blank screen.

At first Brigitte appeared motionless. But when Mariel looked again, she saw the woman was trying to control her shaking shoulders. Grief was overwhelming her and there was nothing Mariel or the doctor could have said to comfort her.

A long exhalation of cold wind blew along the street as Mariel returned on foot to the hotel.

Where had it come from? Hungary? Russia?

It was like the last bitter gasp of winter.

The trees shivered overhead.

Mariel, pulling up her collar, walked on.

Freitag

Friday

2008

Mariel would never know how it happened, how she had managed to confuse cemeteries. She might have misheard what was said to her, or plans might have been changed; did the taxi driver fail to understand the instructions she gave him, or thought she'd given him?

Or was this state of affairs merely fated to be? Kroll always needed to have the better of her, didn't she?

By the time she had headed south from Hietzing to reach Zentralfriedhof, the Central Cemetery, the funeral was over. The hearse and cars had gone. The last mourners were dispersing.

A man in a green loden coat, *that* man who had welcomed her to Graf-Rhena-Strasse, raised his hat to her before turning away.

Mariel found a mound of wreaths and cut flowers, supplied and discreetly tagged by the best florists in Vienna.

The flat gravestone was a large, plain black marble slab with gold lettering:

URSULE KROLL

1915–2008

Underneath was a line she immediately recognised from von Hofmannsthal's libretto *Arabella* – a curious choice – '*Hab' ich geträumt?*'

'Have I been dreaming?'

The plain ledger offered no concessions to religion. No mention of the calling of the deceased, let alone her achievements. The name only, because everyone who made a pilgrimage here to the grave and read the words from Strauss's opera would *know*.

Mariel turned away at last.

Half a dozen elderly figures, elegantly dressed in black, stood together. They were the same sinister sorts to be encountered in all big German-speaking cities, or in South American hideaways. They were considering her, Mariel felt, not in a threatening way but out of intense curiosity.

Had they recognised her?

She had been spotted leaving Kroll's graveside as if she was acknowledging her inheritance, as if Kroll's ghost was walking by her side, as if the spirit was preparing to transmigrate.

No, she couldn't oblige them. That was a role she was *not* equipped to play. But as she walked away she was aware that, even with this botched ending, she was written into the tale, whether she liked it or not. She couldn't exempt herself. She had made her bargain long ago. The rewards had come to her tainted, but the world in its ignorance viewed them as advantages: she would always be called successful, and lucky in life, even if that flew in the face of what she knew to be the truth.

Then – her heart juddered in her chest – she heard footsteps behind her. She jerked her head round to look.

'Brigitte!'

The woman, wearing a dark coat which might have been Kroll's, was holding out a plastic carrier bag.

'This is for me?'

Brigitte didn't speak.

'You want me to take this?'

A brief hesitation. Then the bag was pushed into her hand.

'I think *you* must have it now.'

'Yes?'

'You will know why.'

Mariel looked inside. A wrapped book-shaped object lay at the bottom of the bag.

She waited until she was out of everyone's sight before she opened the package. She remembered Brigitte's final uncertainty about giving it to her.

She removed the sheets of tissue paper.

They had been protecting a silver photograph frame. Mariel stared at the two figures in the photograph. Ursule Kroll and Adolf Hitler. The singer, with her famously aristocratic mien, was wearing stage costume, in this case the high fashion of the 1860s; she was being greeted by the Führer in his most charming mode. Or alternatively, an excited and bright-eyed Hitler was being given his long-wished-for introduction to the brightest singing star of the age, in his favourite of her great roles.

On the back was some writing, in Kroll's hand. The words were quotations from somewhere.

'All those who serve German music pledge him, who is their leader, loyal following to prove themselves worthy of him as far as is in their power. We beg from a higher power all happiness for his life and work.'

Mariel started walking along the long straight avenue of limes, towards the entrance gates in the distance.

To left and right were the bronze and stone likenesses of Vienna's great and good, now mostly forgotten names. Draped urns, angels plucking harps or blowing trumpets.

Somewhere lay the bones of Beethoven, and Brahms, and Schubert himself.

Overhead the trees were coming into bud. The green was so sharply green.

She fixed her eyes forward. To the future.

What next for Mariel Baxter?

She pictured a girl hurrying along East 87th Street. Nervous, glancing at her watch, making doubly sure that she has what she needs in her music case, checking her appearance in a plate-glass window and looking again. This is her first lesson.

Upstairs in her apartment, the woman who will teach her is nervous, glancing at her watch, making doubly sure that what she needs is to hand, catching her reflection in a mirror and looking twice.

Schubert in Manhattan.

Mariel's feet continued to carry her along the avenue of the cemetery. Would she ever be back? The city existed in her head, where it was just as real as the gravel beneath her shoes, or the files of ridge-barked trees, or – overhead – the blue sky as wide as the Hungarian steppes.

The young girl meanwhile is exiting from the elevator. Her teacher is standing behind her front door, waiting for the bell to ring, ready to count out ten seconds until she opens it.

Mariel slowed as she walked between the two lines of trees. Did she have the courage for teaching? How much of her knowledge was she willing to give? Even the presence of someone so young in the apartment would be an awkward adjustment to make. Youth has an aura: a quality of physical intensity, like a charge of electricity. The sizzle of youthful sparks in return for the solemn knowledge of the years?

Was that a fair exchange?

It was sunny where Mariel was standing. The place didn't feel deathly any more.

She turned and looked behind her at a sound.

A bird was singing somewhere up in the trees.

'*Tit-looeet!*'

A lark, which might have been equally at home on the meadow's slope. But here it was, in the city, on the branch of a linden tree.

Lines were being pulled together, Mariel was aware. An order was being imposed. Rationality. It was also the American way, accentuating the positive.

All because a songbird was trilling.

She moved beneath the tree, letting the quick spring shadows play on her face. The woodlark sang over all the other voices in her head.

'*Tit-looeet!*'

This was how she wanted to remember Vienna, and the graveyard, and a day in April.

Sap rose – sustaining the tree – which supported the bird.

And meantime her anxious but eager student was waiting.

'You've come here to learn. About lieder. A tiny, perfect world. Not life, I now know. Greater than life. Art! Are you ready to begin?'

Mariel was quietly hopeful that from obsession and jealousy and betrayal, even from those, could come something good.

Acknowledgements

I first heard about the 'unwritten secrets' several years ago, listening to soprano Gundula Janowitz being interviewed by Joan Bakewell on BBC Radio 3. From that same intriguing conversation came the notion of the 'tiny, perfect world' of lieder.

The most valuable work of reference on the period proved to be the magisterial *Music in the Third Reich* by Erik Levi. The Paul Ehlers quotation appears in that.

The longer translations from German are not my own. The sources are as follows:

Gretchen am Spinnrade (Schubert), unattributed (Polydor International GmbH, Hamburg 1997)
Des Mädchens Klage (Schubert), as above
Im Frühling (Schubert), Norma Deane and Celia Larner: *The Schubert Song Companion*, John Reed (Manchester University Press 1985)
Amor (Strauss), Paula Kennedy (EMI Ltd–Virgin Classics)

I took my quotations from *The Seven Voyages of Sinbad the Sailor*, translated by N. J. Dawood (Penguin 1954).

I owe Mariel Baxter's thoughts on Klimt to a brief description by Gilles Néret in *Gustav Klimt* (Benedikt Taschen Verlag GmbH 1993).

All the characters, except the verifiable 'names', are of my own invention.